Cruising State

...

Western Literature Series

For Phil—
good friends good thoughts
winter — w/ all good thoughts
for the good old day!
Yours
Chris

Cruising State

■ ■ ■

Growing Up in

Southern California

For Rick—
Phil D.—old Pal
from Murray — no longer
w/ us — & this copy turned up
on the internet, oh to Re-
so hope it; oh to you —
sign it to you —
all good
wishes
Chris

CHRISTOPHER BUCKLEY

Christopher Buckley

▲▲
University of Nevada Press
Reno   Las Vegas   London

Western Literature Series

Editor: John H. Irsfeld

A list of books in the series appears at the end of this volume.

The paper used in this book meets the requirements of
American National Standard for Information Sciences—
Permanence of Paper for Printed Library Materials, ANSI Z39.48-1984.
Binding materials were selected for strength and durability.

Library of Congress Cataloging-in-Publication Data
Buckley, Christopher, 1948–
Cruising state : growing up in southern California / Christopher Buckley.
p.   cm. — (Western literature series)
ISBN 0-87417-247-0 (cloth : acid free paper)
1. Buckley, Christopher, 1948–   —Homes and haunts—California, Southern.
2. Buckley, Christopher, 1948–   —Childhood and youth.
3. Authors, American—20th century—Biography.
4. California, Southern—Social life and customs.
5. California, Southern—Biography.   I. Title.   II. Series.
PS3552.U339C78   1994
813'.54—dc20   94-4857
CIP

University of Nevada Press, Reno, Nevada 89557 USA
Copyright © 1994 Christopher Buckley
All rights reserved
Book design by Kaelin Chappell
Printed in the United States of America

2 4 6 8 9 7 5 3 1

Contents

PART ONE

■ ■ ■

Golden State

What was I thinking, running loose on Humphrey Road in the shade and backlit filter of camphor trees? What plays back now is a stream of burnished images, the smooth acceleration of my heart and legs through all that air, through leaves and light, a day being a long ordeal in and of itself.

Our road was no more than a quarter mile long with Highway 101 and North Jamison Lane at the top and the train track on the bottom, on the other side of which lay the beach and Miramar Point. Once I'd memorized our five-digit phone number, 92078, I was let out beyond our gravel drive, and the next year, when I could command my bike, I rode top to bottom at will on Humphrey Road, through a world shaped like a tunnel beneath the overhang of camphors, pines, and oaks, a world so quiet I could hear a screen door open two houses away. So few cars came down our road, we played ball in the street and could, especially in summer, hear the milk truck from Golden

State Dairy turn the far corner at Jamison and begin to make its stops. It was rust-red, and right across the middle—just as on its milk cartons—it had a butter-gold sun with stripes stretching left and right, the same sun, it seemed, that set just beyond the sycamores at the end of our lane. Some milk was still delivered in bottles with paper bonnets over the caps, and my "aunt" Doris—our landlady who lived in the front house and rented us the one in back nearest the creek—always bought two bottles and Big Dip, a half gallon of ice milk. We ran after the truck down the length of our road until the driver at some point on a stop would give us each a scoop of crushed ice from the back of the truck, which we held up cool to our foreheads and lips.

At seven or eight I was not the least concerned about the names of plants or trees, but I knew a few names—Big Dip, Golden State Dairy, and the Daylight, the Southern Pacific passenger train that rumbled by at 4:15 every afternoon on its way down the coast to L.A. Along the right side of our driveway there was a tall hedge of pittosporum, a name I did not know until years later when we had moved away, but I knew it then for its hard pumpkin-colored berries, which were great for throwing and "beaning" friends. Toward the road, there was a line of palms along the other neighbor's drive, and their dry branches, when felled and their hard dates shaken loose, were easily made into pirate swords by sawing an angle on the top and a notch for a handle at the bottom. Venturing beyond the track and down to the beach, especially at low tide, I discovered sea anemones that spouted water when poked, the sea slugs leaking a deep purple ink. We had cats that lived under the porch and who soon multiplied to a dozen or more, and I made up names for them all.

First grade was coming to an end and I was one of the last to learn to read, so I endured the humiliation of receiving my Dick, Jane, and Spot reader after most of the other students. But by fifth grade I was doing well. I remember being let out of Sister Julie's fifth-grade English class, the last one of the day, and immediately sitting on the steps outside and writing out the twenty sentences of grammar homework. I loved sports but ran out late to work-ups or kickball on those days we had English homework. Of course, I wanted approbation and had found something at which I could shine, though grammar had to be boring. Most of the time, I placed the right words in the right order and often received B+'s in the class. That year, I wrote a poem for Mother's Day in *abab* quatrains; it was about clouds, sunlight, blue air, and birds. I crayoned tulips and the purple enlarged hearts of the birds as they flew about the sky. Early on, I learned to hear and imitate the music of language but was not much aware of my ability then. I knew only that I wanted that sky, that day I carried around gloriously in my mind, to transfer to the construction paper on which I wrote and drew. Sometime during college, going through an old trunk with my mother, I came across that large card and remembered in a flash its light and sound.

Eighth grade, and, essentially teenagers, we were railing against most everything. It was a difficult year, especially with our principal, Sister Vincent de Paul, hammering us with some New Math no one understood. It had something to do with "set theory," algebra, and even geometry—words that would equal confusion and failure for me for years to come. We had begun as well to study science and perform some small experiments, which only a few of the "brains" could manage, coupled as the science was with the math. Spring was on us, and the ocean and our usual Mediterranean climate was warming up. All we could think about were the upcoming graduation parties and getting out on Fridays and riding our bikes to a friend's beach house for bodysurfing. On one of the last days of the year, I rode bikes with a few friends up Hot Springs Road to the top of the foothills just so we could coast downhill for the minute or so the ride lasted. Few cars on that road, and four abreast we headed down, balancing with no hands, doing twenty-five or thirty miles an hour, throwing our arms above our heads as we coasted between a small orange grove on the right and a line of olive trees on the left. As we neared the classrooms and office, we began to scream our full and wind-stung lungs out. I shouted, "Cirrus, cumulus, nimbo-stratus"—all I could remember from science class that semester—the Latin names of clouds whose sound alone made sense and committed them to my heart.

Our brake pads complained against the rims of our tires and the acrid smell of burning rubber rose as we came to a stop before the cross street in front of school, busy East Valley Road. We then took off again, zigzagging the junipered lanes until we reached our friend's beach house. There we changed into swimsuits, and some of us grabbed fins and masks left there the last weekend we'd gone skin diving. Then, in unison, we stormed out and jumped into the surf—six or eight of us, floating free as the kelp and eel grass, riding the riptide and shouting out Latin names for clouds, elemental chemical compounds, and the odd algebraic equation—all in no particular order, a nonsense of noise and music to reprise the crashing of the waves, just to hear ourselves sound out. We were all heading for high school, two or three different ones, but for now that was the far side of everything. We were joyous, fearing nothing, with no idea of what we wanted or could expect, understanding little more than the fishes in those blue tides, who, in their watery and diffuse brains, wanted simply to be.

Years of school would follow, and almost the next thing I knew, I was teaching at the university and turning in grades for the third year in a row. After handing back three classes' worth of final compositions, I had a flashback, a very clear memory of the paper planes I had become so expert at making during the spelling bees in grammar school. I recalled how well they flew as, one of the first to miss my spelling word and return to my desk, I'd launch a plane to the other corner where Tuck Schneider or Peter Sozzi were sitting. While Mrs. Hanson read out the words, pronouncing each one twice, a pointed air combat was released across the back of the room, two or three sorties per word. When the crossfire subsided, the trick was then to see who could land a plane in the aqua-colored acacia boughs just a few yards beyond the highest open windows out which we were always daydreaming. Rita Carol, Maggie Tappinier, Arthur Knapp, and Susie Norton were always the last ones standing, articulating each letter of "Mississippi" or "marsupial" the way I imagined sleep walkers slowly spoke, until finally the prize word those days, "antidisestablishmentarianism," collapsed in a frothy tumble of letters in the next-to-last speller's mind. . . .

I was handing in my grade sheets—it was 1983—and I was in the whirlpool of economics and career, older and getting more so. Paying rent in Santa Barbara, I calculated that I would need to live another fifty years to save enough for a down payment on a stucco bungalow with its one banana palm, jade plant, or bird-of-paradise, and, given the steady escalation of land prices there, a down payment would probably continue to be beyond all but those of biblical longevity, at least for university instructors. So I moved to Kentucky to take a position teaching creative writing at a state university, where I would stay only a year and a half before returning to Santa Barbara. But while there, I had a good and energetic partner, the fiction writer Ken Smith, and we managed to wangle just enough grant money to bring in a few visiting writers. During a reception for William Matthews, who had just that week published *A Happy Childhood,* one of the older M.A. students who wrote both fiction and poetry asked me why I wrote poetry. I'd had a glass or two of a self-possessed zinfandel, so the usual well-rehearsed answers, the lines quoted from famous writers that many use to explain such a marginal vocation, went out the proverbial window.

I reported that the first poet I was really taken with, whose work I committed to memory and looked up in a library, was A. C. Swinburne, a now unfashionable poet. But, I explained, at fourteen, what did I know of literary style? I knew surfing. I liked Roy Orbison and the Everly Brothers, was a sucker for

smooth music and aching sentiment. I admitted that my intro-
duction to Swinburne, one of the Pre-Raphaelites, came when
I discovered one of his poems printed across a photograph of a
wave in an issue of *Surf Guide,* one of two surfing magazines
published in the early '60s. I took the current issue off the rack
in the Bottle Shop one day, and across two pages in the center
was a perfect wave, one just beginning to peel left to right. Written across the curling face of it was a stanza from Swinburne's
poem "The Garden of Proserpine," the one ending with "That
even the weariest river / Winds somewhere safe to sea." For a
long time then, I said, knowing little about poetry, my voice, or
an American voice, Swinburne was my favorite poet.

But the woman I was talking to wanted more than my first
poetic influence. She was considering a Ph.D. program in writing and wanted real, hard and convincing answers as to what
made someone want to be a writer—especially a poet rather
than a writer of fiction—badly enough that he or she would
endure the hardships, financial and otherwise. Under the influence of Bill Matthews's poems and a California varietal, I
was not disposed to think formally and responded with the first
image that came to mind.

It was a scene from second grade at Mt. Carmel school.
Noontime—a bunch of us taking our sack lunches off behind
the classroom building. The school sat in the lap of the foothills,
and white and perfect clouds meandered through the blue above
us. Some of us—boys and girls, Mexicans and Anglos—sat on
the low branches of acacia trees, some on rocks, some among
the wild ivy, fennel, or sour grass. We'd sit back, eat our sandwiches and Fritos, and watch the clouds that looked like angels
or the lost beasts from books of early history. The crisp light
of late January beamed directly down, and we were comfortable
in our shirtsleeves, quiet as the occasional small winds whish-
ing through the tops of the eucalyptus trees. We just sat there
wanting nothing, I think, to change. A place was ours, glorious

and green among the weeds, among friends. What more could there be?

Looking back at that moment, I told her, I must have known/ felt that I wanted it always; that I wanted to stop time, that I wanted that wave to curl perfectly for a left to right break, and then hold. It must have been clear to me even then that I would be reaching back for that moment, always just out of reach, reaching up to it in all the years to come, like the sun-rich fruit of the loquat on the one tree in the schoolyard. Then, I had no words for it and just let the days form in their silence and somehow form me, pull me slowly toward my life, the way the sun in its bright stanzas called me to the surface as I headed up through the dark sea after a dive, thinking only about air and light, always almost out of breath.

Flat Serve

It was not divorce, nor business partners who stole him blind, nor the fortunes in real estate he should easily have made, nor the fact that he just missed fame as a singer with a big band; it was surfing. Surfing broke my father's heart.

I was given my first tennis racket at age two, and by age four I was dragging it around between games during my father's Sunday matches on the parking lot–like court in Manning Park. This was '52, and the racket was squared off, strung as loosely as a fishnet with what they then called "catgut." I would stand just inside the service line and hit balls lobbed toward me from across the net, and when I connected, my racket would slingshot the ball toward the blue, from where it finally sank to bounce high off the chicken-wire fence. The racket was cheap and built for an adult; the grip was too thick, so I often took a swing with both hands, but was always quickly corrected on my form. And when I was caught smashing acorns on the cement picnic table with it, I received my first lecture on the correct use and care of equipment.

I was soon learning a proper forehand, and when I was able to remember to get to the courts after school, that is, as early as six years old, my father began to hold forth on the moral imperative of a flat power serve. Big Bill Tilden hit it that way, first and second serve, and so would I. He praised Pancho Gonzales as well—a cannonball first server—but couldn't for the life of him figure out why Gonzales put spin on the second ball. As far as I could tell, there was something equally corrupt in a slice backhand; it was for "dinks" and "pushers" I soon learned. Don Budge was the master of the backhand drive, and my father proclaimed the absolute virtue of a flat one-handed stroke. Rosewall with his slice, Segura with his two-handed chip, why Budge would have killed them both! This was a matter of character, and I was going to have it.

Lucky for us both I had what talent I did. The pro, Byron DeMott, said I was a *natural;* moreover at lessons, I hit the ball harder than anyone else and liked it, so my father seemed relieved, if not happy. Weekends I was religiously at the courts. All through grammar school I got off the bus at day's end and walked up the road to the country club courts. I was growing up among the rich, in a rich fashion almost. For although my father was a DJ for a local station and my mother worked as a secretary for the city schools, we lived on a full acre on Alisos Drive, the woodsy section of Montecito flanking the foothills. My parents built our house pretty much on their own, and across the street was a wilderness of scrub oak, acacias, laurel, and eucalyptus, even the out of place palm tree by a pool or creek. I knew the trails and the borders of ferns, the maroon shade or the air stunned with sunlight atop house-sized boulders, which just sat outright on the land like worn idols from a chapter heading in Bible history. I took it all simply on faith; days passed slowly as drifting clouds and were full of coveys of quail, wild peacocks, chipmunks, lizards, gliding spirals of hawks before the sandstone face of mountains. It was that simple. No choices had to be made, no judgments; there was nothing and everything to do under the sky. To be sure, there were large private estates, manicured grounds, a fountain or two, a little old money here and there belonging to folks who had made it big in the market and then moved here to beat the Chicago winters. Most mansions were behind the trees, at the ends of long drives we could never sneak all the way up without being run off by a caretaker. Yet it seemed people could live anywhere they wanted. I had friends whose uniform cords had as many rips in the knees as mine, yet who lived in huge homes, ranch houses, two-story haciendas with fruit trees and automatic sprinklers. I'd stay overnight and we would climb the avocado boughs or run down their hills. It seemed perfectly natural to be always running through all that space.

But more and more I had less time for my friends. The pro at the country club struck a deal with my father. Byron thought I was a prospect, and for nothing more than the love of the game and out of his good nature, he talked whoever was in charge into allowing me to hang out at the courts and play so long as my father paid for one lesson a week. I spent all my time there without having to join the club, something we never could have afforded. And although adults could kick any kid off any court, I soon saw there was a difference among apparent equals. Most of the others, after putting in the required time at group lessons or seeing who could hit the most balls over the fence onto the fairways, spent their time racing down to the grill for hamburgers and shakes; they just signed their names on their parents' tab and came away with everything. Even when I went to pick up lunch for Byron and was encouraged to order an ice cream for myself, I never did. Something in the eyes of the waiters made me feel they knew I had no business ordering or signing for anything.

A couple of long summers of hitting against the backboard passed, and in local tournaments I was making the finals, where I lost to Johnny Fitz or Benny Weiss, boys slightly older who'd been playing longer and had had more lessons. My father dropped me off early in the mornings and came by after work, when everyone else had left. Johnny's father, Harley Fitz, was often at the club. I wondered what Harley did. When Johnny was playing, his father coached through the fence, always trying to psyche out Johnny's opponent. One day when I was serving well, I almost beat Johnny, and though he had seen me play before, Harley turned back toward the court as he and Johnny headed for the grill and said to me, "Stick around, kid. We'll make a star out of you too." For a moment, I was flattered for the attention, but soon I felt put down and resentful. I wondered if he had been talking to my father. But my father was rarely at the club and never went to the grill; I don't think my father would have talked to Harley anyway. Harley wore alligator shirts with a blue blazer and gray slacks, and cordovan loafers, sometimes without socks, which I thought was very strange. He was always headed for the grill once Johnny had the match in hand, and toward the end he would reappear—his face red, his thin hair white in contrast, and commenting on the points in his sandy voice. Among the women, there was Benny's mother, who always arrived after lunch in her white convertible Mercedes with a large white chow stationed in the front seat, Benny and his older brother in the back. Her hair was frosted, streaked with long lines of gold over the gray; her head seemed to match the many bracelets and necklaces that rattled about as she played doubles on the first court with Mattie DeMott— the golden blossoms of the eugenia hedge blooming, the omniscient sunlight, a whole bright world spangling in starched tennis whites. They played with a stiff gentility and displayed no desire to put the ball away, even if they had the ability to do so. I hated being kicked off the courts by people who couldn't hit the ball.

One day Byron wanted to teach me a slice serve. My father was not there, so I decided to give it a try, tossing the ball out to my right and hitting around it instead of over the top. There was a swishing ping like a dull harp being plucked, and fluff from the thick nap of the Dunlop ball suspended for a second in the air. It worked the first time, landing in the far forehand corner and abruptly jackknifing into the side fence for an ace. It was quite a trick for someone my age, and I used it especially for the second serve, but I was pressured into hitting both serves flat when my father watched me play in tournaments, or when I went through a full shopping cart of practice serves after my weekly lesson.

My father paid for the racket, the lessons, and my one set of tennis clothes. I had a Lacoste shirt and Jack Purcell shoes, the ones with the large half dome of rubber over the toe, the heavy ones that lasted best. Although more than once I wore my high-top PF Flyers until holes in the soles made holes in my socks, and the knees of my corduroys were layered with iron-on patches, I had the gear for tennis. He just knew I would make something of myself. And at thirteen I had my photo in *World Tennis* for winning a tournament in Palm Springs, and for him it looked like this might make up for something he'd missed out on in the world.

That year I moved down the hill to the municipal courts. There were more and better programs for junior tennis, more competition and tournaments. But I suspected it was because Mike Koury, the pro there, gave weekend lessons for free, that I was told to ride my bike and play there instead of at the country club. Also, by then the club probably wanted us to pay up. I also think my father realized Byron had taught me the spin serve, or maybe he'd seen him hit a slice backhand, or, God forbid, his "Peruvian," a trick shot that amazed kids and club players alike: from the forehand side he would hold the racket face like a plate, flat up at the sky, then hit under the ball with a tremendous backspin, and the ball would drop on the other side of the net and draw back over the net before the opponent could reach it; definitely not stuff for future champions. I improved with Koury. He called me "Bull moose" and worked with me on my serve and volley game. There was always the pressure to win, to beat the boys from the club in tournaments, and I went through a temperamental streak, smashing a few rackets, throwing others into the podocarpus trees that lined the courts. But even when I outgrew that stage, I still went through my Victor Imperial gut every two weeks; the combination of hitting the cannonball flat serve followed by the slicing can openers and high-hopping American twists was deadly for strings. Playing a power game mushed out the wooden frames in a month, so it was a good thing I could earn my own rackets; I was able to garden around the nine courts and stadium and earn a dollar an hour toward frames and strings at Koury's Pro Shop.

I began high school at a prep school in Ojai, California, a small horsey town about an hour and a half south and inland from Santa Barbara. Football was the thing there, so I felt compelled to play in the fall and winter instead of practicing full-time for tennis. There was pressure to conform and produce according to a standard, yet when spring came, I did not go out for training with the rest of the guys in crew cuts but instead played on the tennis team. We had good players and won the tri-valley conference. Things looked good until the summer, when I drew Bob Lutz in the first round of a big tournament, and there wasn't much I could do. My serve won me five games in two sets, which my friends assured me was a good showing. Later that month, playing in both the thirteens and the fifteens, I was clobbered by a couple of other hot players, my father remembering one of them as a young Stan Smith. Whoever they were, I kept things in perspective—those guys were from L.A. and already famous, especially Lutz. Overall, it still came pretty easily, and I played for the Santa Barbara city team on weekend trips against Oxnard, Ventura, and Ojai, and at summer's end against the team from the L.A. Tennis Club.

One year, Clayton Smith and I beat Hobson and Rombeau, two top-ranked players in the sixteens, and that was really the last grand moment in tennis for me. They walked onto the courts in matching Jack Kramer creme-colored whites, carrying about six or eight rackets apiece, joking to themselves about us as if we'd just fallen off the last turnip truck from Bakersfield. Clayton had a Jack Kramer jacket, and we both had two rackets, though they were different makes, which showed we weren't on any "free list" of a manufacturer that outfitted ranked players. Clayton poached well and put the ball away with crisp angle-volleys; my serve and overhead were on. It took three sets for us to beat them, with Hobson changing rackets every couple of games as if losing were a fault of his equipment. Santa Barbara lost the match, but we felt great anyway. That was my summer in between my first and last years at prep school, but when my father could no longer pay the bill, I was allowed to attend the local Catholic high school in Santa Barbara, which was where I really wanted to be.

That was the end of the '50s and the start of the '60s, and next to nobody was surfing, though Santa Barbara had several good spots as I would later find out. Then only a few old guys in their thirties were in the water on planks and "big guns" in Hawaii, or south of town at Rincon Point. They were considered beatniks, and no one thought much about it. But a lot of my friends were surfing. Those days, you could leave your board strapped to a rack on top of your '59 Chevy in the school parking lot, and it would still be there when you got out of class. There were good beaches with lefts and rights and a swell always running, or so it seemed, especially in early fall when school began, and September was hotter than any summer month. The last class would let out, and there would be an exodus for Hope Ranch, The Pit, Hammond's Reef, or Miramar Point.

Surfing meant social distinction as well. It was easy acceptance as long as you really went into the water; everybody knew who the "hodads" were—those who dressed the part and drove their woodies to surf spots without ever taking their boards out of the back. And there was a dress code—white Levis, T-shirts, and wool Pendleton shirts. We all wore blue tennis shoes. If you were really cool you wore Sperrys, and if you weren't, the less popular Keds. But if you were a surfer, it was blue. At the city rec dances you would band together with the other surfers mostly, but at school dances there was no need for group protection. Then there were the movies—for surfers they were the most important social event. Bruce Brown filled the vast Santa Barbara High auditorium time and again with *Surfing Hollow Days*. John Severson had a big hit with *Big Wednesday*, featuring famous surfers Ricky Gregg and Greg Knoll outracing twenty-five-foot walls at Waimea or Makaha. In those days, two- to four-foot swells ran much of the summer, and we were in the water as long as there was light. For weeks at a time we were happy and unbothered in our lives.

The tennis coach at Bishop High School was incompetent, a fact he tried to hide with an officious and authoritarian manner. I was the one player he could do without, because I would expose the fact that he had no idea what he was doing. I was a threat. His condescending attitude and verbal cuts clearly conveyed that to me. I went out to the first two practices, hit some forehand and backhand drives past his ears, and never showed up again. He lost the best player he had, but he was smug and happy about it. He then could work the other, mostly beginning players without too much embarrassment to himself.

I took a part-time job at the local grocery chain, and that paid for my car, a new board, and gas to go north or south looking for waves. On the Feast of the Immaculate Conception or the Feast of the Assumption, we'd load our boards in a friend's VW bus by 5:30 A.M. and be pulling off Freeway 101 as the sun came up, determined to have Rincon to ourselves while all the public school guys wrestled with algebra or sweated out biology. On days I didn't want to drive that far, I hit Hope Ranch, a beach break with no rocks, where I sometimes ran into three or four friends I used to play singles or doubles with at the municipal courts. It was good to be a local and know people; then there was no fighting over the waves. We were all, in our rice paddy baggies, civil to each other and were concentrating on trying to ride the nose with that casual aplomb we'd seen Phil Edwards display in the films. Phil was the first one to ride the Banzai Pipeline in Hawaii, the tubes steaming in overhead and breaking on a shallow bed of coral, which accounted for the shape and power of the waves. We'd all seen Edwards crank a hard left bottom-turn, crouch about a foot from the nose, and come flying out of the curl with the wave spitting spume close behind. Or at Malibu, on waist-high sections, there was Phil, nonchalant as you please, riding six inches from the nose, feet parallel, both hands clasped casually behind his back. Ultimately cool. We were all "stoked" and spent hours wiping out and "pearling" off our boards in our attempts at imitation.

My father silently gave up on pushing the tennis. Since I was paying for all my own expenses, there seemed to be nothing he could do. He just offered his half-despondent look when I began loading the car with my gear.

I was in the water at every opportunity until I went away to college at a small Catholic school in northern California. There I played a little on the tennis team, but the captain was obsessive, a real "come-on-guys" type, and the school did not furnish rackets or clothes. We were given little more than gas money and greasy sandwiches and told to drive to some state university for a match. For the rest of college, I took up golf and played on the team and with friends. But during graduate school, especially during the summers, I was playing tennis again, largely out of economic necessity, as I could land jobs teaching at courts around town in the city's summer program. By summer's end, I was usually playing with friends who had been at it all year. Yet one kid I had beaten with regularity years before had become a celebrity of sorts, winning tournaments in Los Angeles and in the East. Word was he had just signed with Philadelphia for World Team Tennis. For me, well, it was just too late, though I could make it through a couple of rounds in local summer tournaments. My father knew this, though he hadn't seen me play since I was fourteen. Nevertheless, I was offered a job at one of the local clubs. My old pro, Mike Koury, seemed to be making the recommendations, and he put my name in based on my ability as a teacher, I guess. I then had a choice between more school or a permanent job in the sun, playing the other local pros a couple of times a week, watching the station wagons pull up summer mornings and the kids pour out like Myrmidons across the courts while the mothers went off for lunch on the terraces or patios beneath the blue shade of oak trees in Montecito. It was a choice between a life of writing or years of saying until I reached sixty-something, "Better racket preparation, Mrs. Johnson. Bend your knees, left shoulder toward the net. Now, follow through all the way. . . ."

Even though I wasn't going to make the World Championship Tennis tour, even though Bob Lutz had just spin-served and half-volleyed his way through the best players in the world to win the U.S. Pro Indoor title, even though his knees would begin to give out the next year and I'd never get another shot at him, my father was truly disappointed when I turned down the tennis job. From that day forward, although I took my degrees, published and taught at universities, he would continue to shake his head sadly and tell anyone who would listen how surfing had ruined my career.

Radio Towns

About cities we lived in before I was four and came to Santa Barbara, few impressions remain. I do remember my grandfather's farm in Brandenburg, Kentucky, and my other grandparents' house in Ohio, which was modest and white, boxlike amid the vacant fields. Those days, my father always seemed to be on the road chasing down a job at a new radio station. My mother and I were mostly on the farm, or sometimes with his parents in Washington Court House, a small town between Columbus and Chillicothe. So cities, downtown areas I should say, are mostly a blur—all similar in recalled image, strange from a child's point of view, low to the ground and the long cars of those days. Each place gives back a widespread grey, and each street is much the same, with buildings shouldering up to each other and blocking out the sky. The glass storefronts with manikins, the dull or glimmering stuff of the world went by overhead with little endearment or lyricism to mark it or make it remain and resonate in memory.

One town that does come back a little is Charleston, West Virginia. I still see a pink fog from the neon call letters aglow above the doorway of the station where my father worked. I still see the glass boothlike room where he sat in front of the microphone, which rested on a table; it looked like a huge bronze star with a metal halo around it. I was just tall enough to see over the bottom of the booth to where the glass started, so I could watch as he finished reading the news—*The Five Star Final*. After that, we would all drive home in the Buick, a light green boat of a car with a line of silver ovals along each side of the hood and a figurine on the front. With its wings spread, with all that shiny chrome, the car looked as if it was taking us somewhere very fast.

After Charleston, my father had an offer from CBS in New York, which he turned down in favor of a job in Santa Barbara that offered a lot less pay and prestige. Perhaps he was thinking that a sleepy little coastal town was a better place to raise a child, and if so, that was the most unselfish thing he ever did. Upon moving to Santa Barbara, I immediately noticed that the main street downtown, State Street, seemed more open to the sky; most buildings were shorter, two stories only; there was a wider and more constant light. There were only two stoplights the entire length of State; over the street's wide four lanes they hung on wires stretching across the blue. One of my earliest memories is of huge artificial Christmas trees, thirty feet high at least, with round candy cane–like bases. They were placed in the middle of the street each season, and drivers had to slow down and swerve a little in the middle of each block to avoid them, but no one seemed to mind. There must have been speakers in those trees for piped-in Christmas music, because somehow I always remember hearing "Silver Bells" by the McGuire Sisters in the air.

There were only two really tall buildings, the Granada Building and the Balboa Building—the first I knew for its movie theater on the first floor, and the other I knew for the radio station. The Balboa had red letters on one side spelling out "KIST" bigger than the windows; it also housed KTMS, the station where my father had just taken a job. This was the '50s, and everyone smoked; it was glamorous in the movies and magazine ads. The '40s had not altogether lost their hold, and people still wanted glamor, romance, and were largely oblivious to the future and to consequences. The big room at KTMS looked like a newspaper room with desks lined up and all the phones. On my father's desk there were always pipes in a big circular ashtray, a red tin of Velvet pipe tobacco, and one of those funny rubber U-shaped wedges on the phone to cradle it against your shoulder so you could talk and still use both of your hands. I played with the pipes and sometimes got a sheet of paper to put in the old Underwood office typewriter; I would punch out capital letters that seemed familiar in groups of threes and fours until these finally gave way to a long string of nonsense, which still looked fine and important to me.

Later, he worked for another station, KDB, which had a small round office and a broadcast tower in an empty field on the beach side of the freeway—there too a layer of smoke and men drinking many cups of coffee. In the years following, he switched back and forth between stations and jobs. The clearest memories of this time are of those Saturday mornings when I'd go with him to the Copper Coffee Pot, a cafeteria-type restaurant downtown, where one of the stations hosted a weekly roundtable program. He would emcee, and various members of the Junior Chamber of Commerce would talk about the pressing issues of the community in 1953. I sat at the far end of the long table with a plate full of waffle, beyond range of my father and the conferring men at the head of the table. I remember that same outer-space microphone on top of the table in front of him, his camel hair sport coat and green knit tie, the white shirt stiff from the laundry with stays in the collar and the cardboard pulled out by me. I can still see his cordovan wing tips, beneath the table among the wires, where I scurried about. I was four or five, and these were businessmen serious in their suits. I was quiet and hardly seen or heard. This was business in the '50s, the bedrock of America; this was High Mass in the small social and political order of those times, so, aside from the diversion of a waffle, this was no place of real interest to a child. But this still hums over the air waves of memory because it was a place I got to be with him, at least once a week for a year or so.

Our car radio was always on. Those times when we went places together, it seemed the radio—chromed, large and glowing the yellow of an autumn moon—was often the center of things. Songs. He knew who had a hit, who could really sing and who couldn't, kept a running count and made pronouncements to my mother and me to that effect. And then commercials recurring, claiming some portion of consciousness—*Mr. and Mrs. North* was "brought to us by" Halo Shampoo, and before every episode of *Gunsmoke* someone would shout, "Call for Phillip Morris." I recognized my father's prerecorded voice when it promoted some product or local service, but I understood little else and wondered how it could happen with him sitting right next to me, driving our car. He would sing along if it was a ballad and not a "rock song," or he would whistle and tap his college ring in time on the steering wheel. His ring was large and gold with a cut green stone, and the plastic wheel had three chrome inserts at intervals, which he would tap with the narrow underside while Perry Como or Gordon MacRae were singing. He never sang along with Sinatra. Although in his youth he had been a singer with a big band, he always let Sinatra do his own work, respectful of his style, his phrasing. Not long before that, during the late '40s or early '50s, Sinatra had lost favor with the public, not because of his singing or selection of material, but because the public, in its collective moral wisdom, had taken great umbrage at his relationship with Ava Gardner and perhaps his social life in general. My father was one of the few DJs who continued to play Sinatra's records then; the art and romance of the singing for him were more important than the social climate and mores of the times. Only music could so move him beyond convention and politics.

But politics didn't leave him untouched. After years of working with engineers, he built his own radio station, the first FM stereo multiplex station in the United States, KMUZ. He was committed to what was called "easy listening" and to "soft-sell" ads. And also committed—more each year it seemed—to a conservative political agenda, which he used his editorial and public service spots to promote, often against some active local opposition. McCarthy was gone, but the Communists were still there, still coming—at the borders of Mexico, in the UN—and my father was vigilant and devoted to pointing out each clear and present danger. It wasn't "Politics" for him really, Left or Right. It wasn't as simple and fatuous as George Bush using phrases like "The L Word." No, it was Good and Evil. It was absolute. And, well, those Liberals were either "dupes" for the Communists or sinister, or worse. For him, these were questions of the highest order. All of this combined to keep him away from home most days and nights, down in the basement of the Carillo Hotel cuing albums on the large flat turntables, cupping his hand over his right ear to announce the promotional spots, lining up the huge spools on the tall machines for taped programming—Mantovani, 101 Strings, Keely Smith with "You Go to My Head" and "I Wish You Love." It all would play for half an hour or so and reach all over the tri-county area, sometimes to San Francisco. And even though he still gave airtime to Sinatra, he would, after the music, read a speech by Barry Goldwater from the *Congressional Record* to alert the listening public. And then he'd again bend his ear over with his hand, slowly and sonorously pronouncing the call letters—KMUZ—and say, "The sound of music," while in the background, the recorded surf was breaking and you could hear sandpipers, a gull or two calling out.

After my parents divorced and my father remarried, he was still away about as often. Radio business—the selling of commercial spots and a brand of music—were his real and only joys. I was getting to that age when radio/music would become important, but of course not his station. All the kids listened to rock stations—KACY from Oxnard, KIST locally, and a station broadcast from just over the border in Mexico that first had Wolfman Jack as a DJ, a station whose call letters now are lost along with most of the lyrics to those fifties teen tunes I then knew by heart, those dreamy repetitions of love lost and found from Kathy Young and the Innocents, the Fleetwoods, the Flamingos, Dion and the Belmonts. Listening to doo-wop and the harmonies of heartbreak, I passed solitary evenings, avoiding math homework, staring out to a dark blue sky blinking with distant light, light sourced in the dark centers of galaxies that were also sending out radio signals, inscrutable then as now. As the '50s ended and the '60s set in, Roy Orbison gave us "Only the Lonely" and "Blue Angel," and though a group of us were always together, we all had a vague feeling that it had something to do with us and the years just ahead.

With my own car for the last two years of high school, we cruised State Street religiously, and always with the radio on. I drove a '59 Chevy with wide winglike tail fins, and usually Orsua, Schiefen, Rosales, or Bonilla rode along. There was really no place to go then—one pizza parlor up on the Mesa, Me 'n Ed's, which was great, but you had to buy pizza and couldn't simply sit around most of the night and talk. There were no malls or other such places to hang out. So, with gas about twenty-five cents a gallon, we cruised up and down all night, three or four to a car, switching stations to find a new song by the Beatles or the Rolling Stones, perfectly content to drive the wide four-lane main street for hours. Now and then we would all sing along with some popular refrain. I can remember rolling down every window in the Chevy, boosting the volume up all the way, and all of us shouting more than singing, "*G-L-O-R-I-A*—GLOR-I-A" along with Van Morrison's first group, Them. We were more and more on our own and found meaning in most any lyric or tune, though with cars passing slowly on every side of you, each one with a different station blaring, there was often a cacophony hanging above the street like the neon lights from the theaters. We drove along punching a new button on the radio after every song. I hadn't heard my father on the air in years.

Sometime during my first year in college, through a series of bad business deals or some involvement in politics that was never made clear to me, he was forced to sell his station to an arm of Kemper Insurance. They got it for a song, you could say, and knew it—paying about one-tenth of what it was worth. He moved to Arizona and took time off, and after over twenty years in the business, he never returned to radio. And soon radio moved into the background of the times. Vietnam came through the TV each night. Armstrong walked on the moon, and we saw it live one afternoon, without commercial interruption. For years thereafter, '40s and '50s music disappeared from the air; the easy listening and popular melody, the lush romantic stylings of Julie London and Mel Torme were gone. Dialing around, you never ran into Perry Como, Julius LaRosa, Steve Lawrence, and Eydie Gorme, the slightly too sweet instrumental versions of Broadway tunes; only Sinatra kept his head above water, trying to adjust, and not too successfully, to the late '60s. Folk music, protest, Jimi Hendrix, Dylan, and the Doors were what was wanted, what was coming in now over larger speakers with volume and with force. Life, more harsh and more real, was immediate now, and the music was part of it—much less romance, next to no nostalgia. The Stones had had a big hit that repeated, "Hey, you, get off of my cloud!" FM stations from L.A. had whatever audiences there were, and most were playing the first heavy metal music. No one was going to turn on the radio and relax, sing softly along.

Often driving 101 between San Francisco and Santa Barbara, I'd dial around for a station when I found myself in one of those remote areas where there were still no housing tracts or businesses, where the land was flat for miles except for the sea greens and blues of eucalyptus groves planted as windbreaks for fields of broccoli and cauliflower. Punching one of the buttons, never finding something slower with melody or romantic flare, I'd turn off the radio and think of my father driving that old Pontiac station wagon, tuning in a June Christy ballad, or I'd see him in Arizona watering the little grass and rocks of his backyard in the late afternoon, whistling something, lamenting how business and music had changed, knowing nothing would ever again sound the same.

In Montecito

There, between the trees and the sea, we were almost an island, one lost or left off the maps. There was no real traffic on the woodsy suburb roads. Hills were hills, and let go to tall wild grass—creeks, canyons, a resort of clouds and air where we could travel at will. There were some secluded estates with long driveways and even a country club, but on our bikes, oblivious to any social standing, we pushed our noses right up to the wrought iron gates and rode through the private lots. Not far off was Santa Barbara—white Spanish-style homes, the municipal buildings with red tile roofs glinting in the constant sun, the violet lines of jacaranda trees along Mission and Carillo Streets. A bay and breakwater, a harbor and boats, beaches, and a wide blue hoop of seaside light surrounded everything. There were oaks and eucalyptus, palms and bougainvillea, birds-of-paradise and pines, and large sandstone boulders that had almost worked free from the foothills and from which, having climbed on our own to the top, we commanded a view of it all. It was the '50s and no one seemed to know or care that we had all this, in Montecito.

My parents built a house in those foothills. Along with nine other families they bought up a parcel of land and bulldozed a road. It was a ranch-style home with a huge patio opening onto the brush where quail and chipmunks trafficked and wild peacocks called each twilight and dawn. My parents did most of the building themselves. I remember a vast shell of a house with open beams, my father varnishing the ceiling and putting up paneling, my mother wallpapering the two bathrooms and fitting tile. They had cleared most of the poison oak from our acre lot, and after a while I seemed immune to the coppery red leaves and made it my job to cut them down and to collect bark from dead oak limbs for our BBQ. Right across the street were the hills and fields, outcroppings starred with pale green lichen. I wore trails among them hunting the blue-bellied lizard or roaming the wide rooms of sun between the shaded woods.

Montecito was a suburb of Santa Barbara, and altogether it was a slow and sleepy place two hours up the Pacific Coast Highway from L.A. We spent a lot of our time by the beach, and the main attraction in Montecito for those tourists who did find us was the Miramar Hotel, where really anyone could walk on the boardwalk and beach and use the facilities reserved for hotel guests who had paid to escape Los Angeles. I went often with my friends and rode the waves on rafts, swam out to the float the hotel provided about fifty yards offshore. There was also a tennis court we'd use, and no one ever checked to see if we were guests. Mainly, we rode our bikes along the paths that threaded through the blue-roofed bungalows. Whenever one of us came up with a nickel, we'd ride to the boardwalk, drop our bikes, and hit the concession stand for a pack of rootbeer Lifesavers; they came individually wrapped in cellophane and were easy to share. We knew by sight all the custodians and maids who we saw daily pushing carts of food, dishes, and linens to the rooms, and they had seen us riding through often enough that they let us go unbothered.

One day, my friend Murphy turned up with several books of Green Stamps he'd taken from the glove compartment in his mother's car; he wanted to take them over to the hotel and try selling them to some of the workers. I didn't think anyone would buy them, but I rode along. I figured these people didn't have much money as they were always working; adults I'd seen who had money rarely seemed to be working or going off to work. Murphy was a wild kid and, though younger, seemed to be able to run loose a lot more than I. Looking back at it now, I think his mother usually started the cocktail hour about 3:00, with what must have been martinis—I remember clear V-shaped glasses with a kind of green and red olive we never had. Just about any time we came in the house she seemed to have one in hand and gestured with it for us to head out the door again to play. So it didn't seem too incredible when she never missed the stamps. Murphy sold them to the first man he tried and thought it was a great deal. It was more money than I'd ever had in my hands— lots of ones and two fives—so much that we didn't really know what to do with it. Murphy thought a minute and then rode to the boardwalk and instead of Lifesavers or a Three Musketeers, he pointed to a cardboard display with rubber-tipped arrows and a bow, and then a plastic raftlike thing that looked like a sea serpent. The guy behind the counter knew us well enough to be suspicious and to ask where we'd gotten the money, and Murphy, without missing a beat, said it was from his birthday. The man's face told me he knew better, but this stuff had been sitting above the counter all summer, and he must have realized this was his chance to unload it. He took most of the bills and handed over the things Murphy had pointed out, the cardboard and the raft a little bleached out from the sun. We rode away awkwardly with the things on our handlebars and went to another friend's house nearby. We showed him the spoils and, after a short while, hid them in some pittosporum hedges at the back of his yard. Unused to this kind of money and knowing we would be discovered if seen with the loot, we just let it waste away in the bushes. Ethics aside, I was not even practical, never said, "Gee, we should save some for later," so far was I beyond my depth. I knew it was wasteful and tried to forget how stupid and guilty I felt for going along with Murphy and buying that useless stuff for nothing. All that money we hadn't done a thing to earn, more than we could think up uses for—we were kids with no plans, nothing in our heads beyond riding our bikes through the light of the next day.

There were private schools and one public school in Montecito. Our Lady of Mt. Carmel was the only parochial school, and there, for the most part, everyone looked to be about the same; we all wore the same uniforms, brought sack lunches, used the same equipment. We were only vaguely aware of the poor, who were obviously none of our friends or schoolmates as we saw it. Some hobos lived near the bird refuge, and there were winos by the train station under the huge Morton Bay fig tree, and panhandlers on the lower part of State Street downtown. These were the poor, not the busload of mostly Mexican and Filipino students who arrived each morning from Summerland, the little spot just south of Montecito next to the freeway. One girl, a grade ahead of me, used to refold her brown paper lunch bag and take it back home. With a squished banana or half a smashed tuna sandwich still in them, we crunched up our bags and with hook shots tried to hit the garbage cans five tables away when the nun wasn't looking. We were oblivious to our waste. Quite to the contrary, we walked around feeling conscientious because we had worked in the drives for "pagan babies" by selling holy seals. We were encouraged by being able to win holy water fonts or plastic saints by selling top amounts, by being able to choose names for these starving African children for whom we'd collected dimes and quarters. We named them after European emperors and kings from the Dark and Middle

Ages—Constantine, Pepin, and Charlemagne. It seemed noble and educated, and we never for a moment realized our lack of charity and sense in such choices. Our real goals were centered on ourselves, on gaining religious trinkets and prestige in the class for making our sales quotas; we went blithely about neighborhoods making nuisances of ourselves as we hocked religious stamps. We were not focused, finally, on helping starving children in another land. We knew that this girl, along with others, was bused in, but it didn't strike us that taking your lunch bag back home meant something—we didn't see that there were disadvantaged kids among us all the time. I still remember an eighth-grade boy saying something behind the girl's back as she emptied out her bag and smoothed the sides, making a comment supposedly to his friend, but loud enough for the girl to hear. Dark and slight, always neat, she just folded the bag twice and carried it back to the classroom before rejoining her friends; she never looked around to acknowledge the remark of a boy whose family had never had to add up the costs of such small things as they drove away from Isaiah Brothers Market in their Chrysler Town & Country station wagon.

Although I was not as callous as the boy who made fun of her, I was, like most everyone else, impressed with those who we figured were "rich." Still, it wasn't easy to tell whose family had money, except when some parents drove into the yard to collect their children after school. I remember one classmate with three brothers who had moved here from the East. Each day his grandfather would pull up in their Chrysler Imperial, a car with fins fanned modestly but significantly along the mauve/silver sides, fins with ornaments over the taillights that looked like the rings of Saturn. This car was as big as the Cadillacs and Lincolns we occasionally saw driving around Montecito, and it easily had as much chrome and prestige. The grandfather would sound the horn that had to have come right off a diesel train, and the troop would come running. It was big enough for all of them and more; they cruised away on wide silent whitewall tires. One day a friend told me about a kid's father in the grade below us, how he had just gone into the local showroom of Washburn Chevrolet and bought a new Chevy Impala right off the floor— white as milk, covered in yards of chrome—and had simply written out a check for $2,000! Then, that was unbelievable to the group I hung around with; yet we knew it was certainly possible for some in Montecito, and we were impressed.

Yet most families were doing fine—they had a car, owned a house. Anyone and everyone, it appeared, could live in Montecito. My father was a DJ for a local radio station, and my mother was working as a secretary for the school district. We had our home and TV, lived among the trees, but I knew that certain cars and charge accounts at the country club meant a little more. I was just beginning to see the other side of things. There were a lot of us with Fords and ranch-style houses, and then there were the wealthy. The middle class was composed of merchants and employees, almost anyone who worked, men with one or two good suits and an idea for a business of their own someday. They were our parents. Their money bought iron-on patches for the knees of our blue corduroy uniform pants, bought wax paper to wrap tuna or peanut butter and jelly sandwiches, lunch bags to throw away without a second thought. Money in Montecito was old money, money quietly inherited over the years, money used as quietly as the oak trees grew; it was not money that had much effect on everyone else. Aside from the occasional long black Cadillac, old money was not conspicuous. It wanted to be left alone behind the tall borders of eucalyptus and Italian cypress lining drives so long you really couldn't see the mansions at the end, where the trees were smaller and finely trimmed. Old money wanted to arrive discreetly in Lincolns and at the Valley Club or the Montecito Country Club. It lunched discreetly at the Biltmore while the kids were attended to at the Coral Casino across the street—the huge private swimming complex built right on the beach. It didn't then seem strange or ostentatious for all of us to go around in the same space; we went to

school with some of the wealthy children, had no desire to belong to clubs, and ran around in all that sun-stropped and hilly
space.

Although I sometimes wore holes in my PF Flyers high-top
tennis shoes, times seemed pretty good to the child I was. All of
us managed the routine economics of hocking pop bottles to buy
two-penny sticks of licorice, getting friends to share. Sometimes
one of us had a dime for a "Suicide," the top-of-the-line drink
at an actual soda fountain down the road from our school; the
rest of us would go along and sit there even if we did not have
any money. You could sit at a counter and order your Suicide,
and one of two twin brothers who worked there would hold
an old-fashioned soda glass, a heavy tall V-shaped one with a
round foot at the bottom, and go down the line with one shot of
everything—cherry, lemon, Coke, and chocolate syrups—before adding soda water. Against the wide mirror that backed the
counter, there was a wooden wheel set up with holes around its
circumference, each with a 5¢ COKE, CHERRY COKE, 10¢ COKE,
or SUICIDE label under it. After you bought a drink, you'd wet
the end of your straw wrapper, blow into the straw, and shoot
the wrapper across the counter space trying to land it in one
of the holes for a free drink. In all that time, I think I saw only
one kid hit anything, so it was a safe come-on for the brothers
who owned the shop. That shop was a vestige of earlier times
and hung on in a sleepy outpost like Montecito for as long as it
could. By 1961 they could no longer make it economically and
sold out to a shopping center developer.

While the focus of our discretionary income was usually that
fountain, we did try to come up with the little cash it took to
stay more or less current in the various "seasons" at school. In
addition to the usual football, basketball, and baseball, there
was marble season, yo-yo season, and in March, kite season.
These were more important than sports for most of us as only the
seventh and eighth graders played sports against other schools.

Marbles and yo-yos often lasted a year or two, although there was always some new model of yo-yo—one year a fluorescent green one with rhinestones in the sides was the one to have. Kites never lasted. Most sold for fifteen cents and usually held together for a week or so. There were more expensive models, but after a week or two we had lost interest anyway, so one fifteen-cent kite usually took care of kite season for most of us.

Unannounced but somehow known to all, kite season arrived in the fifth grade, and a bunch of us walked down to the soda fountain to buy kites after school, but there were none. They had all been bought. My friend Cameron had his father check in town at Otts, the big department store, and they too were sold out. At school the next day, only one or two kids brought kites, kids who had bought them the first day of the week. No one else could get one. So instead of staying after school and running across the wide football field trying to get a tailless triangle of crinkly paper airborne, I took the bus home and after changing clothes decided I would go across the creek to see what my neighbor Seth Hammond was doing. He was not a popular kid at school, but living right across the creek, we got along OK, though he did have a few strange habits, I thought, for a kid. He'd eat mushroom soup cold right out of the can, and no one I knew would even touch a mushroom let alone a can of cold ones in soup. Seth and I were sort of friends until the next year when he went to a private school and we moved from Humphrey Road to our house in the foothills. Home from school, I told my "aunt" Doris, who watched out for me, that I had no homework, and then took off across the creek to the Hammond Estate. It was an estate, though that meant little to me then. Plenty of people, rich and not so rich, had big houses with lots of land around them all over Montecito. Coming up from the creek, I had to cross a few acres of lemon trees before I hit the clearing with the yard and main house. There, I think his housekeeper told me Seth was down at the airfield with his father. I took off down the dirt road for the beach, past the other Victorian house set back from the road where his grandmother lived. Years later I'd realize that all that land that ran right down to the sea had belonged to the grandmother, acres and acres that would later be leveled and clotted with condominiums.

Seth's father had a small hangar on what would best be described as a golf course fairway. Spread along the sand, there was a huge level green lawn where he could take out his small plane and lift into the sky above the ocean or the town or the oak-covered foothills. There was also a little beach bungalow and next to it a long green wood building that I discovered was a one-lane bowling alley. (I went there on a rainy day with Seth and another friend, but the pins had to be set back up by hand, so we soon lost interest.) As I turned the corner to the landing field and the trees were behind me, I could see what looked to me like a hundred kites in the sky. There were Seth and his father, going from pole to pole, reel to reel, attending to all these kites they had bobbing and weaving in the air. It was a blustery day, and they were all up there—box kites of red and blue, of green and yellow, regular kites of all shades, and even several of our favorite fifteen-cent kites, the light yellow and light green ones with red dragons imprinted down their length, and all at various levels in the air. Many were attached to deep-sea poles staked into the ground, and some of the lines spun from large cable wheels with a handle on the side for cranking. Seth and his father were busy running between each, letting out string, pulling it in, keeping the whole armada up. It reminded me of the Ed Sullivan TV show, that act in which a man starts plates spinning on rods balanced on a table, gets two or three going, then runs to the end of the table and starts a fourth before racing back to give the others another spin to keep them going before running to the end of the table to start some more—seeing how many he can keep up and spinning at one time. Seth and his father were busy. No sooner had they said hello than they put me in charge of a kite, a flag-patterned regular one that seemed to be holding its own; I was to make sure it didn't come down in the sycamores over the creek. I was so amazed by the spectacle that it wasn't until I was walking home in the dusk that I realized that this was what had happened to all the kites in town. Seth had said nothing at school. Maybe he didn't know about the kites until he got home from school; maybe he was too smart to mention them to the rest of us, who were pretty perplexed by the disappearance of all the town's kites. It was not a malicious act; Seth and his father were not intentionally depriving the rest of us. They just did it for fun, because they could. I'm sure they never gave it a second thought.

There were private schools in the area—Crane Country Day School and another called simply the Howard School. Kids from those places seemed a bit more formal, but regular kids for the most part. However, later on, in about sixth grade, it struck me that my friend Tuck Schneider's father had been a golf pro at the Valley Club, but Tuck and his family were not members, never went out there. I soon began to see more closely how that portion of society lived when I was allowed to play on the tennis courts of the Montecito Country Club.

My father worked a deal with the pro there, who thought I had potential as a player, and as long as my father paid for one lesson a week, I could hang out at the courts without membership. I was not quite accepted by the members' children who were left there on weekends or after school. They hit tennis balls over the fences onto the golf course and ran around the eugenia hedges throwing ice cubes at each other from Cokes or orange juices, which they picked up at the grill simply by signing their parents' name. I can still see those large white waxed cups with their blue stripes, hear them popping as the kids stomped on them in the parking lot just as someone was beginning to serve on court 1. They seemed uniformly bored and were always killing time, playing tennis or taking a lesson as a last resort. I was serious about the game—my father saw rigorously to that—and practiced for hours against the backboard and helped Byron

DeMott, the pro, pick up balls after lessons and put them in his shopping cart. As I moved a little closer to the fence and looked over into the yards of the rich, as I rubbed elbows with the tennis crowd and their children, I became aware of a difference in what was once called "station."

Fifteen years later in graduate school, I realized that the poet Randall Jarrell had a firm notion of all this, had spent time in my hometown and knew the quaint and slightly elevated rites of the rich sequestered in such beautiful surroundings. He wrote the poem "In Montecito" sometime in the late '50s, and it was printed in his collection *The Lost World.* No longer in the thrall of a child's vision of the world, Jarrell saw clearly into Montecito and enunciated by example what that world, at times, had become:

> People disappear
> Even in Montecito. Greenie Taliaferro,
> In her white maillot, her good figure almost firm,
> Her old pepper-and-salt hair stripped by the hairdresser
> To nothing and dyed platinum—Greenie has left her
>   Bentley.
> They have thrown away her electric toothbrush, someone
>   else slips
> The key into the lock of her safety-deposit box
> At the Crocker-Anglo Bank; her seat at the cricket matches
> Is warmed by buttocks less delectable than hers. . . .
> And Greenie has gone into the Greater Montecito
> That surrounds Montecito like the echo of a scream.

I saw "Greenies" all the time. The convertible Mercedes parked next to the first court with two standard white poodles in the back, their owner playing doubles and serving with a half dozen silver bracelets and bangles clattering along her left arm each time she served or ran out to attend the dogs between sets. A woman very tan with frosted hair and coral lipstick sitting in one of the white wrought iron patio chairs with a cigarette and

something in a tall paper cup, weekends and weekday afternoons, watching, never playing herself. The men coming up
from the grill, looking businesslike in blue blazers and cordovan
loafers, appearing serious and official after an afternoon of cards
and martinis. Almost daily I was kicked off one of the courts
by members in starched tennis whites, people who could barely
move about the court. They had paid for that privilege and I
had not. My resentment then was for their lack of skill and not
so much for their ostentation or their lack of manners. I did
feel something else was up with that world, but I never took it
consciously to heart. So many of us lived then among the rich,
a child was not keenly aware of the contradictions.

While I was in high school, my mother remarried. I no longer
lived in Montecito. The man my mother married came from a
wealthy family who had moved to Santa Barbara long ago from
Chicago. Old money. H.W., the family patriarch, had been in
on the ground floor of such stocks as IBM, Kodak, and Iris
Foods. To me, Frank, my mother's new husband, seemed ex-
travagant but wonderful, driving around in his long white boat
of a Lincoln with a two-way radio, compasses, gyroscopes, and
an oxygen tank in the car. He was a lawyer, a bright and serious
man, but also one of great good humor and generosity. He owned
a huge white house in Montecito more or less across from an
even larger estate owned by his mother. His children were often
away at boarding school, and I can remember him allowing me
to hit wiffle golf balls off practice mats across the wide back
lawn. There was a long hall and entranceway at the front of the
house and a very compelling bust in white marble of a fierce-
looking man set in the alcove as you came in. Years later I would
learn that it was a bust of Robinson Jeffers and that Frank was
a great admirer and collector of his work.

Frank was not one to make much of his money, and it was
clear to me that he really did not like all the formality expected
by his social class. He did not care for the formal dinners with

family, preferred his celery and carrot juice, rare lean meat, and enjoyed being alone with my mother in his house. Yet when there was a dinner and social occasion at the Valley Club, he would go and fit in. When his niece had her coming-out at the debutante ball, he was in attendance. He bought white dress shirts with large collars so he would not feel choked by his tie and circumstances. I was sixteen, and he bought me a tuxedo so I could attend that debutante party; I wore that suit only that one time. I remember one former ambassador and head of an insurance company, Kemper, who came to town and dinner, with his entourage lining both sides of a long table. I had to attend and sat with a stepbrother at a table far removed from where the ambassador's followers were toadying up. Frank seemed the only person there as uncomfortable as I.

After he had moved to Redlands and Palm Springs, Frank took care of the estates of his sisters who continued to live in Montecito. He worked hard on their accounts and on his mother's, so much so that he did not have his own affairs in order when he was stricken with cancer and died suddenly in 1969. What there was was mostly taken by probate lawyers and taxes. I especially remember helping mother go through files and papers, and a host of lawyers coming by, giving curt instructions, and then heading for the golf course. In their dark well-fitting suits, they were every bit a bunch of crows hovering for the good pickings. At least my mother was left with the house in Palm Springs, where she and Frank had moved for the dry climate necessary for her lungs. Frank's house in Montecito had been sold years before.

My aunt and granny by that marriage would invite me over to say hello or to have dinner once in a while when I was home from college. One summer, my aunt informed me that Frank's son, Frank Jr., would be coming into town and that she would like me to meet him for lunch at the Coral Casino, her treat. I had not been there since I was very young and invited to a birthday party, and I did not want to go now, knowing at this point in time that I did not belong. Nevertheless, my aunt had always been kind to me, it was a free lunch, so I went at the appointed time to meet a stepbrother who never seemed to like me much. Arriving a bit early, I walked in and immediately saw my friends from high school Mike Alvarado and Larry Blanco; they were doing the gardening and sweeping up, wearing dark green twills with their first names stitched in red on little white ovals sewn to their shirt pockets. It was only a summer job I guessed, and it was good to see them and joke around a little. I wasn't living in Montecito, nor would I ever again—they never had. Economically, lines were beginning to be drawn more clearly, and I would be on their side of that line. I hoped then that I did not appear to them to be different or superior, but I couldn't help but feel embarrassed, inconsiderate, as my friends went on sweeping and trimming and I walked off to the lunch counter of the upper class.

That was the late '60s, and soon there would be People's Park, courtesy of then Governor Ronald Reagan, and not long after, the burning of the Bank of America in Isla Vista, the small town—an apartment community for the most part—around the University of California, Santa Barbara. People's Park was a city block of dirt and weeds in the middle of downtown Berkeley. The university had decided to use the land for a parking lot, but a number of hippies and some students adopted the place, planted flowers and, as an act of defiance to the state and powers that be, resisted police and work crews who tried to move them off the land. Had Reagan waited two weeks, the school quarter would have been over, and there would have been next to no resistance. However, his points in the popularity poll were down, and by sending in the National Guard to rough up a few unruly student agitators and take over, he grabbed the headlines and his popularity soared. The Bank of America, one of the true symbols of power and commerce in California, a bank heavily invested in the political status quo, was burned one evening in June of

1969, as much in protest against the Vietnam War as against the government in general. The burning set off a week of unrest and curfew in Isla Vista. The later trials documented a good deal of police brutality, and all but one of the eight or nine accused of setting the fire were exonerated. This was the climate of confrontation, and it was as strong among the youth in California as anywhere else in the nation. People were becoming polarized; the upper-middle class had developed, and Santa Barbara and Montecito were places they chose. Upper State Street, which had been all lemon orchards and a dairy when I graduated from high school, was now a shopping mall with a Robinsons and a Sears. Goleta, the little community north of Santa Barbara that had been 90 percent avocado and lemon groves, that was known to us during high school only for its vestigial Bams Auto Court set off on a dirt road by the main street, was developed into housing tracts for the workers at General Dynamics, Raytheon, and other defense industry subsidiaries. The house my parents built in Montecito and sold for a tiny profit at $24,000 was worth $400,000, or more, by the late 1980s.

Reagan became president and bought a ranch in the valley in back of Santa Barbara. Bo Derek and other movie stars became neighbors there, and eventually Michael Jackson also bought a chunk of Santa Ynez and moved in with his exotic animals. During the early and mid-1980s, I taught at the University of California, Santa Barbara, starting at $17,000 a year. Almost all of my paycheck went to rent, and in addition to teaching full-time, I had a gardening job to keep my head above water. On occasion I would drive up the roads in Montecito where, as a boy, I rode my bike and praised the acacias, bay laurels, and eucalyptus. More often, I drove the freeway to school in the morning and frequently saw the California Highway Patrol parked on the overpasses, walkie-talkies in hand, patrolling the footbridges and watching the cars. This happened every time Reagan came into town. Who were they looking for? Who were they trying to keep out?

And it was getting harder and harder to drive around Santa Barbara. Streets designed for a substantially smaller population were always crowded with the ubiquitous BMWs, Porsches, and Mercedes-Benz. Long ago the four-lane street in the heart of town, State Street, had been narrowed to two lanes, the sidewalks tiled and widened to revive and receive business. Running an errand before classes, I wondered why so many people were on the streets and not at work, but then I realized that they were here now because they did not have to work. New money from L.A. had moved in for the foothills and shoreline, the jacaranda-lined streets. By this time the town had at least three times the people it was designed for, and the developers and real estate agents were clamoring for more.

Whatever it was I realized, I had realized it too late. In the early '70s, when a standard stucco California bungalow was going for $3,000 down, I was putting my money into schooling. A few years went by and land prices skyrocketed, and prices would remain, for the foreseeable future, beyond reach. Downtown, real estate speculators would take two full blocks for Paseo Nuevo, three stories of shopping and department stores with a Nordstrom and a Buffums. Car parks would rise as high, and still it would be difficult to squeeze through side streets—De la Guera, Arellaga, Canon Perdido—at noon. After twenty-five years of debate, an underpass instead of an overpass had finally been agreed to. One was built at the bottom of State Street, the main street, and led directly to the beach two blocks away. This eliminated the stoplights—the only ones on all of Highway 101—where State, Chapala, Anacapa, and Garden Streets had crossed the freeway and tied up traffic for years. In the process of all the roadwork, rows of palms, oleanders, and lantana were leveled along with many old businesses, including Reynolds Yater's on Grey Avenue, one of the first surfboard shops in California. The rescue mission was converted into a local brewery and pub, the appliance shops on lower State Street turned into quaint croissant and coffee places, and on the corner of Cota, the last thrift store held out like a remnant from a foreign culture. The crowds, the imported cars, the real estate companies, the movie stars and all the president's men, the Mexican restaurants with giant margueritas and bland food, all had arrived. We were beyond modern times, beyond growth and satellite communities.

Those of us who had grown up here could never go home again, but not because we had gone into the wide world and the scales had fallen from our eyes, not because the boyish, embellished perspective of our town had shrunk. No, just the opposite was true. We could not go home because the place itself had grown exponentially with the mix of money and sun and conspicuous consumption, and thus there was very little left to hold onto in what had once been a small and almost private place. This was no longer an island afloat in a sea of oak and eucalyptus a hundred miles above L.A. This was now the "Greater Montecito" that Jarrell saw all those years ago—the old money, austere, quaint, retreating further behind the discreet demarcations of its trees while giving way to the new—all of it adding up and then subtracting from the sky, pushing everything else out of the way so that it could reside there along the sea and shine as the emblem of our collective loss.

Days of Black & White

Some things you know. I didn't have to be a rocket scientist to know I was going to get beat up my first day at a new school if I arrived wearing short pants.

The parochial school I had been attending took boys only through second grade, so by midyear, I was the only one left—with little to do at recess. I kept trying to talk the one nun I liked into tossing a ball around. No luck. She suggested a new school to my parents. So there I was my first day, in my old uniform—white shirt and blue sweater, brown shoes, and blue short pants. I'd been after my father to buy regular pants for me to wear to school as soon as I heard I was transferring. But my father, as I years later came to understand, first and foremost wanted to spend his money on himself; he insisted that there would be plenty of other boys there wearing shorts. Even at that young age I knew I'd lost the argument when I began to be steamrolled by clichés: he'd "bet me dollars to donuts"; it's "as plain as the nose on your face"; "as clear as black and white"; "there's a right and a wrong. . . ." Wrong.

I didn't have to look around. I knew what was coming. And it did. I'd no sooner been pointed toward the classroom and put down my sack lunch on the steps than I turned around to meet G.G. Colson. Seven years old and he had the hairstyle of a '50s hot rodder—wiry, greased back in wings along each side, a little waterfall effect working to a spit curl in the middle of his forehead. Inches away, he breathed his salami breath in my face and said, "Hey, I wonder what this new kid looks like when he cries?" As I looked over his shoulder to see who he was talking to, he sucker punched me in the stomach, knocking every bit of air out of my breadbasket. The other kid was Tuck Schneider, and he came over and told G.G. to lay off. Though I'd spent the last three months with only girls in my class, I'd been around enough in the neighborhood to know what was what. I'd been in a fight or two. I knew boys at other schools wore long pants and didn't look as ridiculous as I. I'd seen Colson's type. And although the punch was a surprise at the moment, I knew it was coming—if not from G.G., then from someone. Out of air and doubled over, I couldn't fight back. Had I been able to straighten up and face him, I would no doubt have taken a few more shots. This was, after all, someone named "G.G."

That same day, Peter Sozzi, a boy who would become a life-long friend, led a group of girls and boys past me on a strafing run. I was standing alone, obvious in my blue shorts, when eight of them descended from a hill in back of the swings yelling and waving sweaters above their heads helicopter-fashion. They roared by inches away on either side of me. A new kid. In funny clothes.

It was all clear, expected—it was open season on me in the schoolyard. I pointed this out at dinner as I refused to eat my cooked peas and carrots, and next morning I put on my suit trousers to wear to school. I think also that one of the nuns made a phone call to my father, who shelled out for the uniform pants that week.

Tuck clued me in on Colson and others, which nuns to watch out for, and this gave me some confidence. I was as big or bigger than most, and that seemed to be the main factor at that age. A week later, a tough Filipino kid named Rudy Ortegon from Summerland, south of Santa Barbara, started something over a game of four-square. We wrestled in the dirt, and I pinned Rudy's shoulders beneath my knees. That victory, coupled with regular uniform clothes, put an end to my status as target. Rudy, of course, turned out to be a good guy.

The entire school fit into five new classrooms, constructed in a mock adobe style, a stucco version meant to match the church, which was built in the Pueblo tradition of New Mexico. Whole eucalyptus trunks lay across the tops of walls for roof beams, the ends of the beams protruding a foot or two beyond the exterior walls. The building was pink and green, a horrific combination, but no one was paying much attention then. This was the first year in the new classrooms, and the old white board schoolhouse stood empty in the yard, a high eugenia hedge around it, the new building with the classrooms on one side and a large field on the other. Below it were a blacktopped volleyball court, tetherball poles, and a basketball court with two hoops, then the rows of lunch tables beneath trellises of trumpet vines. Below that, the rectory backed up to the church and parking lot. Tuck showed me through the old schoolhouse, pointed out the loquat tree at the top of the field next to a gnarled acacia. One prize was to arrive early to school in the late spring and pull a ripe loquat off the tree, eat it, and spit out the large smooth brown seeds before you were caught. It was sweet and tasted of sun, and there were never many to go around. The eugenia hedge produced berries which, when ripe, were ammunition for after-school attacks; a clear hit with one of those left an indelible purple blot on a uniform shirt and assured trouble for the wearer at home. But you had to be careful on both counts as the nuns were ferocious about rules and "deportment"—an actual category on the report card.

We lived mainly for before and after school, when we played

work-ups or other games. In between, we followed the glacial progress of the hour and minute hands until we were released for lunch or recess. We arrived early and left late and loved to stay after for the older boys' or girls' games—baseball, football, and volleyball—against other schools. We felt part of things, contributing with our yelling. We sat on one side in our blue pants and blue-grey checked shirts that matched the girls' skirts, while the other school sat across from us in their grey corduroys and green checked or white uniform shirts. It was easy to know what side to be on and where you belonged, which call was fair and which was not. The seventh- and eighth-grade girls' volley-ball game was as important as a football game, and the whole yard on game day was electric as groups of us watched the sta-tion wagons pull into the yard, swing around, and doors and tailgates open. Students from Dolores, San Roque, or Guada-lupe poured out—a fierce, cold look of concentration in their eyes as they stared right past us and took the field to warm up, encouraging each other with "Way to go" and "We'll kill these chickens." Other cars arrived with referees in striped shirts, parents and nuns from the other schools looking as if they were on their way to a Vatican Council. Only four catholic schools in the Santa Barbara area and rivalries were intense. Our team, having warmed up, stood at one end of the field, arms folded across their chests, eyeing the visitors' practice with contempt. I can still see our team jerseys, white sweatshirts with three-quarter sleeves and once blue numbers on the back gone grey. Boys all wanted to wear one of those, but by the time we could, six years later, they'd disintegrated from washings and bleach. When it was our time, we played in white T-shirts, happy, con-vinced of the importance of a game, of us versus them, there in the isolation and carelessness of the '50s.

Once a month we had hot lunches for fifty cents; occasionally it was hamburgers, but too often it was a drab spaghetti, which a few of the fifth-grade girls named "worms and ground hus-bands." Each First Friday of the month we were compelled to fast before taking communion at mass, which meant no breakfast. After church, a double line for cocoa and glazed donuts snaked in and out of the auditorium. A quarter bought one of each, and another dime a second donut. After that, it was no wonder we were uncontrollable in the classrooms for the next few hours, and it wasn't sanctifying grace we were charged with—it was plain sugar-loading, American style. I can still see Jimmy Darcey eating four or five donuts every First Friday and turning his eyelids inside out, his shirt backwards, and walking up the classroom aisles stiffly like Frankenstein.

Especially in the younger grades, we were frequently dismissed from class and marched to church to pray at funerals for someone no one knew, but who must have been a big contributor to the church for all of us to be in there instead of at our desks. We were also let out of class to practice for the Christmas play—Dickens, Bible stories; half the school was in costume at one time or another. At the end of my first half year, the nuns organized a minstrel show for the annual spring performance. Two of the most popular boys from the eighth grade told jokes and sang some songs in what I'd later learn was vaudeville style. The old schoolhouse was converted to a theater—folding chairs were arranged across the lawn, and the old porch became a stage. It was a beautiful evening—floor lights and floodlights, stars like little pats of butter spread across the foothill sky. I had memorized all the lines that Bernard Lambert and Troy Janzen would deliver and knew even when to pause for laughs. Summer's long beach afternoons awaited, then third grade and cursive writing—exotic, suspenseful, and far away.

The eighth grade hovered over the distant horizon, and since it was going to take forever to get there, we never worried about when or how we'd arrive. Parents were parents; older sisters and brothers were already older; when they graduated and went on to high school, the order of things did not really change. We were fixed in place and our choices were simple—we stayed within the lines, our days so prescribed that everything felt almost always present tense. Schoolwork rolled along in patterns—Palmer Method practice in penmanship and the sour smell of the ink, weekly spelling tests, SRA reading kits, countries colored in on our dittoed geography maps, memorizing the major exports and imports of Brazil and Venezuela, long division and fractions, diagramming sentences, choosing the correct suffix or prefix, the correct helping verbs in our twenty sentences of English homework.

And to all of this was added a mild backdrop of terror, integrated as religion was into our daily routine. Once, at my desk near the window, in fourth or fifth grade, my attention was drawn from our reading to the cloudburst pouring down on the asphalt, so thick and heavy for a while that I couldn't see across the schoolyard. Phil Witucki, sitting next to me, always had a serious expression, even when he was joking. As he looked at me and said, "It must be the end of the world, by flood again," a biblical terror and anxiety grabbed me for a few seconds, steeped as we were in Bible history and the vengeful hand of God. After a minute or two the downpour let up; I then remembered the agreement was that the world would not end by water next time, and relaxed. Also, there were the "pop quizzes" on our faith when, once every month or so, the pastor or assistant pastor would drop in during religion class and pick randomly from the Baltimore Catechism and from theology in general and call on individuals to stand and recite. The blue book had all the answers, and we were to know by rote the responses that reduced and summarized the tenets of the faith. Name the Spiritual and Corporal Works of Mercy. Why did God Make You? What one sin cannot be forgiven? And some unlucky student would be called on to stand and stammer out the compound sentences about God, while the rest of us opened our books beneath our desks and tried to find the right page and answers. The priest left the room giving us all a blessing for which we knelt in the aisles, this just after a final reminder about the temperature, dark discomforts, and lurking proximity of Hell, as if it were a place close by that you could get to by the smallest mistake, like missing your stop on the train headed out of L. A.

Schoolwork, recess, and sports aside, it seemed we were always being herded into church—for funerals, First Fridays, and Feast Days, which seemed to occur every other weekend. The lines of children headed out of the building, class by class, coiling around the yard and down the flagstone steps by agave plants on the side of the church. There, spread out along the path, we'd rehearse one hyperbolic hymn after another before marching up the center aisle. A procession it was called, led by flower girls throwing invisible rose petals during our practices—youngest grades parading in front, the oldest at the rear. The Epiphany, Transfiguration, Feast of the Ascension, Immaculate Conception, Assumption, all of the Christmas programs, and the redundancy of Lent. Every Friday during the forty days, Stations of the Cross. The whole school crammed into pews repeating the robotlike moves—stand, genuflect, kneel, sit, kneel, stand. All the lights out, a tomblike atmosphere. The priest down the center with altar boys on either side carrying candles and incense, and on the aisle against the wall three other altar boys with a metal crucifix and candles—all in black cassocks and white surplices. Fourteen stops, with the same prayers, the same thick nerve-numbing incense and old story. At six years old, from repetition alone I was able to articulate "ignominious." Inevitably, the smaller children at the front of the church succumbed to the waves of incense, especially if there was a High Mass during which the censer was loaded a second and third time. Sitting in the middle of the church in fifth or sixth grade, I'd watch a snaky length of incense waft from the altar toward the second and third graders in the front pews. Then—particularly if it was early in the morning and some had not had breakfast—it was only a matter of minutes until two or three passed out, fainted dead away like tiny saints in a trance, their heads often sounding against the long wooden pews with little reverberations. Kneeling, woozy, no one dreamt of excusing him- or herself for some fresh air. We were strictly watched by nuns in black and white pirate-flag habits positioned behind us every ten pews. The only way out before the end of the service was by fainting.

And each month, confession. One class at a time marched down in silence for the procedure. The priest in the center box, with a stall on either side, where each of us would take a turn kneeling. The line along the walls stopping a discreet ten yards away from the stalls so none could overhear the sins of his or her classmates. Until your row stood in line, you had twenty or thirty minutes to "examine your conscience." You spent most of the time looking for something to confess—which venial sins to trot out once again. Bored and in dim light, we traced the red, ochre, and aqua colored Indian designs along the walls; we counted the tin candles and mirrors fixed at higher intervals, the little stabs of light there angled from the few high windows. Most of us were in and out in a minute and returned to kneel and say our two Our Fathers and three Hail Marys. Everyone watched to see who was held up in the confessional. There would be whispers especially if Terry Mills, the girl in our class who had that sultry Gina Lollobrigida look in her brown eyes, spent any time at all in the confessional. She was not too secretly going steady with an eighth-grade boy. Anyone in there longer than usual would come back and kneel for only a minute to give the impression that he or she was not in fact the Mary Magdalene or Herod of sixth grade. To save face—there being, somehow, no rule for how immediately penance must be said— a long penance could be said at a later time.

We spent so much time in church, it's a wonder we learned anything else. What we did learn was language, music, the sound and rhythms of Latin. We put in our time memorizing litanies, responses in Latin, the long names and praises of saints during whichever holy day. This all in addition to the Kyrie, Tantum Ergo, Pange Lingua, and the glorified procession songs we sang in English. We were a school of organized praisers if ever there was one.

For no reason I recall, it seemed important in fifth grade to be in the boys' choir. Perhaps it was that Sister Julie led the choir and was one of the only nice teachers in the school, perhaps because we were excused from math? Before one practice, Sister Julie gave a lecture to the group to say that none of us *had* to be in the choir, that if, examining our consciences, we found that we were not really committed to singing, then it was no disgrace to quit. It was not hard to figure out what she was getting at. Some of us sang consistently off-key. Although I felt a little guilty, I knew I was not a grievous offender. I snuck a look around, and as no one else was making a move to leave, I didn't either. Besides, I only had problems with the high notes, whereas others were flat and had to be carried or drowned out. I could at least keep to the tune. So I doubled my concentration to perfectly memorize the Latin lyrics so that on the high notes I could effectively mouth the phrases. The next practice, the tin-eared did not return, and overall we were passable. Whereas we wouldn't receive a call from Ed Sullivan when the Vienna Boys Choir canceled from his Christmas show, we did sound a bit better, there close as we were to the ceiling with the accompanying reverberation of the eucalyptus beams.

We were banking sanctifying grace, naming pagan babies, contributing to the wheel of prayer, praise, and faith around the world. Nothing was called into question. Although we were regularly told a series of preposterous tales about mystical apparitions—rose petals falling from the sky, St. Theresa of Avila living only on air, levitation by monks in Peru, and defilers of the sanctuary struck dead or burnt on the spot—the real difficulties of the world at large were held off beyond our attention and imaginations. For all we knew, we routinely experienced the true uses of the mind.

At home one evening in the fall of 1957, I did pick up some

inkling about where we as a nation stood in the world. The black-and-white picture on our large Sylvania TV was interrupted by a snowy haze and alternating beeps. My father, who worked in broadcasting, knew what this meant: a bulletin was coming. It announced that Russia had just launched a satellite called the Sputnik. The artist's rendition had it looking like a baseball stuck with soda straws. Despite its silly appearance, my father worried out loud about it, said he knew Russia was going to beat us to it. He was clearly shaken and concerned. I was too young to appreciate the political and military connotations he was reading into the Sputnik, but I picked up on the notion that the Russians were the guys on the other side of the field. We were not long past the McCarthy era, the House Un-American Activities Committee was still meeting, and all the parents seemed to "Like Ike." The Catholic Church had an "Index," a list of forbidden books, and there was "The Legion of Decency" for movies, each listing which ones we were not permitted to read or see—and eternal fires awaited those who did not observe these prohibitions. There were no grey areas, nothing to confuse.

We arrived, finally and incredibly, in eighth grade in the fall of 1960, and later that school year Alan B. Shepard was shot 116 miles in space in a suborbital flight. In no time, there wasn't one of us who couldn't identify the black thimblelike, barely man-sized, Mercury space capsule. The United States was in the "Space Race," and we were told to be glad for it. President Kennedy was making speeches about a man on the moon. Most people then appeared to support Kennedy, although there had been a good deal of division among families in the school/parish, a fact that was backed up by the results of the "elections" each classroom held. Just before the real election, the nun would count votes for each candidate for president and total them up on the board in those little stick-rows of five. Of course, each student voted exactly as his or her parents did. I remember in the Eisenhower/Stevenson election there'd not been enough votes in my class for Stevenson to cross the single ones and make five. This was a Republican area, and the '50s was a Republican era. But in 1960 there was a wide defection to the Democrats, especially with Kennedy being a Catholic. The vote in class split between Nixon and Kennedy—due to Liberal/Communist dupes, my father kept repeating. I remember the pastor visiting each classroom while the election was in swing and admonishing those who had been holding up Kennedy stickers and yelling their support at passing motorists from the school driveway after classes. Perhaps he wanted to keep politics away from the church, to appear objective—perhaps he supported Nixon? We never knew.

We were struggling with New Math, set theory algebra. Everything was changing. The pear-yellow light of spring streamed in the transoms, not like revelation, but radiant with indolence. VDP, as we called Principal Sister Vincent de Paul, called on us for answers from our math homework. Almost to a person, we were a mafia of math criminals. Sitting there, as if before a Senate subcommittee, we went down the rows one by one and instead of "I refuse to answer on the grounds that I may incriminate myself," we replied, "I didn't get it," which had the same effect. We didn't get it and didn't care. It was new, difficult, different, and our hormones just wouldn't sit still for it. Graduation was coming, and suddenly we were being pushed out of our lives, out of the last unaccountable outpost of youth, which was the eighth grade. We knew we'd go on to high school, but emotionally we didn't know up from down. We were children of the '50s, but the '50s and childhood were fading fast. We were still debating the virtues of Brylcreem versus ButchWax or Wildroot Cream Oil for slicking back our hair, how close we could come to the Elvis ducktail or the James Dean jelly roll before the nun threw us out of class. And now we had to learn to dance.

We were taken out of study hall into the auditorium, brought in on weekends and coaxed by parents volunteering to teach us the fox-trot, the waltz, and the cha-cha-cha, but we wanted to dance fast. We were listening to rock 'n' roll radio, Duane Eddy and his twangy guitar instrumentals, Dion and the Belmonts, doo-wop; we raved for the doubled-up rhythm of "Barbara Ann." We stomped along in mild rebellion, happy at least to be socializing with the girls, holding them, if only at arm's length while they wore gloves. We had our orders. Boys appeared in blue business or olive-green poplin suits from J.C. Penney, wearing our fathers' discarded ties. Girls teetered in heels, in stiff armored dresses of star yellow, minty blue, and green. They wore nylons; we sported constellations of razor nicks. Our heads were swimming. We were looking for an unchaperoned moment to convince a girl to take a walk behind the classroom buildings. Parties became important, though they seemed overorganized. We watched the known couples to see if they could be detected inching beyond prescribed physical boundaries—in a dark corner of a long-suffering parent's recreation room, someone's head on someone's shoulder as Paul Anka entreated on his hit single. Now we were encouraged to socialize, boys and girls together. Even the nuns knew that in the real world of high school, dances lasted until midnight and kids drove around in their own cars.

We developed a camaraderie from all the pressure and orders, and from just the general revolution built into the genetic code of adolescence. We bought cameras, Kodak Star Mites, that took little black-and-white photos, and all that last spring we snapped pictures of each other at pool or dance parties, at the school carnival and at games. The world looked like the one we'd always known—cars with huge tail fins, baseball, rules and ritual, county fairs sponsored by the Junior Chamber of Commerce. But another world was out there now. Questions of politics, social and moral questions, were coming from Selma, Birmingham, Little Rock, filtering through just enough to awaken us to questions we were almost ready to ask. A war that would divide many friends then lining up to march down the aisle between folding chairs was only four years away. Like sleepwalkers, we took our practiced steps. Following the ceremony and speeches by the priest and VDP, the light grew dim behind us as we walked down the aisle and stepped into the dark outside, into the flashbulb of a parent or friend.

We looked stunned in those photos. We were. We stood around in groups, adjusting ties or petticoats, in our haircuts and bouffant hairdos, with no real sense of what was ahead. There was a bowl of Hawaiian Punch and little squares of cake; there was Linda Underwood in her white satin dress with the coral corsage at her waist, all the available light surrounding her. The schoolyard was dark, but that night I filled in what had vanished or changed over the years. The eugenia hedge, the volleyball court, the wild banks of grass, the loquat tree now gone from the top of the field, the old white schoolhouse—all of it was streaking by the mind's space capsule as it burned through the night to land in the dark by the new L-wing of classrooms, the dirt yard and its bright dust lifting to the level of the pepper trees somewhere in the past.

Home that night, unable to sleep, I looked out the window to a full moon receding in the sky like that dot of light holding for ten or fifteen seconds after you turned off the TV. I thought back seven years to second grade, that last week of spring and the minstrel show—how we were kept in the back of the old schoolhouse as jokes were delivered out front to our parents, how the waves of laughter rose and fell and were washed away under the serene night sky. In overalls and red kerchiefs we waited for the ending line of dialogue. We stood backstage silently, without thinking—waiting in blackface with white gloves on our hands, to be called out dancing for the final number.

Double Feature

My earliest memory of being left at the movies all afternoon was in fourth grade for *20,000 Leagues under the Sea*. There was a free matinee at the Arlington that Saturday, largely to promote technology and the nuclear future, because the U.S. Navy had just christened the *Nautilus*, its first atomic-powered submarine.

The future was on us, and though we all belonged to that group later known as baby boomers and soon would have television sets in our homes, movies were still a big part of life. We would grow up with TV, but there weren't that many programs to watch, and most of us had limited viewing time. Moreover, a double feature matinee was the small salvation of working parents, giving them their only chance to spend an afternoon alone together. Santa Barbara was a small and drowsy city then, but it kept three theaters running on the same main street through the '50s and well into the '60s—the State, the Granada, and the Fox Arlington, all with wide rainbows of neon humming and pushing the dark back for blocks around. One drive-in a few miles out of town by the airport did a roaring family trade charging by the carload, and profited from teenagers looking for a relatively private place to go on a date. Most everyone's parents still went weekly to see a film, a holdover from their younger years when going to two or three movies a week was not unusual. *Life* magazine flourished with movie stars on the cover, and *Photoplay* carried all the news about Tinseltown. We were always sneaking a look at the glamorous in glamorous poses on the news racks as we walked by. Except when we were sent to special showings of Disney hits like *Old Yeller* or the Davy Crockett films, we were rounded up a little before noon and hauled downtown. We were routinely dropped off on the corner of Micheltorena and State Streets for whatever double feature was playing at the Arlington. There, Saturdays were always given to children's films, and though that meant an opening fifteen minutes of cartoons, it also often meant John Wayne winning World War II again, Audie Murphy leading a charge at Iwo Jima and only occasionally in the saddle for some technicolor western. It meant *Battle Cry* with Van Heflin and Aldo Ray, and even Gregory Peck in *Pork Chop Hill* more often than it meant Danny Kaye in *The Court Jester.* There was little choice.

Yet despite the fact that the films were not all that interesting, I looked forward to Saturdays. Dropped off, I'd wait for the other station wagons to pull up and for Fowler, Cooney, or Witucki to jump out. We were always early enough to stroll around the streets awhile, to be a few minutes on our own in all the world we knew, seaside among the white stucco and red tile roofs of our Mediterranean town, alive in our little principality of blue air and sun. We'd check out the import shop from Mexico, the guitars in Bennett's Music Store, or lean against a wall watching freshly waxed Chryslers and Buicks pull up and stylish women saunter in and out of I. Magnin and Lou Rose with coral and ivory shopping bags. We'd wait until the last minute to buy our ticket at the booth, walk up the long tiled corridor that resembled, with its fountain and sprouting plants, a garden from the Alhambra, and finally go in. We enjoyed just hanging out in front, inspecting the sidewalks for cracks and the starry mica shining up at us. We each had a dollar, and the ticket was seventy-five cents, which left only enough for Jujyfruits or Junior Mints, perhaps a popcorn without butter. Hitting the candy counter, being on your own with friends, was much more important than whatever films we would endure for the next four hours.

But it was not long before we worked out an alternate plan. My younger friend Archie Korngiball and I were the first to figure this out; we lived next to each other and were often dropped off together for the matinee. Further down State Street, west on Canon Perdido, was another theater, the California. On very rare occasions they had a film for kids, but generally they showed first-run dramas followed up with second-run B movies. The neon out front was not as ornate or profuse as that of the other theaters, and there were no loge seats to try and sneak into. The advantage was that if you were under twelve, you could get in for fifteen cents, twelve or over, fifty cents. Archie and I gave this a try one day when we were left off earlier than usual uptown at the Arlington. We walked down to the California, verified the fifteen-cent admission, and walked back to Woolworths on Anapamu Street to load up with candy before the movies started.

We didn't know cinema, but we knew candy. Even with fifty cents to spare, you could run out of funds for the concession stand before the second feature began. Going to Woolworths beforehand, we could buy candy by weight, almost a pound of M&Ms, and still have change left for admission and popcorn. Woolworth's had a row of large glass cases with a half yard of candy in each. The clerk slipped a chrome scoop into the M&Ms, candy corn, or chicken sticks, and then set it on a scale, weighed it, let a few slide back into the case to make the weight exact, and then tipped the scoop into a white paper bag, a bag too big to fit comfortably into our jacket pockets. We carried our bags almost like lunch sacks but tried not to be too conspicuous. I passed on the procedure to my other friends, and as soon as we were dropped off by the Arlington and the station wagons were heading back into Montecito, we began walking toward Woolworths and the California Theater. In a time when someone with a dollar in change felt free, we'd flip fifty-cent pieces and strut along the sidewalk. For a half year or so, most of us were under twelve, and even those who had to pay fifty cents came out ahead on the sugar-loading.

At the California there were no cartoons, although a few years earlier they had run matinees on Wednesdays in the summer with two cartoons and a drawing during intermission for fishing poles or skin diving masks and flippers. We couldn't tell film noir from adult romance, but that freight of sugar so thoroughly embalmed our veins that we were largely oblivious to whatever it was that Liz Taylor and Montgomery Clift were up to. We didn't even mind when the second feature with Robert Mitchum and Yvonne DeCarlo was all in black and white. We knew there was going to be the requisite number of burning silver profiles when someone was kissed—Joan Fontaine and Zachary Scott supported by Joan Leslie and Mel Ferrer in *Born to Be Bad*. We guessed that what we saw went on somewhere in the world, though we couldn't say exactly why or how. None of our parents drank martinis or flew to Mexico or Singapore. There was good and evil, and somewhere in the middle of both there was romance, but somehow it didn't quite add up. As often as not, the second feature was an RKO film. Mostly, I remember the predictable letdown when that RKO Broadcasting tower began to buzz out its signature radio waves—we knew we were likely in for another war film or black-and-white romance. But with our cargo of various confections we made no complaints. We sat quietly and watched our watches to know when to leave and walk back uptown so we were standing in front of the Arlington as our rides appeared.

As we became older, the California was still a good deal, fifty cents versus seventy-five cents, and some of the newer science fiction features played there. *The Blob* and *The Fly* were two that Tuck Schneider and Zale Coffman talked about all year. But my father would not let me see such films, fearing they would terrorize my impressionable mind, disorder my imagination, and skew my vision of the world. My father also forbade me to watch *Superman* on TV after he heard about a boy who tied a bath towel over his shoulders and tried to fly out an upstairs window. He never trusted my judgment, it seemed, and figured I'd somehow, with more stars in my head than sense, forget my part in gravity.

As we moved from seventh to eighth grade, we were allowed more say as to which movies we would see. While I was still not able to see most of the science fiction and horror films, I clearly remember Rick Slattery and I going one day to the State Theater to see *On the Beach* with Gregory Peck, Ava Gardner, Anthony Perkins, and Fred Astaire. This too was in black and white and all the more real for that. The scenario presented was the aftermath of a nuclear war and a submarine surfacing to find that it had missed the conflagration. It heads to Australia, the only place, it seems, where a population has survived, but the people there are just waiting for the winds to bring the radiation that will kill them all—in a matter of a few weeks. This filled me with terror, more so than any B movie about *The Thing* or *The Mummy* ever could. Like many my age, I grew up with a nuclear neurosis, like a low-grade infection I could never be rid of.

As it began to show more weekend movies for our age group —historical adventures, second-run westerns—we went more often to the California. Yet the adult drama was still the main offering there, for both features. Six or eight of us would meet up and sit in the cavelike glow of 1960 still knowing next to nothing about our lives despite our first year of social studies class and the newsreel shown at the start. We had scant idea of what was playing out before us but watched whatever was shown, happy to squeak our high-top PF Flyers over the sticky floor, to be there together on our own, and, on those weekends when there was a kids' show, happier to flatten our ten-cent cardboard popcorn boxes and sail them into the blizzard of boxes that rained down through the air the minute the lights were dimmed for the first presentation.

The last film we saw at the California Theater was in 1961, another Saturday matinee, the whole crew of us dropped off from various cars for an "epic adventure"—*Alexander the Great,* —starring Richard Burton. Some of it we knew from ancient history class—his father Philip of Macedonia, his tutoring by Aristotle, his conquering of Persia and Darius Mede. But we had come for the bloody technicolor battles, the saw-toothed blades protruding from the wheels of the Persian chariots, Alexander's phalanxes as they shifted formation so that the chariots could pass between their ranks and be speared from behind. We didn't know Alexander died at thirty-three. It never occurred to us that that was dying young. Everything was far away. We didn't know adjustments would have to be made, that change would arrive quickly and as sharply as the light that stunned us when we left the theater. After four and a half hours, we walked out into a flat white sun slipping down over the Mesa. Momentarily we were blinded, walking up the ramp alongside the theater, our hands shielding our eyes from all the bright and familiar images, sharp as tinfoil, which were soon to disappear.

A little while, and the theater would be torn down and re-placed by a drive-through bank. One day in high school when I heard that the theater's doors had closed for good, my memories of the California did not turn back to the neon loops and colon-nades of the marquee fizzing and popping in the dusk, to war films, or even to *Alexander the Great* and that battle to extend the reaches of the civilized world that had raged all through an afternoon. I recalled instead the face of Kim Novak, blond and tragic in a love scene, as Kirk Douglas walked out on her a year or so before, and there and then thought I understood the complete depth and extent of loss, coming soon, out of the dark.

Work-Ups

Baseball and the '50s

By the time I was two years old, that is, as soon as I could tell a baseball from a beach ball, my father had trained me in the proper batting stance and often would show me off to adults who came over to visit in the evenings. I have a clear memory of standing in the living room in pajamas—white ones with red and blue baseballs and bats printed all over them, the kind with feet built in—and stiffly assuming the batting stance before heading off to bed. This was 1950, and by then the country, and baseball, had moved into modern times—stadiums in the major cities of the East, kids playing sandlot or city league, grammar school, high school, and college. Actually going to a major league game was a real event, and it seemed almost everyone listened on the radio, shared a lineup of heroes and a jargon.

For decades baseball was big news spring and summer, and the '50s, to a great extent, were a carryover of the '40s. My social studies textbook still had scenes of men in hats and baggy coats and trousers, women in suits with squared shoulders and wide lapels; the "metropolis" was crawling with Hudsons, Nash Ramblers, and checkered cabs. In the auditorium for a geography film, the same four-prop "modern" plane landed each year on a strip of dust in South America. We'd seen *The Babe Ruth Story,* starring William Bendix. Joe Dimaggio was married to Marilyn Monroe. It was traditional, even reasonable, that a pennant race was a major topic of discussion every fall. There was the big black-and-white cover of *Life* magazine with a shot from a late inning of the Series. To us, as to many, not much was more important than baseball. Not bikes or grades, not a dime for the soda fountain after school. Baseball was social tonic, a counterpoint of common joy set against routine. It was one thing most everyone understood together.

Eighth grade began the '60s, and like a batter looking for the off-speed pitch and getting the Heater, we just weren't ready for what was coming. TVs were in most every living room, and the whole technological and commercial space-wired juggernaut was gearing up just over the horizon, yet it was not obvious to us then. Standing in the rush of 1960–61, fresh from the '50s, the bat was still on our shoulders. Our mind-set was a content and dreamy one. Everyone liked Ike, but no one really paid attention to his parting speech about a military industrial complex. We didn't for a moment think we'd be some of the last kids riding bikes to school or around town with baseball mitts always threaded over our handlebars. We had no idea that many of our generation would become "long-haired hippie-radicals" marching in the streets of Berkeley and Chicago, opposing the government and another war before the decade was over. We couldn't see that we were slipping calmly over the edge of a world with our inherited small-town values of camaraderie and plain dealing, values that seemed a part of baseball whether it was played in Ebbets Field in Brooklyn or a schoolyard in Santa Barbara.

Although Los Angeles was only two hours away on the three-lane Pacific Coast Highway, we were pretty much off the map. The tourist industry was almost nonexistent; the saying we knew even as kids was, "Santa Barbara—for the newly wed and nearly dead!" Few movie stars lived in Montecito then, and all the president's men were twenty years away. Rock stars were far off too. Elvis, or from the camera angle, half of him, had been on the Ed Sullivan Show, and I remember that in 1959 or 1960 Tuck Schneider's older brother Joe had been suspended from Santa Barbara High School for combing his hair in a "ducktail." That was as close as we got to any rock 'n' roll fallout in those years. A couple minor leaguers assigned to the Dodgers' Single A farm club that played at Laguna Park were still years away from the big leagues. And baseball thrived. We had semipro, little league, pony league, CYO school league, the neighborhood games, and when not enough kids could be rounded up for teams or work-ups, a few of us would play hit-the-bat, three-flys-up, or over-the-line. Baseball was a portable ritual, where a hit or home run allowed you to momentarily run the bases like any one of the known pantheon of major leaguers—and almost everyone could play.

The World Series was played every September, so fall found us arriving at school with mitts hanging from our handlebars and bats balanced on top, found us playing catch, or "burn-out," before class, then coming in and hanging our gloves up on the coat hooks in the back of the room. Ball gloves could contribute to your status. Some had them and some did not. Many had only hand-me-downs, gloves from older brothers or sisters. It was always an event when someone got a new glove—it happened rarely enough that the new owner was the center of attention for a week or two at least. We did not know many brand names then, but it meant a little to have a Wilson or a Rawlings. I had an inexpensive second baseman's mitt. Having, when I was seven, lost my father's "professional" fielder's glove—the one preserved emblem of his youth—I had to make do with a glove that was too small for a number of years. But at the beginning of seventh grade, I embarked on a campaign of complaint so relentless that after a month or so my father, much to my surprise, gave in. I was sure my ability to perform was hampered by the old glove—pocket too small, no good in the outfield. I was going to be a starter on the school team, and the other starters all had decent gloves. I wanted to be admired, wanted to make a move up in that society, though at the time I thought my reasoning was only practical.

One evening then, after work, my father presented me with a new fielder's glove—a Wilson Bob Feller model—and the requisite lecture about responsibility. He'd picked it up at Otts, our town's only department store, for about thirteen dollars on sale, a fair sum of money in those days, but with the best gloves selling for twenty-five or thirty, it was a bargain, and he knew it. It was large, perfectly shaped, and made of supple yellow leather. The next day I took my week's allowance and went to Jedlicas, the western supply store, and bought a piece of rawhide to restring the top of the fingers, pulling them tighter together with the thicker, stronger string. I rubbed Neetsfoot Oil into it and left it with the fingers tied around a softball overnight for a week to form a pocket large and permanent, soft and responsive, one that would close like a Venus's-flytrap over any ball it touched. It was easily the best glove I ever owned, the best I ever saw.

But this was still 1960 and we trusted people. One day toward the end of eighth grade, heading home with my mind on Linda Underwood or Virginia Cortez, I let a friend's younger brother borrow the glove. A work-ups game was still going on, and he promised to return it to the classroom and hang it on a hook in the back of the room. He didn't. Timmy Armour—I still remember his name—just tossed it on the walkway next to the classroom, where we often threw our lunches or sweaters. He honestly expected it to be there the next day. It wasn't and was never seen again. My father was not about to buy me another one. I'd given my old mitt to my friend Sozzi, a kid who had four older sisters and had never had a glove of his own. There was no way to ask for it back.

I would get by borrowing. We still left our gloves in the field just behind our positions when we came to bat, so if we were playing teams, it was easy to come up with a glove. Everyone, however, wanted to use Harry Fowler's glove. It was the biggest glove anyone had ever seen, bigger than any I've seen since. Harry's father was a contractor doing well and obviously decided to get his son the biggest ticket item on the rack. It was a Nakoma, and its fingers were so long and stiff that the mitt really didn't have a pocket like most but operated on the hinge principle, one half collapsing toward the other over anything in range. It was not nearly as quick or as sure as the wonderful glove I had lost, but it was *the* item on the field. Everyone wanted to use "the vacuum cleaner." Harry knew its worth, its prestige; at the same time, he was generous and allowed lots of kids to use it. With few things to be jealous about in those days, ball gloves could be a point of contention, but playing work-ups, switching positions often and borrowing gear, there were no real problems. The game was the thing—just running the bases, taking your chances on a steal, accelerating steadily around third and sliding into home, never caring if you ripped the knees out of your uniform corduroy pants.

Baseball—softball as we played it in the Catholic school league—was not just for the boys. In spring, the boys fielded a team to play the other schools in the league, and the girls had a team playing on the same schedule, and often we traveled across town in station wagons together. Although there were two or three guys known for hitting homers, I always remember Peggy Dormier, a tall, dark, sinewy girl who could hit the ball as far as anyone. Playing center field on the lower diamond while the girls practiced on the upper, I turned from my position when I heard that blunt reverberation of the bat when a softball was really being tagged, and would look up to see one sailing high against the blue, off the grass onto the asphalt where the smaller kids were playing four-square. I'd see Peggy then slowing down as she rounded second base, realizing it had cleared everything. She was quiet and modest, mostly because her popularity on the ball field did not carry over to the classroom or cliques. She was poor, and though we all wore uniforms, hers showed wear while the girls who were better off, more blond or more popular, wore blouses starched and ironed, white as March clouds. We knew baseball, but not much else. Later in the '60s, most of us would become aware of the fact that because of class, money, or race alone, and despite all religious protestations to the contrary, participation in and access to our society and its rewards had been, and would be, denied to many.

But baseball was an equalizer of sorts. Some girls, like Peggy, were great hitters, some could play the infield well, and I recall Maggie Tappinier being one of the best pitchers, boy or girl. Playing work-ups eliminated any favoritism of position or batting order; it eliminated being chosen for one side or the other. In work-ups boys and girls raced together out of the classroom after school and tagged up on home plate; the first three or four were batters, and the rest called out the positions they wanted in order of their arrival. When a batter grounded out or was tagged out, he or she went to right field, and everyone else moved up one position: the catcher becoming the fourth batter, the pitcher moving to catcher, first base to pitcher, and so on. The only exception was when someone caught a fly ball—he or she took the batter's place and the batter took that person's position in the field. So even if you were one of several stuck in the outfield, you had a chance of getting your "ups" before the bell rang to go in or the last bus pulled out of the yard. Everyone was in it together.

The lower grades fairly idolized seventh and eighth graders who were the star athletes on the team. At the beginning of the year you could approach them, actually talk to these heroes by asking what position they were "going out for." There was no coach until spring and no official tryout process. Each player just declared his intention and somehow a lineup evolved. Positions on the team were a main topic of conversation; it was almost like a political caucus. Myths developed too, and in the insular world of our small parochial school, they perpetuated themselves; repeating stories was our way to prove that we knew what was happening. And things happened that, to us, seemed wonderful, grand. One of my first memories of being a second grader at Mt. Carmel school was a baseball game across town in old Pershing Park. A nun took me and a couple of other kids. Sitting there on weathered wood-slat bleachers, the green paint pealing off in the sun, I wasn't quite sure what was going on. I do remember that the eighth graders playing in the game seemed huge, about the size, in present-day comparison, of starting forwards in the NBA. I think we were behind until one of the Sosa brothers hit a line drive into left center, which must have won the game, because everyone jumped up off their splintery seats and went happily out to the cars. Years later, kids still talked about the Sosas pulling it out in the late innings, and we felt good that we all knew the same tales, had seen or said we had seen that game.

It was said that Tote Borgatello, the pitcher for our school team, could make the ball drop. Now this was a thirteen-inch softball, underhand pitching, and the pitcher's rubber could not have been more than thirty or thirty-five feet from the plate, so the laws of physics did not provide much room for a ball to break sharply in any direction. Nevertheless, watching a game, seeing an opposing batter whiff at a third strike, we all concurred that Tote was putting something on the pitch, making it dip somehow at the last instant. Tote had dark hair and eyes, and when asked how he managed the trick pitch, he would just smile and say nothing, his dark eyes sparkling. Perhaps all pitchers have that in common, school league or majors? I still remember the day after one of the games between the fifth and sixth grade when Tote volunteered that a backhand stop he'd seen me make at shortstop was pretty good and I should think about going out for the team next year. I was beaming for days. That was a signal that I'd almost made it, and it meant everything in the limited context of school, sports, and those few years.

We played baseball almost all year long out there alongside the acacias, eucalyptus, and pines that bordered the blue sky and the edges of our field. The grass grew steadily and green, and we were playing work-ups before and after school, jumping the fence into the Vogels' yard to retrieve foul balls. There were no league championship games then, only the National and American Leagues and the World Series in September. One girl in our class had a portable TV. Those who owned TVs had large Philcos or Sylvanias, housed in mahogany or blond wood cabinets, that they were paying off on time. A portable in 1958 was a second set, and hardly anyone owned one of those. The nun blackmailed our class into promised good comportment through to Christmas if we were allowed to see the Series. So one morning, right after the salute to the flag and after each grade filed back into their rooms from the yard, the girl's father drove his big Buick across the asphalt and right up to the door. He got out, opened the trunk, lugged the set in and put it up on the nun's desk, adjusting the rabbit ear antennas until the snowy black and white came clear and there was only the smallest hint of "ghosts" behind the players. We knew we were lucky— no other class got to watch—and with the exception of two or three students, we all followed every pitch, even staying inside to eat our lunches at our desks. Undoubtedly that year it was the Yankees beating some National League club; the World Series script did not vary much in the late '50s; nevertheless, we were enthralled.

Our biggest year for the Series was 1960, when the Pirates won on Bill Mazeroski's homer. Santa Barbara was a long way, in every way, from Pittsburgh—East to West, industrial to pastoral, large to small. Nevertheless, most of us supported the National League, so we backed the Pirates; everyone was tired of the Yankees winning the series almost every year. Everyone except Tuck Schneider that is; he was a die-hard Yankee fan who bet all takers and to whom a bunch of us had to pay up every September when the Yankees won. The bet was a quarter, and a quarter then was a week's spending for Big Hunks or Milky Ways. At the end of each series, everyone grudgingly paid off in pennies, and Schneider always had a heavy bag to lug home. Our collective revenge arrived while Bolduc, Wesley, Witucki, and I were moving tables and chairs in the rectory under direction of the monsignor, who, fortunately for us, had his transistor radio tuned in and positioned in the window for the best reception. When Mazeroski connected for the game-winning homer, we let out a subdued cheer but could hear a roar rise from our homeroom two buildings away where they were watching. Schneider made himself scarce, and we did not have to hear about the Yankees for a while.

The Dodgers and Giants set up on the West Coast while they were waiting for their stadiums to rise. The Giants played in old Seal Stadium waiting for Candlestick Park, and the Dodgers made do with the L.A. Colosseum while the city council forced the last poor families out of Chavez Ravine. The colosseum rigged a high netlike fence in the short left field. I went to a couple of games there with my father, whose favorite team was the St. Louis Cardinals. The Dodgers had just made a trade with the Cardinals for outfielder Wally Moon, who, though his power and career were running out of gas, was made to order for that short porch in left. He hit a patented high fly ball to left that cleared the fence for a home run, a ball that in any other park would have been an easy out. I remember Stan Musial, Red Schoendienst, Enos Slaughter, as much from listening to my father and trading baseball cards as from anything I actually saw them do at games; even in those days, it was hard to get seats close to the field in L.A. It was especially exciting in 1959 when I raced home after school to watch the playoff between the Milwaukee Braves and the Dodgers at the end of the season. I remember Warren Spahn, who always looked lost inside his baggy uniform, and I had once seen Lew Burdette turn a triple play to get out of a jam. Playing catch, kids would imitate Burdette's tics, his routine of straightening his cap, his jersey, his throwing hand going to his mouth, his belt, before he threw each pitch. Eddie Matthews, the Braves' third baseman, was from Santa Barbara, but along with Aaron and Adcock he could not overcome the Dodgers that year. Duke Snider, Gil Hodges, Drysdale, Koufax, Carl Furillo, and Charlie Neal became household names. We all knew pretty much what there was to know about the sport at the time—who led the league in homers, Sandy Koufax's ERA, how many times Hank Aaron had repeated on the fifteen-minute TV show *Home Run Derby*. And, when trading cards were only worth trading, we knew the value of a Cookie Rojas versus a Cookie Lavagetto, a Charlie Neal versus a Jimmie Foxx, or a Musial versus a Mantle. It all meant something to us, and we were content; the times still seemed to run on such intangibles.

By our last season in eighth grade, we were sure our league was going to change to ten-inch, a game somewhere between softball and hardball. A ten-inch ball was only one inch larger than a regular baseball, but rubber coated and lighter. It was, however, pitched overhand, though not from a mound, and the catcher needed all the usual gear. I had a live arm and some control, but I had no game experience pitching and also had to bring all my imagination to bear to actually *see* my curve ball curve. My friend Cameron Carlson, who was catching assured me that, yes, my pitch had curved, a little. We didn't know what we were doing, but we'd seen pitching and catching overhand plenty of times on TV, and were still young enough to believe that we could do it, or at least manage a version of it that would play in our league.

I was in a bit of a pressure cooker as we headed for our first game with arch rival Dolores School—we didn't really have a backup pitcher if I lost it out there. I knew from previous years how hostile the parents of Dolores players could be, how vicious the little kids were along the sidelines. We arrived at the school feeling confident nonetheless, knowing we had been practicing ten-inch while other schools had been playing softball. I fully expected to burn it by the batters, hear Cameron's official hard-ball catcher's mitt pop as strikes were called out. As we began to stretch out along the first base line and I loosened up my arm, a Dolores nun ran from the distant white classroom building and descended on home plate like a dark rain cloud. She announced that she had a telegram from the archdiocese forbidding ten-inch games and overhand pitching. No use now for Cameron to squat down and give me a different signal each time for the same pitch; we were back to softball and I was out in right field with little action. Schneider came in to pitch and Sozzi covered second. I did get one memorable hit that day using a thirty-five-ounce Louisville Slugger I had brought. I sent a fly deep to center field. The kid playing there turned clumsily and took off, running out of grass and onto the hardtop of the schoolyard. Without looking, and with his back completely turned to the diamond, he stuck out his glove and the ball fell directly into it from over his right shoulder. He was as surprised as I was stunned. I'd broken into a trot rounding second, sure it was gone, and just couldn't believe it when he held it up above his head; the ball and mitt wiggling in the air, the fielder looked like some kid holding up the first fish he'd ever caught. Longest ball of the day, and this kid pulls off a catch like that, a real *sapo*—a local Mexican term we all used for unconsciously, unbelievably lucky. For what little consolation it was, I even heard one of the Dolores mothers saying it was a real *sapo* catch.

There were other games that spring of 1961, but nothing stands out in memory. As a class we had pretty much quit play-ing work-ups the spring before. Now our interests were more focused on records, radio, who had the new 45 by Dion and the Belmonts, the Fleetwoods, the Ventures. Who was having a party, who was going for a walk with whom behind the buildings after the nuns and teachers had left. When we stayed after school now, it wasn't to run across the grass and tag up for positions on the diamond. There was no one skipping the first bus home and waiting for the next one an hour later so he or she could get their "ups." The dust of the ball field had settled and faded away with the '50s.

Our world had changed as all do, but the new times had a pronounced spin to them as well. Baseball became less important, less relevant. It no longer defined a collective experience, and as a topic it became, in an ironic way, one of many that produced friction, signaling the much publicized "generation gap." Vietnam took over the TV. Staying in college—not going to Vietnam—became important. Staying alive once you found yourself in a jungle became more important. The game was rigged by LBJ, Westmoreland, and the Pentagon, but diving into a sandbag shelter to escape a mortar attack, ducking your head in a firefight, was no game. No one in Vietnam was wondering how the Dodgers were doing. We lost a lot of kids there while folks here went to the ballpark, while dividend checks were sent out to shareholders of Shell Oil and Colt Manufacturing. In four years of college, I watched only two games of the World Series, and those during my freshman year.

One friend, a first baseman who could really dig out the low throws, went down in a gunship; he survived, but it took seven operations to make his glove hand 20 percent useful. Among others who came back, some felt edgy, out of touch with past and present. For others, the aftereffect snuck up on them years later—a little like what happened to that pitcher for the Pirates in the late '70s who, after a solid career and a championship season, just couldn't get the ball over the plate anymore, who had something snap in his nerve, in his radar on that sixty-six-foot path to the plate, and who ended up selling college rings.

But by the late '70s, I'd come back to baseball. Teaching part-time at community colleges and universities, I became a "freeway faculty." Driving forty-five minutes between various campuses and home, I started to listen to Dodger pregame and postgame shows, interviews, and baseball talk shows on one of the few stations my AM radio could pull in. I listened to what part of the games I could, and often would turn on the set for the late innings when I got home. Facing weekends with seventy-five compositions to respond to, I started sitting down in a big chair with an armful of papers and working Saturday and Sunday from one game to another—network games, ESPN, TBS, and anything else I could tune in. It was a way to break up the mind-numbing repetitiveness of seven or eight hours of grading. The games were slow enough that you could divide your attention between a men-at-the-corners, two down, hit-and-run situation and a lack of coherence and the comma splice. The background patter of a broadcast became a mental liniment for the cramping muscles of the part-time teacher trying to pick up a living. Time passed and I landed a good full-time position, but I kept up with the games—by then a habit, an unconscious comfort that connected with my youth, something I was becoming more conscious of losing having lurched into my thirties.

At this point in time, with a sizable portion of seriousness and loss behind me, politics and change look to have come and gone almost seasonally, and all we finally got was older. Headlong into the '90s, things less certain, living far from my friends and home, I begin to doubt the worth of a great deal that has had to do with career, getting ahead, the hundred additional concerns taking up time, energy, and spirit. On TV, I much prefer games on natural grass. Years ago, I never thought I'd use, automatically, a term like "natural grass"—by definition, there was no other kind. It doesn't matter much who is playing, but if the game is played on a real field and not AstroTurf, I'll watch.

Now and then I see a '57 Chevy with its swanlike fins, or a two-tone '56 Chevy Nomad wagon with those thin chrome strips on the fold-down tailgate, and it brings things back. All that time ago, there was something sustaining in expecting less.

You got along. A lot less was conspicuously consumed—fewer models and styles—there were fewer pressures, and fewer of us. More time to play ball. Of course, the choices then were easier, but maybe that's a point in favor of the past? Even a constant pastime like baseball now faces problems of "smaller market" teams being unable to compete and possibly survive. As a result of smaller shares of TV revenue, the teams can't afford the high-priced free agents, and a losing year means even less revenue. But baseball made a comeback in the '80s, and attendance has climbed yearly since then.

I know it's simplistic, but nine out of ten days, all I want to do is drive an old Chevy again, lean back against the wide bench seat, switch the AM radio to a game, shift that three-speed on the column, and cruise with the windows down. I'd like to drive it home, up Cabrillo Boulevard or down East Valley Road toward my old grammar school and get a bunch together for work-ups. I want to pull up to the field and open the four doors or the tailgate and let folks out to tag up for positions— happy to be there, alive among people who recognize the same trees and grass and clouds I do. I'd be happy to just stand there awhile worrying about nothing more than whether I'll be able to bend down far enough to field a hot grounder hit my way. I'd like to be positioned in that center-field grass, sun holding on in the west over the blue line of the eucalyptus, and see Peggy Dormier at the plate—see her connect and send one flying deep, see that moon-white softball almost breaking into orbit before spinning down in the direction of my glove, and then hear my old friend Sozzi calling, "I got it. I got it," as he cuts in front of me for the running catch and carries it in toward home.

Playing for Time

An only child, I spent a good deal of time on my own, and pool tables turned up where I was left to fill the hours. The smooth sea of felt, the almost mechanical clicking of the balls, the colored stripes and solids moving in conjunction like atoms in a science model, the confident patter of older boys and men as they made a bank shot or a combination cast a spell over me from the start.

Early on in grammar school, I walked the half mile to the Montecito YMCA on the corner of San Ysidro and East Valley Roads each day after school. For a couple years, my father paid a partial membership so I could stay there, do homework, and be more or less under supervision until he and my mother picked me up after work. The Y closed at 5:00, and often I sat out in the dark, waiting on the steps until they pulled up at 5:30. Few boys my age went to the Y, and the regulars were a group from the public high school who came by to shoot pool in the afternoons. Instead of working on arithmetic or spelling, I sat in the room with the tables—one pool table, and one snooker table no one used—watching. These guys were confident, cool. No wonder—they got away with wearing blue jeans to school and most had their hair combed into Elvis Presley ducktails or jelly rolls like Freddy Cannon. They had jalopies, and one rode a motor bike. They were independent and, for all I could see, in complete command of their lives. For the '50s, they looked like toughs or punks, but in truth they were regular kids and nice enough. Mostly, they played rotation, a game that required the balls to be sunk in numerical order, the winner being the one who had sunk the most balls at the end of the rack.

I had become a fixture in there, sitting on the bench against the wall, watching hour upon hour without a word as the balls rolled smoothly and fell, making a tiny clink as they hit the wooden disk at the bottom of the leather pockets. They let me collect the balls and line them up in the racks on the wall. I never was allowed to play but was happy enough just learning the jargon, absorbing the many mysterious skills of this intriguing and, to me, exotic pastime.

One day the high school guys failed to show up for their usual game of rotation or Eight ball. The nice old fellow who managed the place, seeing me sitting in the room alone, tried to show me how to play snooker; he handed me a cue and demonstrated a few shots. But it never held my interest—small balls, small pockets, and the long table that required me to use the bridge or "granny stick" to reach many shots. It was largely a defensive game, he said, but all I could see was that it lacked the speed, clash, spin, and immediate satisfaction of pool. It didn't appear to have the nonchalance and ritual proceedings of straight pool.

I made mental notes while watching games of pool: blue chalk was applied to the tips of the cues with two or three quick, squeaky twists of the wrist; a white cone of chalk was occasionally fingered by the left hand. I studied the two methods of forming a bridge—fingers fanned out on the felt and the thumb against the index knuckle to form a **V**; or, better, the index finger curled to touch the tip of the thumb to form a circle through which the cue would glide. Though I never spent a minute on a table, I knew the games—rotation, Eight ball, 14.1 call-shot, and Nine ball. I knew the splash of sound and color as someone broke a rack, and it all fascinated me and consumed the long hours of the afternoon.

At an eighth-grade party, instead of joining the boys pursuing the ever popular Linda Underwood or Yvonne Thornburgh, my friend Tuck Schneider and I shot pool. A rich kid was hosting the party at one of those huge houses you see only in movies, and Tuck and I had found the "billiard" room. The table was in fact a billiard table, but it had substitute rails with pockets that could be snapped into place. It was a rare opportunity to play and test our imagined skills. When we'd miss a shot, we'd say we were out of practice, that we usually made those easy ones. In truth, it was an opportunity we rarely had. We almost got through an entire game of Eight ball before we were discovered missing by the chaperones and called back to join the others.

My first real playing time came while I was attending boarding school. There was a basement with four tables, one class assigned to each; the seniors, of course, had the best table. You had to know the tilt or "table drift" of the freshman table— the fact that any ball would slide at least an inch off line to the right—if you were ever going to make a shot. It was difficult to get on a table. Pool there was about peer one-upmanship and pecking order, but on weekends with the day-hops gone and most of the boarders away, the tables were free, and shooting pool held, for me and many others, a lot more interest than Latin or algebra homework. I spent almost as much time on the tables as at the books. One Friday afternoon I was not out on the lawn waiting to be picked up for a weekend home. My father figured out where I was and came down to the basement. I was sizing up a difficult shot—the blue striped 10 ball almost in the middle of the table and the cue also centered, almost on the dot used to set up a ball when you "scratched." Both far corner pockets were blocked, so my only shot was a paper-thin kiss that would cut the 10 ball into the right side pocket. I took my time, did not overpower the shot, and shaved it just enough to have it trickle in.

I did not return for the second semester of my sophomore year—a matter of unpaid tuition—and ended up back home at the Catholic high school. I began to spend my free time playing pool, spent most evenings and weekend afternoons at the Fiesta Bowl. Table time was about $1.75 an hour, and the mildest form of wagering was to play for time—that is, the loser would pay for the table charge. You picked up a tray of balls, and the man behind the counter punched a card with your starting time. The loser had to collect the balls, take the tray back up to the counter, and cough up a buck or two once the ticket was clocked in. Older kids from school played there, a number of the local car guys, and there was always the regular crew of old boys who played billiards at noon.

The Fiesta Bowl had six pool tables and one billiard table, and afternoons I'd shoot for an hour or two by myself. I'd practice the break for Nine ball. Placing the cue ball a little closer to the rail than many would, I held the stick at the hilt and rested the shaft on the rail. Then, guiding it between the first two fingertips of my left hand, which barely curled over the cushion, I took one, two, three pendulum-like strokes to build up momentum before striking the cue with all the power and giving it all the topspin I could manage. I followed straight through with the stick in my right hand still pointing down the middle of the table. The cue ball crashed into the diamond-shaped rack of balls and recoiled a few inches before the overspin took hold and shot it back into the remaining balls for a second hit. Six or seven goes at it then I moved on to some other aspect of the game as the old boys began to look over as if to say, "Kill the noise."

Young players often hit shots much harder than necessary,

slamming balls into the pockets. I learned to concentrate on my stroke, an even follow-through instead of a jab, a stroke that would keep the cue ball moving after the shot to leave you "shapes." Leaving "shape" was important. A slammed shot usually stopped the cue dead where it struck the object ball and left you blocked from another shot. A cue ball with good stroke had plenty of spin to move around the table and leave you a clear line to another shot. A good stroke left you good "shape." I also worked on "draw," that is, backspin. This was simple. You struck the cue ball low in the center, careful to stroke through it but also careful not to run a long rip in the felt. The cue then hit the object ball, usually a ball on the edge of a pocket, and backed up, thereby avoiding sinking and "scratching." I worked on bank shots to the side pockets, bank shots the length of the table into corner pockets, cut shots on a spotted ball with high inside "English" on the cue. When a ball was frozen against the rail, I knew the cue should catch the ball and rail at the same time; the ball would then "walk" down the length of the rail and drop in the corner pocket. The shots were always easier practicing by yourself, but after a while, I started "canning" the shots when playing for money or time.

Tired of practicing, I'd watch the old men. A postman, Frank, who punched in table time and collected money, and who was always releveling one table or another while chewing on an unlit cigar; another man smoking a pipe who reminded me of an Irish priest out of uniform; and a white-haired man with the clothes and mild manners of a doctor—they played billiards, a game with no pockets and only three balls. I began to see that this was a game requiring much more skill than pool, a much more proficient stroke and a more protracted sense of geometry and imagination—a game of sophistication. Billiards has a red ball and two cue balls, one with a small black dot so that each player has his own cue. You have to strike your cue, hit either the red ball or the other cue, then take three or more rails before striking the remaining ball. The variation on the basic shot is to make your cue take three or more rails cleanly and then hit both remaining balls in succession, no rail intervening. You manage either one of those shots and you get a point and can shoot again. You fail, and it's your opponent's turn. I shot billiards by myself when the table was free, and although I was never as proficient as the older men, I could run off ten points or so in a half hour—good enough to beat any of my pool opponents but not good enough to compete with the old-timers. The main advantage that struggling with this game brought me was a much improved stroke on the pool table, and a new variation on the hours, those afternoons on my own when the air in the room was still.

Soon enough, I was playing for more than table time. The money game was Nine ball, played to usually 10 or 15 points, with points awarded for sinking only the 3, 6 and 9 balls, or the Spartan variation with points only for the 9 and 5 balls. To get to one of the money balls, you had to sink the others in sequence. Only nine of the fifteen balls were used, racked in a diamond shape—one, two, three, two, one. After the 9 ball was sunk, the balls were reracked and a wide-open break given to the player who had sunk the 9. The break was a big advantage as you didn't have to play it safe as in 14.1 call-shot. In Nine ball you blasted and hoped to sink some of the money balls on the chaotic collision or "slop." You could play for a dime or a quarter a point, plus time, and you could win or lose two to three dollars in half an hour.

I was careful with whom I played and bet—usually friends, schoolmates, guys from other schools whom I had at least seen shoot before. Hanging out by myself those days, I was an unknown quantity to many. I didn't play with the older guys usually, and in high school there were cliques—people played with their friends. I knew the big-money players, and I'd sit against the wall and just pay attention when there was a match. Some evenings, moving from the Fiesta Bowl to the Orchid Bowl out in Goleta, I'd run into a different group. Often they had had a few beers and were cruising the pool rooms just to see who was there, to shoot a few racks and have something to do. Some wanted to play for money instead of time, and beer accounted for confidence. There was a stretch when I took regular money out of the Orchid Bowl.

I had bought a used Brunswick cue, a twenty-one-ounce break-down stick with a white and black plastic joint. One of the regulars at the Fiesta Bowl was going to a new brass-jointed cue, and his used one, in weight and balance, fit me fine. After I'd screwed it together, rolled it back and forth across the table to check that it wasn't warped, after I'd shot a rack of Nine ball and checked the tip, I handed over the sixteen dollars he was asking. I caught a lot of flak for having my own stick, and some friends wanted to shoot against me for only that reason. I had no case, no colored thread wrapped on the hilt. My cue was, comparatively, unpretentious. Still, it must have looked self-important to guys pulling cues off the racks. Usually, I'd win—I had put in many hours by myself at the tables. I don't think that stick had much to do with it, but having my own cue felt great, I thought, and that alone gave me an edge.

One evening Teddy Ruiz, who had come to meet his usual crew of older guys, got tired of waiting and asked if I wanted to shoot. Ruiz was steady, smooth, made all the shots he should have and did not leave much shape. I broke, almost ran the first rack, and had a lead of a couple of points when Andrack, Tagney, and a few other of Ruiz's friends showed up. They wanted us to hurry up, to just finish what was on the table. A quick check of the points and the remaining money balls told me I couldn't lose, so when I looked at what might be the last shot, I was loose and tried a shot I'd only done a time or two in practice—a massé shot, in which you put "English" on the ball from the top—in this case the top right. I had to punch quickly down and through so the cue ball would scoot around the targeted ball in its direct line and then, when the spin grabbed, curve back. I also had to have the cue ball bank off the rail and come back to the corner pocket and hit a ball hanging on the lip. The sign on the wall said NO MASSÉ SHOTS—ONE FOOT ON THE FLOOR AT ALL TIMES, but Frank was behind the counter gluing new tips on a bunch of sticks. I figured out the shot, figured I could do it and had nothing to lose. It went perfectly, snaking around the black 8 ball directly in front of me, biting into the rail and coming back to the near corner to kiss the 6 ball in. Ruiz said, "Ah shit, man, you ain't that good," and went up and paid for the time on the table. His friends had already selected cues and pulled the balls from the trough below the table. I was just in my junior year and had nothing else pressing. With time on my hands, and though not a member of that group, there I more or less fit in. I was comfortable with the routine and so unscrewed my stick, content to sit awhile and watch them play.

The only time I really lost money, I deserved to. I'd been shooting around for a while—a few racks of straight pool, a little billiards on my own until the regulars came in. I went back to the pool table to try to run a rack, and a guy a few years older came up and asked if I wanted to shoot some Nine ball. I'd never seen him before and had heard enough stories and seen enough movies to know better than to shoot with someone from out of town. Still, he looked young and not too slick, I didn't have a game, so I took a chance. He won the toss and just before he broke said, "You want to go for a quarter a point?" I had enough sense right then to say, "No. Ten cents like we said, and time. Fifteen points, then we'll see." He looked around. A little after noon, I was the only one there other than the billiard men, so he said, "Sure," broke, ran the table, broke again, and in the middle of the second rack missed a shot. At that point I felt he probably missed on purpose, realizing he might run off his mark, but he didn't leave me much. I made a couple balls before missing a difficult combination bank shot on a money ball. He sank the rest and had 15 points before we'd played half an hour. He asked then if I wanted to play some more, go to a quarter a point. I just laughed and said I planned on leaving the room wearing the shirt I'd worn in there. My caution had saved me from really being skinned. I'd only lost a few dollars—the amount I usually won over the course of an hour playing in my own league. The next day I saw the same guy playing one of the hot local players. Young and old sat on the benches around the first table, and it was quiet and tense. They played for over an hour until the local player threw some serious folding cash on the table and walked out without a word. "Cleaned-out," I heard one of the old fellows say. No one ever saw that hustler again. I still loved the game—the many possibilities and varieties of shots, the cheap grace and immediate glory it could provide— but a little of the romance and mystique fell away that day as I realized I was only good playing for small stakes, playing for time.

Soon after that, I made some friends and was working on cars, cruising, going to dances. I just didn't have the time to shoot regularly anymore. So I gave it up—the low cloud of smoke fogging out the lights, the satisfying double click of a combination shot, the lingo punctuating the long green drifts of concentration, the comfortable hours in command of an easy fate. I sold my cue to a sophomore, a kid who seemed to keep to himself a lot and who said he was going to invest some time getting serious about the game. I never really played again. I sold the stick for sixteen dollars and broke even.

Old Spanish Days

All I really knew was that I had a new hat, a straw sombrero we bought two days before at Woolworths—it sported red, yellow, and green flowers machine stitched around the brim. I also had a red sash tied around my waist for some reason. My mother's brilliant auburn hair was pulled back in a ponytail, and she wore a white blouse and a flared coral skirt, and shoes with straw bottoms, black canvas tops, and ties, which I later learned were espadrilles. She had a hot pink hibiscus pinned behind one ear. We were walking downtown to meet her friends, to stake out a good space to see the Fiesta Parade. I carried a folding canvas camp stool and tired of it within a few blocks. My attention was captured by the girls along the sidewalks dressed in pomegranate-red and lime-green dresses edged with lace; in their black shiny hair they wore tiaras and tall combs with rhinestones glistening from the sun. Each had a basket of confetti eggs for sale. I'd seen one girl crack one of these eggs on another's head and the colored bits spray into the air.

We walked quite a ways down the main street and found a place on the corner of Canon Perdido. I snapped open my stool and sat right down waiting for something to happen, but as soon as the dancers leading the parade were near enough for us to hear the clicking of their castanets, people crowded in all around me and blocked the view. Over the level of the adults' heads I did see some floats, as I heard people call them, go by with more dancers and musicians. One had the front of the Old Mission with its entrance and two bell towers made completely from flowers. This went on for a long afternoon as I pushed my sombrero back from where it consistently worked its way down over my eyes. My mother kept pointing out to me things I could only barely see—a group of Franciscan padres, a tribe of Indians, a whole squad of riders on palominos with the sun flashing off the silver-dollar saddle work. I was clueless. Why exactly grown-ups were dressing in costumes and riding horses down the middle of the street escaped me.

I was too young to have a context, a mental picture, of what the Fiesta Parade and Old Spanish Days were supposed to represent. I didn't even know who the Spanish were. They weren't friends of my parents and didn't go to my school, where, among other things, I was learning French. That, at least, I knew was another language, a code of lovely sounds that I was doing well at imitating. The Spanish didn't go to the private school where I attended kindergarten, but neither, except for the nuns, did the French. I heard lots of people that day of the parade saying, "*Viva la fiesta*," which I managed to parrot in no time. And though it didn't sound like French, I would often follow it up by saying, "*Le livre est sur la table. La fenêtre est ouverte.*" I thought I might be really getting the hang of things, but any response I received from strangers on the street was due, I think, to the strange sounds coming out from underneath a sombrero that largely hid my face.

This was still the '50s and I had grown up listening to radio. My father worked at radio stations, and on trips in the car my parents listened to *The Jack Benny Show,* and another one called

The Whistler. I always recognized Benny's voice, though I never picked up on the humor aimed at the adult audience; and similarly with *The Whistler,* I didn't follow the mysteries but always felt a chill on my neck at the beginning and end of the show when I heard that eerie whistling. Saturday mornings I listened to *Big John and Sparkie,* a kids' program whose main attraction was Sparkie, an elf who talked with Big John and made jokes. I had an image of them in my mind, though the crazy thing was that somehow I felt they could see me!? Big John had a "spyglass" with which he looked into the homes of the kids listening and reminded them about their chores. One morning Big John said he was looking into "Chris's house" and that my room wasn't picked up. When I heard my name, I popped out of the big chair I was sitting in and hid behind it. No good. Big John immediately said, "No use hiding behind that chair, Chris. It looks as though you've combed your hair this morning with an egg beater!" How *could* he see into our house? What in the world, as my father would say, was going on?

Two years later, we'd rented a house about a block from the beach. A few months later, I came home from school one day to our first television—a large blond wood cabinet with a big Sylvania screen inside and several knobs I was not to touch. Things began to slowly come into focus. Weekend mornings were filled with cowboys and the landscape of the old west— Hopalong Cassady, Wild Bill Hickok, and the Lone Ranger. B cowboy movies played all day on one of the L.A. channels— a posse in white hats riding after desperados in black hats in speeded-up sequences, firing dozens of shots from their six-shooters as they raced through the then undeveloped hills in back of Malibu and Thousand Oaks. My favorite show was *The Cisco Kid.* Cisco was smart and clever, a fast draw and a straight shot, and Pancho was full of good humor. Perhaps here at last were the Spanish? My favorite part came at the end of each show after they had once again defeated the *bandidos,* saved the *señora,* and protected the *hacienda*—I knew, unconsciously, at least a handful of Spanish words. They would ride to the top of a small knoll, Pancho in his great sombrero and buckskin jacket, riding his golden palomino, and Cisco all in black on his white stallion. They would trade a line or two about their most recent adventure, and then Duncan Renaldo, as Cisco, would say, "Oh, Pancho!" to which Leo Carillo would respond, "Oh Cisco" before they both laughed together, reared their horses into the air, and spurred them off into the sunset. If these were the Spanish, I thought, no wonder there were parades. It would certainly be worth sitting through an afternoon on the street to see them.

Of course, there were Mexican kids attending my new school, Mt. Carmel, but at that young age, in that place and time, I had no idea who they were, who I was, and that there were supposed to be some differences. That next year, when my parents mentioned going to the Fiesta Parade for Old Spanish Days, I was ready and willing to go. I had heard at school that the Cisco Kid was riding in the parade that year. My father was in the chamber of commerce and worked at one of the local radio stations, KTMS. He would be broadcasting live at the parade from the curbside patio of the Copper Coffee Pot restaurant farther up State Street, but he saw that I was able to see Cisco. One of the businessmen who owned a shop on State Street was having people up to the second-story offices to watch the parade go by. My mother and I stood out on the balcony, and I waved at Cisco for as long as I could see him, and I was sure he waved back, shouted a "Viva" directly to me, his hand waving just above his white felt sombrero.

In the years that followed, Leo Carillo became a real fixture in the parade riding his great palomino. One year he was *el presidente* of the parade, and in many others he just rode along waving, throwing a rose or two into the crowd or some of those spiraled streamers of confetti. There is a story about Carillo in the late '50s, riding his horse right into the old Barbara Hotel on lower State, grabbing up a highball from the long bar there and riding back out to his place in the parade without missing a beat. For the years he rode in the parade, Carillo was the real thing, had the real spirit of a fiesta, and as a Mexican celebrity he was the exception.

The year after I saw the Cisco Kid, I ended up in the Children's Parade, which took place the day before the main Fiesta Parade. Every Saturday I had attended a school of sorts. A woman took us children in every Saturday, and we put on costumes and made up plays and also worked on our elocution and articulation. I was told I had a "lazy mouth" and remember the drudgery of "Susie sells sea shells" and other tongue twisters endlessly repeated. Our group was asked to perform in the parade. Someone's father, or some fathers, built a skeleton of a pirate ship with handles sprouting from the spine. We all dressed up—bandanas on our heads, eye patches, earrings, sashes, and swords—and took our places inside the ship, lifting together and carrying the thing down the street. I liked the pirate part, but the lifting and marching along was tiresome. Strangely, we had also rehearsed a song to sing as we went along, "Cielito Lindo"—a very popular Spanish song I had realized by that point—and yet I never wondered if pirates actually sang that song. We had learned it by rote; it was a fun melody with its refrain of "Ay, ay-ay-ay . . . ," and since in school and church I often sang Latin hymns whose meaning largely escaped my ability to translate, it did not seem too unusual that none of us singing really understood the words. After all the parading that day, I was tired and went off to bed without argument, the full moon out my window shining like a large piece of eight, a mariachi melody drifting toward it.

I was getting an idea of who the Spanish were. I soon recognized them on the Fiesta posters plastered all over town in summer. A woman in a fiery red fancy dress, a mantilla over her dark, dark hair, usually clicked castanets in both hands above her head; a man in tight black trousers, short jacket, and shiny black hat posed with one hand on his hip and one saluting the air—one of them always with a rose in his or her teeth. Jose Greco's flamenco dancers came to town during Fiesta one year, and I was dragged off by my mother and her friends for an evening of swirling, clicking, and stomping dancers at the Lobrero Theater. From watching *The Cisco Kid* and all those westerns on TV, I recognized that the facade of the Fox Arlington Theater was Spanish. The Arlington was everyone's favorite, with its ceiling domed and dark as the night sky and an appliqué of stars sparkling constantly above you. On the side of each aisle, there were white stucco walls leading to a second-story balcony with red tiles overhead; rough-hewn timbers and beams supported the roof, or so it appeared. No one, of course, was ever allowed up there because it was all for show. I found out later that all of downtown Santa Barbara had a building code that required that all buildings be constructed in the Spanish or Mediterranean style. From the hills, from the sea, driving down the main street, ours looked for all the world like a Spanish town.

As soon as I entered my teenage years, I was predictably disinterested in such things as parades. Like most of my friends, records and radio, cars and dating, work and surfing occupied my time. Then, before we knew it, we were out of high school; it was the mid-1960s, and we were faced with work and college and were developing a social consciousness, among our age group at least. At first, we only knew we wanted to avoid Fiesta—the crush of tourists. Working grocery in the summers, Tuck Schneider and I would plan crosstown routes on our motorcycles to circumvent the parade and parking. Jordanos markets closed down for two hours on the afternoon of the big parade, and we just wanted to eat lunch, get a beer, and perhaps take a short nap. We knew we were missing only the rich horsey types who were riding in the parade by virtue of their fancy horses and saddles, and their small-town social connections. There were precious few Spanish in the parade, few Mexicans, and none of the indigenous Chumash or Canalino Indians. This came really as no surprise at this point. A few years later, as temperaments radicalized in the early '70s, my friend Sid Flores wrote a scathing letter to the editor in the *Santa Barbara New Press* decrying the Fiesta Parade as a racist and elitist celebration that preserved and proclaimed oppression of "La Raza," the Mexican peoples and what few Native Americans were left in our region. He was, of course, correct, but such obvious truths then had little effect on the majority of people in the city or the organizers of the parade. The Old Spanish Days represented the wealthy landowners who traveled in fancy carriages, rode beautiful horses, and enslaved the Indians and Mexicans. Sid went on to, as the saying has it, put his money where his mouth was—literally. For, once he had escaped the general prejudice of the educational system that said as a Mexican, the best he could aspire to was two years of city college, he took his B.A. and was admitted to Bolt Law School, and from there took an LL.M. at Harvard. To talk to a lawyer with the extra degree from Harvard, fees started at $125 an hour. Sid, bright as he was, could have commanded more. Instead, he moved to San Jose and gave his time for the most part to community legal services for the Chicano population.

The year of Sid's blast in the local paper, my friend Orsua and I, along with Schiefen and Rosales, decided to attend the parade. We knew it was a lie, a confection spun out by the chamber of commerce for the greater glory of the business community. But we were out to have a good time raising a little hell. Instead of fighting for the best spaces along upper State Street, and certainly passing up tickets for the reviewing stand along Cabrillo Boulevard, we decided to take a position on lower State not far from Mission Billiards. When we arrived down there, we found room on the tiled fountain in front of the Bank of America on Ortega Street. We sat there and jeered at most of the ornate floats and the rich folks from Hope Ranch. We kept our bottles of Ripple cool and clandestine in the fountain pool, and Orsua took off his shoes and cooled his feet there as well. Lack of respect was our theme.

The parade was as boring as we knew it would be, but we were making a statement in our own small way. Late in the afternoon, as shadows started to spread like water through the street and the confetti and streamers began to foam up over the curbs, a battalion of street sweepers brought up the end of the parade. There were a few people with carts and brooms, but mainly a half dozen old-fashioned and mostly rusted "street sweepers"— the large tanklike machines driven by one man with wide and whirling brushes front and side. Now a dull and oxidized red, we could remember when they had been bright as candy apples. The street-sweeping crew was all Mexican, and Orsua knew some of those guys who were friends of his uncles. As soon as they approached our position, Orsua stood up on the fountain and started to applaud loudly. As the street sweepers swooshed up in front of the bank, the rest of us did the same, whistling and clapping as if we had seen the prizewinning float, or some famous TV star was riding by. This momentarily amazed those around us, but then a few rowdy types across the street joined in, and then the regular folks there took it up too, realizing at once the irony of the applause and at the same time the fact that these workers deserved it. The street-cleaning crew could see and hear us as they slowed down so as not to overrun the last floats in the parade. In their city uniforms, they had no fancy hats or sombreros to tip or wave, yet they smiled broadly, and then, after a few moments of consideration, and as the applause increased, they raised up a little in their seats and gave salutes to each side of the street, surprised, no doubt, that someone had acknowledged them.

PART TWO

■ ■ ■

Cruising State

We grew up watching our friends' older brothers comb their hair into jelly rolls or ducktails, take a last rebellious drag off a cigarette, flick it into the street and then, in blue jeans and a white shirt or jacket, get in a souped-up hot rod and blast out of sight like Jimmy Dean. We lined up to take our own places in a tradition we had seen evolve from the main streets to the movies, from the '40s to the '50s and throughout our boyhood. As soon as we were able, we were on parade beneath the lights or hugging a dark curve under the stars, being as sophisticated as we knew how in a small town large enough for everything, it seemed, we'd ever need.

Santa Barbara was blessed then with many things, foremost among them State Street, the main drag. State had two lanes to cruise up and two lanes down, and popularly designated turn-arounds top and bottom so we could repeat the process endlessly. So many cars, so many colors J-Waxed to a blinding gloss. Such ritual. Nothing more easily confirmed our lives then than simply being mobile, getting in line and motoring slowly in a friend's Chevy, new or old. Powerful or dog-slow, it didn't matter as long as you were there and kept moving, nodded with appropriate reserve to those you knew or admired in the next lane. Mexican kids, white kids—you were as cool as your ride, and cruising usually two or four to a car, your friends were your friends, Mexican or Anglo. It was simply important to be seen, especially on weekends after working on your car to see if you could draw a little more attention next time out from gloss or rumble. Late '50s, early '60s, there was time for such confection and aimless ambition—all the time in the world it seemed. This time and place was given to the automobile, the ostentation of fender skirts and fanned-out fins—swanlike, sharklike—set off by red constellations of taillights, bright bands of chrome. Paint was cheap; Earl Scheib would paint any car for $19.95. Used cars were cheap, parts from Solomon's Salvage Yard or Garcia's Auto Wrecking cheaper yet. The air was still good, and none of us, rolling down a window while idling at the light, had any idea what it all might come to. The lanes were wide with coughing jalopies, resurrected Mercuries and rebuilt Fords, late-model Chevys or someone's parents' new Oldsmobile hot off the showroom floor. The streetlamps glowed, four neon galaxies from movie marquees whirled above, and the latest Top 40 drifted from car radios all around. We rode along in the wonderful unquestioned and unqualified emblems of ourselves. To us it seemed an age that would never end, for wouldn't cars always be at the heart of things in California? Gas was cheap and the living was easy. Cruising was all means and no end. We were going nowhere fast, and that was fine with us.

I began to really pay attention to cars in the fall of 1956 when the new models for 1957 were just coming out. In only fourth grade, my friend Tuck Schneider and I were competing to identify cars. Compared to today, there were precious few makes and models, but one way to be revered among your peers was not only to recognize, but to know details about the latest cars. Tuck was the first one to recognize the new '57 Chevy and point out the tail fins spread like a swan's. No wonder. His father had bought one, a two-tone, black and yellow. But Tuck knew all the other cars as well, new and old. From his older brother, and his sister's boyfriend, Louis de Ponce, he learned a good deal of car lingo. While we were supposed to be working on geography, filling in the major exports and capital cities, or diagramming ten new sentences for English, Tuck would festoon the margins of his binder paper with fire-breathing dragsters smoking their way down the quarter-mile strip. "Tons of torque," he'd say, or "Oversized slicks grabbing for traction," he'd tell us, and explain how crew members poured bleach on the track around the tires before the start so the slicks would take hold. He knew the Indy drivers and their cars. Eddie Sax was one of his heroes because Sax always went all out and survived, for a time, many crashes. Tuck read road racing magazines in the El Camino Pharmacy and knew European races with exotic names like Le Mans, Nurburgring, and Targa Floria; he knew that "GTO" stood for *Gran Turismo Omologato* years before Pontiac produced their high-powered production model sedan.

By sixth grade, the attraction expanded from identification of year, make, and model to the reading of *Hot Rod Magazine,* in which we saw Duce Coupes and roadsters customized to accommodate huge engines, bored and stroked with blowers rising out of the hoods, and chromed exhaust headers fanning out like ribs. Roadsters were raised or lowered, anointed with a glistening purple or green paint job with metallic flakes, or, with gold flakes, candy-apple red. Another year or so later Tuck's mentor, Louis de Ponce, had bought a '58 Chevy and installed a three-speed on the floor that would wind out the standard 348 truck engine despite the low gear ratio. The '58 models had dispensed with fins in favor of understated concave scoops along the flanks, giving the models a curved box shape that highlighted triple sets of taillights, and this was new and therefore impressive.

Louis went to Santa Barbara High School, and whereas we were in class at Mt. Carmel school until 3:30, the high school let out forty-five minutes earlier. Almost every day during last class period, quietly writing an essay or parsing sentences, we could hear the gearing up and a high whine building as Louis came speed-shifting along East Valley Road. Tuck would give me a knowing nod or nudge with his elbow at the first far echo of that green monster peeling out along the quiet afternoon roads of Montecito, proud that, tangentially at least, he was connected to all that roaring significance.

Styles were changing too. Left behind were cars of elegance like Harry Fowler's mother's black convertible 1955 Cadillac with the white flip-top and red interior. Coming on the scene was a futuristic look we first noticed in the Cooneys' Chrysler Imperial, a mauve '59 with little concentric chrome hoops set on modest tail fins, surrounding the red cones of the brake lights like the rings around Saturn. Our last spring in grammar school, the Tappiniers arrived in a new 1961 Buick. That four-door was square and large as a tank, but it had more chrome than any of us had ever seen. We marveled at the handful of thin silver streaks running the length of each side of the car, the jetlike hood ornament, the grille and front bumper, which were a solid grid of chrome. On the back, where large tail fins would have sprouted a year or two earlier, there were two thin chrome strips standing up like feathers on a metal arrow, one running from the top of each taillight to the corners of the back window. That car virtually shone in the dark, and we couldn't begin to guess the cost.

Yet despite all this radiant machinery, the immediate future for us would have little to do with the money or class that cars usually signified. We were, most of us, off to Bishop High School, where social standing was going to be a matter of cliques and personality. Many students drove old cars, and there didn't seem to be much difference between one "bomb" or "heap" and another—Ford, Chevy, Dodge, sedans and wagons, rusted import or primer-covered domestic clunker—as long as it moved. We were closer to getting ourselves firmly behind the wheel of our glittering and rumbling aspirations, but for the first year and a half in high school we were too young to drive. So it was important to have a friend with wheels; for a while, it was enough just to ride along. The same guys would catch rides together; the same cars cruised State Street Fridays and Saturdays, though the vehicle itself might be ragged inside and out.

Many girls did much the same. We would, without success, try to get the phone numbers of girls from San Marcos or Santa Barbara High School cruising by in their parents' Buicks or Chryslers. The only guy I knew who ever got a date that way was Eddie Nagleman, and he drove around in a beat-up black and white '54 Ford—a bucket of bolts—but he was smooth and had pretty much movie star looks, so cars didn't count for everything. One senior girl from our school, Connie Francesca, always cruised in a '57 Chevy that might once have been silver with a bright red top but now looked more primered with a top faded to a drab cranberry color. Every morning she'd deliver six or seven girls out of that two-door, and though it looked abused, we'd see her cruising by herself or with one friend, hear it running OK as she threw some shifts on the column three-speed, see it passing a carload from another school.

An older friend, Danny O'Riley, inherited his grandparents' 1950 Oldsmobile, an automatic almost as wide as it was long, which rolled side to side on worn-out shock absorbers like the proverbial boat. It was what was then known as a "lead sled." The once green paint had oxidized to a shade dull as salt water in a tidal pool. It didn't matter that we were seen in the most gutless and outdated of cars—we got around. Weekends, I'd give Danny a dollar for gas and we'd get to a game or a dance, the one pizza joint in town, or we just drove around punching the buttons on the AM radio, looking for a Beatles tune.

The first guy in our class to turn sixteen and come up with a car was Richie Hoag. For thirty-five dollars he bought an old

Buick "Straight Eight"—a car from the '40s that got its name from its eight cylinders all in a line instead of in a V as in modern engines. It was as long as anything I'd ever seen, the hood protruding yards in front of the rest of the body. A "gangster" car we called it, large enough to carry eight or nine of us and still have room in the back for a card game. It probably would not have made it out of town, but it managed to chug north to south, Goleta to Montecito, especially when the school sponsored "drives," those money raisers that had all the students out selling chocolate bars at a buck fifty. There wasn't any choice in the matter. Each of us was given a huge box to unload. At a dollar-fifty each, I think we could have more easily sold certificates for sanctifying grace, but a bunch of us piling into that old Buick and careening around corners as if we were in some *Untouchables* episode took the edge off the ignominy of going door to door.

One kid took his cars very seriously, aspired through them to some sort of elevated social standing, something akin to a state of grace. A harmless enough guy, Eddie Marsango had a Chevy Impala our sophomore year, and later an olive-colored Pontiac GTO. The Impala was white with a red interior and all the chrome. He kept both so washed and waxed you could use the doors as mirrors, even the wheels and hubcaps gleamed, and for that matter, the tires gleamed, black as fresh oil, and the upholstery too reflected back the sun. Eddie was like his cars— starched shirts, and his hair, always Brylcreemed and perfectly combed, was slicked up along the sides, spiffy as his cars. He kept after his cars the way the priests and nuns lectured us to keep after our souls.

Before Francis Orsua became my friend, I knew his '51 Chevy. It was a low "floater," dull black and beat up, but it was a ride, and that's what counted. Francis had paid his father a hundred bucks for that Chevy with a Power Glide automatic transmission that had pretty much been worn out on construction jobs. To really "trick out" his car, Orsua had put fender skirts over the back wheel wells and had heated up the front coil springs to lower it, to make it look sleek on State. He never went as far as to put a fuzzy wrap around the inside rearview mirror or hang a big pair of Angora dice from it. Going slow and "low riding"—the driver's nose barely above the dash and the passengers' heads just above the level of the windows—that was one thing Orsua was known for. A car that looked to be driving itself down the street usually got acknowledgment from the other cars—a couple quick honks, sometimes a high coyote laugh. Orsua had to slow down for dips and corner carefully to avoid scraping, especially with his full load of riders—De Vito, Favro, Desmond Olivera. Orsua got his friends from point A to point B with as much style as limited means allowed—going in a straight line, slowly, but getting there.

For a while, after Orsua's black Chevy had cracked a head, we were forced to get around on my Honda 110 motor bike. Doubled up on my little bike, we made it to the dance at the Earl Warren Showgrounds for the Dartells playing their hits "Hot Pastrami" and "The Dartell Stomp." We parked the motor bike far from the entrance and left through the line of parked cars in case anyone was looking. Soon after, Orsua picked up a bronze and cream '56 Chevy Bel Air hardtop, that model with no center posts between windows, very cool in car-guy circles. Steve Schiefen and Able Rosales also became regulars with Orsua. We four were religious about cruising State after games and on weekends. Saturday nights when Orsua was taking out Susan Miratti, the daughter of the family that owned most of the liquor stores in town, he would borrow his parents' Ford Galaxy LTD, a 390-cubic-inch V-8 with a four-barrel carb, three-speed automatic, leather upholstery, heater, radio, white sidewalls, the works. Those times, he'd turn the Chevy over to Schiefen and Rosales and me and we would drive for hours without the first thought for insurance. If we were still wheeling around late, we'd head up for the Mirattis' house in Mission Canyon, park in the dark below the drive, and hit the headlights after Orsua had pulled in and just made a move across the wide, comfortable front bench seat.

Weeknights when we had shined on algebra or history homework, we often got together to work on the car. Nothing was needed really as the 265 engine was well tuned, but then, we all wanted to upgrade the investment, mechanically and socially. Orsua and Schiefen knew the mechanics. Rosales and I lifted the heavy stuff and handed over the next size ratchet or torque wrench. We soon had a basic education in mechanics and enough car-guy patter to fit into most conversations. I think even Orsua and Schiefen were learning a bit as they went along, but they had the confidence as well as the aptitude to pull the old engine when it threw a piston and to install a new one. We worked in Orsua's half garage on Punta Gorda Street on the east side. Four of us pulled the chains on the A-frame hoist, positioning the new engine on the mounts; it took two weeks to get the timing and the big Holley four-barrel carburetor working. From Washburn Chevrolet, we bought a short block, bored and stroked thirty-thousandths over to equal 301 cubes. A radical Duntov cam had the engine almost missing—a little extra half beat on top of every main beat, then a pause and then two quick beats. We went for the regular Hurst three-speed on the floor, making the necessary changeover from the automatic. To look "sano" and "solid," we put some spacer blocks in the front coils after raking it a little, bringing the back end up higher than the front with some monster shocks. Youth and confidence counted for a lot as we got that car going, got a formidable rumble from under the hood and, after slapping on scavenger exhaust pipes and glass pack mufflers, sounding mean enough for it to be acceptable on State Street.

On Sunday mornings, we'd drive over to Dwight Murphy Field across from the beach, hook up a hose, wash down the car, and then Blue Coral Wax it in the shade of the palm and podocarpus trees. This was applied with a lot of elbow grease due to the two-part application, one a wax, the other a sealer—

some hard work we didn't hesitate to do, attached as it was to our own glorious image. And although cruisers wheeled around under the pretense of looking for a race, most of it was image. Orsua knew enough to avoid "choosing off" with the truly rapid, finely tuned cars that had seen the speed specialist in town, Bob Joehnck, for an expensive "Dyno-tune." Mainly, we'd try one- or two-block races, dragging one stoplight to the next with whatever car had pulled up next to us at the light, punching it, trying to get rubber in all three gears before braking for the next light. The '56 not only gleamed but had good sounds with a reverb hooked to the AM radio. We bounced stiffly along up and down State, and at the top, we'd turn around in the Blue Onion drive-in to head back down, or if there was a parking space, we'd back in car-guy style and order Cokes and fries, which were brought out and clipped to the driver's side window on a tray. That was usually good for a half hour—sitting there, nodding to other cars as they pulled through the parking lot throwing a few revs. Soon enough we'd drive back down and flip a U in de la Guerra Plaza, never tiring of the route.

No matter where you were along State Street in the early '60s, you knew when Bill Brockelsby was out in his black '62 Corvette. Long before you saw it, you could hear the peculiar loud whistle from the Rochester Tower fuel injection unit. We could never figure out if that sound resulted from the removal of the butterfly valves or just a massive vacuum leak at the tower. But then you'd see it, shining like black ice with the dual 'vette lakers exhaust trailing out each side. On the front, gleaming ominously, the moon-tank, the little keg that professional dragsters used on the quarter mile with an exotic mixture of nitro or alcohol. The moon-tank was polished aluminum and not all that functional on the street, but cool, ultimately cool, and intimidating. Brockelsby never received many challenges to drag.

Most dragging was for fun. In Montecito, there was a quarter mile marked on the rarely used Camino Viejo, just off Sycamore Canyon Road. In truth, there was little traffic anywhere in Montecito, especially at night. Serious racing was pointless, as the cars were often far out of each other's class, but it went on, some machismo, some plain craziness. Orsua once raced another kid in our class, Bob Klein, on Camino Viejo. Klein rode around in his mother's 1964 Oldsmobile Jet Star, with a 394-cubic-inch engine with an automatic on the floor. We'd seen him trying to pull wheelies in that Olds, a car that looked at least fifty yards long, and whose V-8 weighed a ton. Klein would stop the car facing uphill on a small incline, rev the engine in neutral until it sounded like bolts were about to fly through the hood, and then drop it into gear and stand on the accelerator, causing the whole boat of steel to lurch a few inches up and into the air. Probably Orsua was being a bit macho, responding to a challenge, and Klein, well, we all knew he was just crazy. Orsua ran his tank almost empty before pumping four gallons of Chevron 110 Custom Supreme from the white pump then dumping in one gallon of 145 aviation fuel. He'd pour in a little castor oil to prevent burning too many holes in the pistons. Thus equipped, he met Klein out in the dark where the white stripe was painted across Camino Viejo and, with the windows rolled down and drivers counting down out loud, took him out of the hole. But having to throw three shifts in a quarter mile let Klein's monster catch up by the end; it's still argued both ways who won.

There was, however, serious racing—for pride, for money, and for the fabled "pink slip." There was Dave Price, the first to have a '66 'vette loaded with 427 turbo and ramlog manifold. For novelty, Alex Diaz had a '60 Ford Falcon Ranchero with Chevy running gear. For looks, there was Luis Salazar driving "Psycho," a black '59 Chevy Bel Air. But if you knew anything, you knew to avoid Chuy Blanco, about the fastest in his stock-car class. A controlled purring emanated from beneath the hood of Chuy's '57 Chevy. He didn't use glass packs or pull the baffles out of the mufflers as many did to sound bad. He wanted things understated. He removed all the ornamental chrome; the mag wheels were stock, the cheater slicks on the back had the required two bands to make the car street legal, and the paint was an unobtrusive beige. But the polish was high—you could read the movie marquees reflected on the fins when he paused in front of the Fox or Granada Theaters. At the stoplight, you could hear a cam turning over tighter than most, hear a little air sucking through the Carter aluminum dual four-barrel carbs. And from behind, you could see that little chrome box on the rear axle—a Hildebrand Quick-Change rear end, ready to convert the 4:11 positraction to a 4:56 or even a 5:12, depending on the race. Once you knew Chuy's car, it looked fast just standing still, looked like even air would pass it right by. If you got a look inside, you saw the Sun Tachometer, the Stuart Warner gauges, the Hurst flat-bar Synchro-lock linkage that took the H out of the shifting. A novice might buy a beast of a machine from the factory, but mechanically it would never measure up; and someone from out of town wouldn't dream of all the hardware hiding under that mild exterior. I don't remember ever hearing of Chuy losing a race.

About this time, Ward Memorial Boulevard—an elbow of freeway off 101 out toward Goleta—was completed. Built to improve traffic flow to the university, it was ages before it was officially opened. After the initial curve off 101, the "boulevard" ran long and straight, long enough for locals to paint two thick stripes a quarter mile apart across the two lanes heading toward the beach. Serious drivers, choosing off to race as they cruised State, would agree to meet out there in a half hour, usually just enough time for a local to get home and change tires or play with the fuel. Most would take the opportunity to disconnect the alternator belt for more horsepower and/or to remove the cutoff headers for reduced back pressure from the engine. The two cars would line up with headlights out while someone down at the beach end would pop out from the oleanders in the center divider with a flashlight and give three even bleeps of light.

Then rubber would burn and front ends would lift as both cars floored it toward the finish line. This race, however, was the exception rather than the rule, an event more talked about than seen. But a little mythmaking kept things in perspective, kept a safe class system that promoted respect for hard work and shine.

And, of course, most of the cars were for show—a paint job and fancy wheels as important as anything. Along the side of a late '40s Mercury, some wide flames in tangerine and yellow looked almost like wings on the metallic purple. There were three car clubs in town—the Dusters, Chevrollers, and T-Timers—and the members were identified by the customized chrome frames around their license plates. Many had the Edlebrock ramlog manifolds with opposing four-barrels, others dual-quad manifolds, and most had Mallory dual point distributors or had had their distributors turned in a Joehnck Dyno-tune. They rumbled and were quick. Marsango went up and down in his completely stock Pontiac GTO, probably stopping after every other pass to wipe off the dust; we always teased him that "all that Goat needs is some high-compression racing stripes!" Our friend Billy Bonilla—nicknamed "Bondo" for his '55 Chevy that had more putty on the body than paint—one day arrived in a blue factory Dodge 440 Charger, called the Wedge. It had three Holley duces and slicks so big in the back that he and Schiefen had to use air-input chisels to cut out the wheel wells for them to fit. Orsua sold the '56 to Schiefen in the fall of 1965 and bought a '50 Chevy, that style called a "turtleback." The previous owner had put a lot of work into it. It had all the chrome restored, reverse chrome wheels with baby moon hubcaps, and a silver paint job that glowed in the dark. The 283 engine had been beefed up with 327 heads and a four-barrel carb. The interior sported a Hurst four-speed, reversed-dish teakwood steering wheel, and Naugahyde upholstery that had been "Pledged to the max"—the tuck-and-roll so slick with Johnson's Pledge that a righthand turn slid your date automatically to your side.

We were still out there inventing ourselves, turning the reverb up as loud as we dared, switching the chromed buttons on the radio from doo-wop to surf, the Beatles to the Stones, Dylan to the Byrds, and then another "blast from the past." At our fingertips were three-minute solutions to love, or at least heartbreak with a beat. But there was some second sense that things were about to change, that something was slipping out of our hands. I think Orsua felt this, and that is why he took this chance and most of his savings to buy that full-on customized Chevy. He hadn't owned the car many months when he totaled it. He was just out driving around with Bondo, cruising one of those long frontage roads not yet completed along the freeway, talking, perhaps searching for a better radio station. Sober, straight as could be, and in the middle of a bright afternoon, he realized far too late that that road did not go through—right in front of him several pylons marked its end. He hit the brakes, cranked the wheel, rolled the car over once, and he and Bondo walked away without so much as a scratch. All that money, that heritage, gone. Standing outside the car, checking out their arms and legs, they finally turned and looked at each other, and with the shock wearing off, started to laugh at just being alive, being able to shake off their loss, there in those generous times.

We didn't have that much—usually just enough pocket change for gas to cruise another half hour or so. But it was a wonderful, blind, innocent time. All we had. All we then aspired to. We cruised beneath the galaxy of light cast by theaters and shops, the fine bright glare rebounding off the chromed bumpers, reasonably content with what we had envisioned for our lives—a vision that came from the '50s. We didn't know that State Street would be narrowed to one lane each way in a couple of years, that the war couldn't be ignored, that no one would be cruising anymore, and that this part of our lives would soon be all gloss, all pity for the past, for a glad and easy way of going.

To say the political climate quickly changed is not news. Yet people do not change all that much. Thinking of cars and those times still shining in memory, I remember a day during our junior year. We were in civics class with Father Bernard, a tough Franciscan who was the school disciplinarian, but who, lucky for us, had a sense of humor and a human side. Having heard from the county probation officer that John Craig, Orsua, and I had all had our driver's licenses suspended within a few weeks of each other, Father Bernard figured a little history lesson was in order. After the usual admonishment about speeding, about taking it easy, he told us of a recent discovery in Egypt. Archeologists had uncovered an ancient tablet, writing that would have then been a newspaper, and one of the editorials in it, some twenty centuries ago, complained about the young people of the city racing their chariots up and down the main street, without regard, endangering life and limb, raising dust. "Some things never change," he told us.

Before our twenty-fifth high school reunion there was a get-together at Me 'n' Ed's, the old pizza hangout, the night before the dance. Parked right in front of the entrance was a brand-new Cadillac Coupe de Ville, brilliantly white with hibiscus-red upholstery, the sales sheet listing price and all the extras still stuck to the back side window. It was, of course, Marsango's, a fact we pretty quickly figured out. I went in to find Marsango and stand near him. Schiefen waited a minute then came running in and spotting me at the bar, shouted, "Futas! Man, you should have seen this crazy guy in the parking lot back up blind as a bat in his old truck and bash this brand-new Cadillac." Marsango's head whipped right around, panic registering on his face for a second until he realized he'd been had.

I remember an evening, probably late 1966. I was home from college for a holiday, Orsua was heading for the marines, Schiefen driving the '56—all of us together there with no idea when we would be together again. Not many cars on the street, and there were no drivers we really recognized as we made the usual turnaround in the Mission Paint parking lot for a final pass down State toward the beach. This was a last time when any meaningful portion of an emotional life would float up from the radio—some DJ with a "golden oldie," the Flamingos with their dreamy harmonies asking simply, "Are There Stars out Tonight?" We were not looking at our stars or anything then hanging just over the horizon in the dark—in our indolence and our own sweet time, we were cruising.

Booze

When I was still fifteen, my mother and her husband Frank came up to Santa Barbara for the summer and rented a little bungalow. Tuck Schneider rode me over there on his motor bike, and the front door was open. We went in, called around the rooms, and no one was there. On a chair was a full box of liquor, just delivered from one of the pharmacies. Only a bottle of Seagram's gin had been opened. Tuck and I thought this was our big chance. We looked out the open door, saw no one, and each took a quick swig. Worst thing I could remember tasting. Fire. Fire mixed with ant spray! Our eyes watered. Tuck stuck out his tongue and fanned it rapidly with his hand. People actually did this for fun? They paid for this stuff? This killed my curiosity for a while.

But then I was sixteen, cruising with new friends, nothing to do, end of our sophomore year. Something had just lit our fuses. We rubbed another layer of sleep from our eyes and wondered what, within reason, was going on. And for us, in the slow spin of the early '60s, reason included booze—something that would only amplify the charged air we were already breathing, something that daily was working its way out of us in momentary jolts of electricity. The high voltage stuff was just beyond our reach, and we were out to discover any solution to that problem. I was wearing my large parkalike jacket, the one I wore riding my little Honda 110. We stopped at a liquor store on the north side of town, that was—no kidding—called Hi-Time Liquor. Francis told me to give him my jacket. He checked the wide inner and outer pockets and said Steve and I should get a couple 7-Ups and call attention to ourselves. We did, and after a little while, we paid for two 16-ounce bottles and walked out. Francis fired up the car and pulled out, saying he had some booze. We didn't believe him, and for good reasons. First, no one we knew had the guts to swipe a bottle in a store. Second, no one had ever done it, was dumb enough to risk being caught. Third, neither of us had seen Francis do anything. We headed out toward the north of town, and Francis opened one side of my jacket with his left arm, like someone on a street corner selling watches. From the inner pocket a pint of sloe gin peeked out. We all yelled out at once, excited at the prospect of finally entering the democracy and secrecy, the firewater and forbidden fireworks of drinking, though none of us had the first idea what sloe gin was. It just happened to be in a display on the front of the counter. In fact, we wondered if sloe gin was just a mix, if it had alcohol at all until we passed under a streetlight and Steve read "sixty proof." We then didn't know what a "proof" was exactly, but we knew it meant booze.

We drove out to the cliffs by the university where kids parked to look at the ocean and make out. It was a cinch we'd be nabbed if we just pulled over to the side of the road somewhere. I do recall rolling down the windows and pouring out half of each 7-Up and then refilling the bottles with sloe gin. Not half bad. Tasted like cough syrup, but the 7-Up covered the medicine aspect for the most part. I doubt we had enough alcohol split three ways to get us very high; there was a fair portion of sloe gin left in the bottle after we filled the 7-Ups. I think we thought we were floating much higher than we actually were. But that wasn't the point. We were flying along on our own, confident we were now part of what was going on in the world. No one threw up or went crazy. We just cruised around for another couple hours with big silly grins.

About a month later, shooting pool at the Orchid Bowl in Goleta, a couple guys from our class and a junior, Mac McGlaughlin, asked if we wanted to drink some beers. We were supposed to be impressed and wonder how they got a hold of beer. We were; we did. They figured we might chicken out anyway. Mac had two six-packs of Coors some older car-guy friends had bought for him, and he looked disappointed when, without hesitation, we said almost in unison, "Sure, we'd love a beer." We all piled into Francis's Chevy and drove out to Sands Beach and parked on a small dirt road off the main road—no lights, no other cars. As we were headed for Sands and our first beer, we looked experienced; Francis had a church key in his glove box, which he handed over to Mac. Mac tore the cardboard off the yellow cans, punched two holes in the tops, and passed them back. We were quiet, almost reverent, as we began drinking. Mac and the others were powering through their first cans and going for seconds. Steve and I in the back acted nonchalant. We'd had only sloe gin before, and that first sip of beer tasted god-awful, like water that had been standing in an old shoe for days. Luckily, the windows were down and the conversation picked up enough that I could stretch my arm out the window and gently let most of the beer trickle out of my can onto the sand without being discovered. We proclaimed to a man that Coors was the best. Much better, I told everyone, than the beer I usually drank, and felt a level up in the world.

But we soon acquired the taste. Getting beer became the problem, the focus of attention and energies. Had we been able to walk in and buy a keg whenever we wanted, I'm sure it all would have been less important than it then was. As things were, we were always looking for someone to buy, and connections came few and far between. Working in a grocery, I could occasionally persuade one of the young clerks to buy for me if I kicked in a few extra bucks. Our stores were pushing LaBatts, a Canadian beer, and my connection would meet me in the back of the parking lot when I got off work, transfer a few cases quickly to my trunk, count the cash, and race off in his old Dodge checking the rearview mirror for the FBI. Although I felt he was overly nervous and it took a good deal of talk to persuade him to buy for me, in these times it was very serious business to be caught with booze or to be caught buying for minors. Once we talked one of the winos in front of a liquor store into buying some six-packs and a gallon of Red Mountain wine for us in return for a fifth of tokay. That worked a couple of times until someone from another school was arrested after that wino had walked out and handed him the bag—undercover cops were all over the lot waiting to swoop down on them.

Steve had what he called his medicine kit, an army backpack with a Red Cross symbol on it. He stocked it with small jars into which he'd emptied a half inch from each bottle in his parents' liquor cabinet—cheap vodka to creme de menthe. This worked once in a while, though with three of us, there was not much more than a ceremony of unscrewing lids and inhaling. You could get a drink sometimes in the back of the only hangout in town, Me 'n' Eds pizza parlor. It was packed on weekends after any of the high school games. Usually in the back, Bob Brown, one of the popular guys from the public high school, had a tall Coke going that was not much Coke. If you knew him well, you got your Coke sweetened—more ritual than substance. But it was what there was to do.

Once George Stark's parents were away for a long weekend, and he took the opportunity to throw a major party—food, music and dancing, Ping-Pong, pool—light early '60s civilization as far as we knew it. But George's connection didn't come through with the booze. Rosales, who planned to arrive later after work, was called on the phone. He had an uncle just a few years older who would sometimes help him out. The party was far south of town in Carpinteria, and it was nine-thirty by the time Rosales drove up. He got out of the car with his eyes looking to the ground and said he couldn't find his uncle, was sorry. Most of the crowd of fifteen or so who had come out to greet him hung their heads and silently began shuffling back up the walk to the house. Steve, Francis, George, and I just stood there looking at each other, out of ideas. As Rosales went around to the trunk of his red Mercury Comet for his overnight bag, I did notice that the car was sitting a bit low in back, and at that moment Rosales let out a great laugh and sprung the trunk open on ten cases of half-quart Olympias. Having waited so long for the beer to arrive, the party to start, most of us made up for lost time and chugged a few too many too fast. In no time a line developed in the hall in front of the bathroom, and George came in and directed some traffic to the back of the house and the other bathroom just off his parents' bedroom. Steve and I, not entirely sober, headed there pronto and I was first in. Steve, shifting from one foot to the other, gurgled out that he was about to burst a kidney and pulled back the shower curtain, aiming at the drain and getting ready to relieve himself. Startled by the sudden light, Francis, who had passed out in the tub a bit earlier as the result of a chugging contest with Rosales, came to quickly with Steve aiming down at him; he threw up his hands half coherently yelling, "Don't shoot. Don't shoot," and on a rush of adrenaline shot out of the tub before Steve had a hernia.

One night after a dance, Steve and I planned to meet Francis and Rosales at a park under a foothill bridge. The park was small, out of the way, and no one went there at night. Even after a social event we wanted to just hang out together, determine the course of daily events on our own, and with the lubrication of a few beers, share our vast experience and views of the immediate world. The road in was dirt and angled down toward a creek. We saw the tire tracks of Rosales's Comet, so in we went. We piled into one car, drank the beers Rosales had picked up, and gave no thought to driving out after an hour of rain had fallen. But as Rosales tried the incline, his rear tires spun. We knew what was needed—traction—and that meant pushing on the rear of the car while someone drove. Steve, being the lightest, got behind the wheel. Francis, Rosales, and I stood out in the rain, and not feeling much pain, readied ourselves. There we were, early '60s sharps, trying to look like the Dave Clark Five or Gerry and the Pacemakers—thin black ties, white tab-collar shirts, red vests, grey slacks, dark sports jackets, and some pointed black shoes called "fence climbers"— our best gear. We pushed down on the rear fenders of Rosales's Comet and, with its good tires, it made it up the grade; only our shoes and cuffs were dirty. However, my wide and heavy '59 Chevy was another matter, especially with its bald retreads. As we pushed and Steve accelerated, mud flew up as if shot from a hose. Shoulders to shoes, we were spattered as the tires grabbed and lurched that lead sled forward—grabbing, spinning, then grabbing again. Steve was cranking the wheel right, then left as the car slid sideways on the narrow road, barely fitting between the two large sandstone boulders that marked the entrance. Up to our ears in mud, but still buzzing, we looked at each other and laughed, brushed ourselves off, and headed to the pizza parlor basically unscathed.

Sometimes with nowhere to go, the four of us would take a couple cases of beer to the drive-in. It didn't matter what was showing; it didn't matter what brand of beer. We'd hook up the speaker on the window and turn the sound off, take a couple sixers out of the trunk, and send someone to the snack stand for BBQ sandwiches. Then we'd eat, drink, and talk while Rock Hudson and Doris Day mouthed to each other on the phone over a split screen. For that little time to ourselves, unhassled, we stayed until the end of the double feature, driving out quietly with the families in their stations wagons and kids on dates in their parents' sedans.

Francis and I were fond of Rainier Ale, the "green death," as it was known. Late afternoons, we'd drive into Montecito, pull off the road and stop among the eucalyptus or lemon groves and open a can. Looking off into the western light above the tree line, we'd praise the attributes of Susan Miratti, Judy Schmeckel, or Kathy Quigley, or we'd enumerate possible futures as if choosing, merely saying so, was all it was going to take. One October evening, on our way to meet some girls and a few guys from our class out at the "haunted house"—an old lemon-packing warehouse in ruin—we stopped off on Milpas Street for some spudnuts. These were donuts made from potato-base flour, and this was the only place in town that provided sugar and grease loading at this high level. We ate some on the way, arriving in the orchard to find that no one else was there. We opened a can of green death and waited. No one showed. We had another, and, feeling OK, we finished the spudnuts, then the ale. As we drained the last drops we realized that the ale, strong enough by itself, had not combined well with the spudnuts. My first hint was Francis's face—almost as green as the Rainier can. I felt as if weasels were playing water polo in my stomach. We looked at each other, threw open the doors, and, crawling out on all fours, recited unholy litanies to the trunks of the nearest lemon trees. That taught us a lesson there and then. We laid off spudnuts for the rest of the year.

We were a bit unconscious, lucky—got away with things— we never drove cross-eyed into a ditch. Before one of the last dances of our senior year, Francis and Steve and I sat in the bowling alley, priming ourselves with a LaBatts beer, a pull or two of Seagram's 7, and then went in once the dance was going. We felt cool, in control, unobtrusive. But Monday in civics class Father Bernard began by pointing out that having served in the navy, he could tell when someone had had even one drink. He was cagey and generous enough to say, "I'm not naming any names for now, but it would be a shame, so close to graduation, to see folks expelled for drinking." I stared straight ahead. I was sure he was aiming at Francis, who'd been slow dancing with an electric guitar, a bit more energized than Steve or I. But we had been right there with him, so it wasn't hard to figure out with whom he'd acquired his swagger. Fair warning and we made good use of it. On campus. Even onboard the bus taking us up to Hidden Valley Guest Ranch for our graduation party, we checked out the chaperones, the bus, and passed on the booze. We had a good evening dancing to Cecilio Rodriguez's band, who played the new Stones hit, released that very week, "I Can't Get No Satisfaction."

One afternoon, driving back from town with a part for my friend Bolduc's Austin Mini Cooper, I mentioned how good just one beer would taste, just something to sip after the greasy job, leaning back against a eucalyptus, admiring the light dusting down into the bay. His younger brother Norm said, "Hey, I can always get a beer." "No," I said. "Where?" How did this kid, a year younger than I, pull this off? He didn't look near twenty-one. He turned the car around and headed back toward Milpas Street. Plenty of liquor stores there, but he didn't even have a fake ID. Near the top, we turned off and drove back a few blocks to a tiny mom-and-pop grocery. Norm asked, "What do you want?" I gave him a buck fifty, saying "Coors," but I was not about to go in with him and get busted trying to buy. Back he came in a minute with four cans. We put the bag on the floor of the car out of sight and headed back up the hill as he explained, "Vera, she sells to anyone." That week I told Francis and Steve about Vera's Market, and said, "Give me some bucks and I'll buy for Saturday night." Puzzled, they still opened their wallets. Middle of the afternoon seemed a good time, cops not as likely to be staked out then, I thought. I drove up in my big old '59 Chevy and sat there trying to work up the requisite courage and poker face. Then I saw Rick Spencer and Norm Henry, surfing friends from the other side of town, carrying two cases each to their car. I recognized a carload of girls from San Marcos High—even farther north of town—who had also just loaded up and were pulling out. Word must really be out, I thought. The only place in town to buy without an ID. I walked up to the small counter and, in my most mature voice, said, "Two cases of Coors." The small Chicana lady across the counter said, "Eleven twenty-five," and that was it. Amazing. There was a big beer truck making deliveries from the tiny parking lot out back. There were four shelves of groceries and then aisles crammed with cases of beer, a cooler stocked with beer, and more cases piled on top of the cooler. This old woman was going to re-tire in style, and soon. You'd think the distributor would have figured it out—the volume out of a mom-and-pop equaling the biggest store on the main street. I stopped thinking, put the cash on the counter, picked up two cases at the end of an aisle, and walked out holding my breath. We hit Vera's a couple more times, buying in warehouse quantity as long as we were taking the risk.

Our friend De Vito, who lived only a few blocks away, walked into Vera's one Saturday morning for a six-pack, planning to watch a morning of cartoons on TV and drink a couple beers by himself. He was nineteen at the time, I think. A plainclothes undercover cop arrested Gary as soon as he hit the sidewalk. For months kids had been loading trunks, vans, and pickups with cases of Bud, Coors, Olympia, Miller, and Rainier Ale. De Vito on a quiet Saturday morning racks up a criminal record for a single six-pack of Pabst. A trial, lawyer, fines, the whole officious mess befell him for a few beers. He had to sell his surfboard and scratch up all his savings to pay the five hundred dollars, and then there was probation. Vera claimed, smartly, that De Vito had shown her an ID, and if he were underage then it must have been fake. But Vera carded no one. If you could say "Case of Coors," put $5.75 on the counter and carry your beer out, you could buy at Vera's.

Summers, we'd sometimes caravan up to Gibraltar Road, high on the ridge above town. Closer there to the sparkling stream of stars, the wide belt of silence over the world, we'd park along the empty road, open a beer, a bottle of cold wine, and lie out in the middle of the road staring up into the firmament as if we were bound to discover the key to some question we had yet to ask. We were killing time the best way we knew how, looking out to a place where there was no time, where a shooting star streaked occasionally by, where whatever went on did so brightly and continuously. Some of our lives, for a while, were just that charmed.

Home from college toward the end of my freshman year, I got together with Steve and Francis. We drove over to a house De Vito and Bruno shared on the edge of Montecito, happy to visit old friends. We sat two cases of Bud down in the living room and walked into the back where we found De Vito and Bruno smoking marijuana—not our thing. We looked at each other, walked back to the living room, picked up our cases, and left. We were now moralizing, judging others. Happy fools that we were, all we'd wanted for the last five years was to speed things up, to be kinetic, on the edge of experience. Here was marijuana, the latest thing, but suddenly we didn't want to go any further, were applying the brake, were not interested in sitars, surrealism, incense, and a looming purple haze. We only wanted to sit around and talk with friends, and we had experienced enough paranoia just drinking beer.

In less than two years, most of us back from Vietnam or in college and opposed to the war, we would become as much a part of the Peace, Love, long hair, San Francisco, Hare Krishna, spare change, tie-dye, Tabasco sauce, and patchouli oil movement as anyone. But right then, time was up—the war waiting, pressure of college, jobs. We were for keeping what little we could under control.

We left and cruised the oaks and eucalyptus groves of Montecito, rode past our old houses on the east and west side, up and down State Street, lamenting the loss of the Blue Onion drive-in and its big blue and cinnamon neon sign, the four downtown lanes of Santa Barbara reduced to a lane each way, the lemon orchard replaced by Robinsons and the town's first mall. We drove slowly, under the speed limit, as if through a city that had just burned down. We drove with no idea really where we were headed, cruised around the rest of the night without anyone mentioning the booze we'd left in the trunk.

Working Grocery

Not a year goes by without that dream. I'm walking past a grocery store—I'm not a teenager, I'm my dreaming age, but it doesn't matter. Someone stops me on the sidewalk. It's Charlie Cantello, the manager, a small man with a military bearing: shave, haircut, square jaw, steely eyes. His grey manager's jacket starched stiff as cardboard, plastic badge pinned to the pocket, name in grease pencil with "Mgr." right after it. "What's wrong with you, boy. You overslept again?" And he lifts his hand as if to slap me upside the head.

There's a momentary confusion, hesitation. I almost recall that I have a life, that there's something else I do, but the truth never works its way fully to the surface. I step on the black plastic runner and the automatic IN door swings open and vibrates to a stop. I walk past the phalanx of shopping carts and know my way between the frozen food aisles—vegetables on the left with Jell-O and pudding stacked above the cold cases; juices and

125

ice creams on the right with cones, marshmallows, and paper plates on the racks over them. Still in disbelief, I walk to the swinging doors at the back and look through the scratched and smudged Plasticine of the oval windows at the dim back room. I move slowly into the room like someone trying to see and feel his way under water.

There's Les, one of the clerks. "Hey, buddy, didn't you check the schedule?" he says and hands me an apron the color of grocery bags. I check the pockets. There's the green wire twist I get from Produce and a box-cutter razor knife; there's the maroon striped tie. I hold the apron at arms' length and my heart sinks—there's the plastic name badge, its red lettering saying JORDANOS, HI, MY NAME IS "CHRIS" in grease pencil. I clip on the tie, stick my head through the strap over the bib, and fasten the back of the apron behind me with the twist.

I go over to the cork board outside the office. The assistant manager, Stanley Rogers, is in there as always at an adding machine checking and rechecking the receipt tapes—click, click, click as he punches the black and white rows of keys with one fat finger, a crunch as he pulls the crank handle down to total up. I flip up the first page of the schedule and there's my name. Shit! A 12–9 shift again! Twenty-some years, and I'm still late for work!

Mercifully, I usually wake up at this point, heart racing, with that sense of terror a trapped animal must know. But in worse reruns of the dream, it's the daily routine. I head to the front to bag orders. I'm clearing carts out of the aisle while the manager, assistant manager, and the third man all stand in the manager's box in their grey coats looking east, west, and south for the first one of us to stop moving, their practiced glares cold as a raptor's over field mice. When business slows down, I'm sent to reshelve a cartload of "go-backs"—items customers discovered weren't on sale or that they couldn't afford once their bill was totaled up. Or I'm sent back to restock the bags: double-time up the wooden stairs, drop down hay bale–sized bundles of 650 barrel bags, 425s and 375s for lighter orders, turn on the conveyor belt, run the bags down, stack them up on the flat cart and push them up front. I have to hurry. Gordon, the third man, is always sneaking into the back for a smoke; he tries to find one of us taking a breather back there as his excuse to be there lighting up a Marlboro. Usually about the time I push the go-backs basket into the middle of the store or get the flat cart loaded with bags, I snap out of it, usually.

Of course, the job didn't start out to be brain-numbing repetition. I had no notion that grocery would permanently invade my subconscious, becoming a psychic malaria whose fever would produce night sweats and neurosis for years to come. In fact, working grocery looked to have an air of prestige. At first, it was just about having a job that didn't look like too much work—it wasn't construction or car wash. I'd seen several boxboys, as they were then called, cheerfully hustling about the front of the store in ties and aprons, snapping bags so they popped open with authority in the air. Like jugglers they flipped tins and jars from countertop to bag. It looked skillful, almost fun, like good work for a sixteen-year-old. I was intent on independence, a car, doing things on my own, and this seemed like the key. What could be so bad about bagging groceries, chatting with customers, coming away every other Friday with a little money to pay for the car or nights out?

There were nine Jordanos supermarkets in Santa Barbara, only two Safeways, a handful of mom-and-pops. Problem was, there were plenty of boys who wanted boxboy jobs. Jordanos' man in charge of personnel had a good part of his time taken up just keeping the boxboy applications and hires moving. My father did business with Jordanos, had, in each of their stores, installed Muzak—basically bad elevator music (movie themes by Mantovani, soft choral arrangements by the Ray Coniff Singers), which was barely audible to shoppers as they deliberated over mushrooms, steaks, or yellow peppers, and which was supposed to subliminally encourage them to relax and buy more. He knew the three brothers who owned the chain, even knew Art Thompson, the vice president who hired and fired. I asked my father to put my name in and expected in a week or two to have a job. Nothing happened. I nagged my father in the coming months to again say something. Six months later, I got a call, but only for fifteen or twenty hours a week, three or four hours a day, no regular schedule, so I couldn't make many plans. Although I wasn't working much, I seemed to always be at work. I had to prove I really wanted the job by giving up most of my days for a paltry schedule and paycheck. Sliding between checkout stands, flipping items from the counter with my right hand to my left, stacking, working fast so cans and jars moved in a waterfall into the bag—I, like all the boxboys, was pushed to hustle, to finish one order and get on to the next.

As low man on the list, I pulled the worst jobs. When baby food or catsup hit the floor, it was, "Buckley, clean up on aisle six." It became second nature to grab a box, pull out my cutter and hack two lengths of cardboard to scrape glass and jam or whatever together, then toss the whole mess in the box, carry it to the back and come out with the mop and bucket to finish up. Once a week, Cantello sent me around with my box-cutter blade attached horizontally to the handle end, edge pushed out flat, and had me scrape up blackened gum and other substances off the linoleum.

His other favorite task for me was unloading water softener salt. Once a month, or for special promotions, a truck full of fifty-pound bags pulled up in front instead of in the back of the store, where deliveries were made. We stacked the bags by the IN and OUT doors or sometimes, if there was a sale, out on the sidewalk. It took a crew of five or six to unload the truck, and though a few had hand trucks that could roll seven or eight bags down the ramp at a time, someone had to bend and unload the bags one by one and stack them. Although it was strictly against union regulations for boxboys to unload any truck of anything, I was always relieved from bagging when the salt arrived.

Nevertheless, being a boxboy seemed a good enough job at the start. I told my friends, flashed some cash, and felt a level up in the world. I'd been working for about three months when one day I came in, clipped on my tie and apron, and walked up front to find my friend Joe Bolduc bagging orders. How did he get the job? His father did not have business connections. Joe said he had just kept calling in several times a day for a week and they put him on, obviously ahead of boys whose fathers had put their names in for them. He seemed eager, and Art Thompson must have figured he'd be a hard worker. And he was, as I was, for the first few months.

We had some education and were heading for more—working grocery was not going to be our life. But it sure was for most of the people there. Bolduc and I were lower-middle class, so the job was certainly not beneath us. We worked hard, hustled our proverbials off for $1.65 an hour before taxes and union dues. We had to belong to the Retail Clerks Union, pay a chunk of our paychecks in dues or no job. We had to put up with the unctuous union representatives waltzing into the store in their sharkskin suits, chatting us up as if we were involved in some great labor movement against the captains of industry. All they really wanted was to check that no new boxboys had been hired without signing up to pay dues. With our wage at $1.65 an hour, we didn't feel the union had actually gone toe to toe with management on our behalf. Where the hell were they when someone pulled three 12:00–9:00 shifts in a row, when the salt truck came around? That's what I wanted to know.

For a buck sixty-five an hour, management wanted loyalty, commitment, dogged work, and an unthinking subservience, and that's what most got under my skin. They were still operating from a '50s mind-set or earlier, when simply being in a position of authority made everyone hop to, no matter what.

Cantello gave pep talks, called us in individually to say we weren't hustling between counters, weren't cheerful enough. Every few months or so he'd complain about pilfering, talk profit margins and the trouble at the top. No one took him very seriously, though he couldn't have been more serious. This was the Bible of business; there was a moral aura over it all, and it was attached to the amount of profit. Few boxboys were really intimidated. One used to routinely slip a carton of cigarettes down each sleeve of his large jacket on the way out of the store, nonchalant as you please. All kinds of things were eaten on the same receipt. Obeying all my immediate commands, I never found it in my job description to protect management in this regard. Along this line, one of the best jobs was to stock the dairy box. There was a pecking order, and after the head boxboy went back to stock it, the next guy would go an hour later. One advantage was getting off the floor, where you had to go full tilt all the time. Working alone in the cool of the dairy box was as good as a break. And usually one of the clerks had left a barbecued chicken or ribs in there, and there was a shelf of loose beers. You could face-up the quarts and half gallons, eat a leg or wing, crack open a crate of cottage cheese, stack the front, and take a swig of beer while your compadres were carrying out or wrangling a snaky row of carts in the sun.

The problem, however, was not so much the work as it was the high seriousness with which the system of hierarchy operated at the market—way out of proportion to what was really at stake. Jordanos employed a "mystery shopper"—a person unknown to management or employees, always dressed in regular street clothes, who went store to store buying things and "invisibly" checking up on everyone's performance. There were two-way mirrors high in the back of each store, a secret police–like setup for watching over customers, *and* employees. This was only selling groceries for wages. We were not saving lives, offering financial planning, healing wounded psyches, or dispensing knowledge. This was getting folks to buy New, Giant,

Super and Improved Tide or Ajax and leading them away from advertised specials on which the store made no money. Yet there was a ladder of command that the lifers lower down just lived to climb.

There was an enforced air of superiority based on position and years put in. But even more than money, what a grocery lifer wanted was to be able to put on a grey coat and tell someone else what to do—when, for how long, and how fast to do it. Store gossip was always centered on who might be chosen to manage a new store or take over for someone who was leaving, who had really screwed up and would suffer the ignominy of demotion back to clerk. There were three managers—*the* manager, who worked the 9:00–6:00 shift and never worked on Sundays; the assistant manager who worked a 10:00–7:00 or 8:00–5:00; and a third man, who worked the late shift, usually 11:00–8:00. But there were always times, late shifts until 9:00, weekends, holidays, and Sundays, when the top people were off and someone had to be in charge. Art Thompson would come around and call one of the clerks into the office to make him fifth man or even sixth man—there was a chain of command for any eventuality. Walter, a man about five feet three inches, was our fifth man and couldn't wait for an opportunity to put on a grey coat (rolling the sleeves up three or four times to finally meet his wrists) and stand up in the manager's box. He'd glare at the boxboys, tell Les to go stock the soup aisle so that he would be left with the easier paper aisle, or, wearing a stiff, practiced grin, direct a customer to an item listed in the ad. On those few occasions he swelled with power and self-importance. He'd order one of us to dust-mop the aisles even though they didn't need it. He was posturing, preparing for difficult command decisions at the top from all the way down at the fifth-man level, and it looked pretty ridiculous to us.

As boxboys we had fifteen bosses at all times, from managers to clerks to checkers; everyone except us had someone beneath them. We were not allowed to talk to other employees. If there was a lull, you stocked bags, collected carts from the lot, or grabbed spray bottle and paper towels and washed down the counters, put up the new ad posters, scraped gum. We were told to offer *every* customer help carrying out his or her groceries. Many people, feeling it was part of the price they'd just paid, would have a boxboy carry out a single bag and put it in their car. Perfectly healthy men would have one of us carry their bags. Tipping was never allowed. Disagreeing with the customer was not allowed. By virtue of simply buying groceries, customers felt superior. They wanted to tell you what was wrong with the welfare system while you pushed a cart full of groceries to their Ford Country Squire station wagon or loaded bags in the trunk of their Buick. I had a saying for these occasions, "Everyone eats." We had to listen to a lot of prejudice and unfounded parochial opinions. It wasn't just the reasonable and informed who came for food.

Boxboys had a dress code—no mustaches or beards, but none of us had long hair as would soon become the fashion. Yet I found myself telling a customer, who had complained to me in a privileged tone about the length of my hair, that that had nothing to do with my ability to bag her groceries and get them into the car. From my friend Bolduc I learned more subtle responses. When it was raining and people had him carry out groceries they could have easily managed themselves, Joe rubbed the bags along the wet side of the car before he put them onto the seat, assuring their disintegration by the time they reached the house. If customers were obnoxious while checking out, we loaded a bag so heavy that no one was going to be able to lift it out of the car once we had put it there. Packages of Lady Fingers, Wonder Bread, eggs, and grapes found their way to the bottom of the bag beneath cans of tomatoes, beans, and soup.

Our store was in the blue-collar part of town but right on the edge of the richer climes of Montecito. Poorer folks usually treated us better, having an idea what it was to lift and heave, to be a subordinate. A pleasant word, a reasonable attitude, was all it took for us to volunteer to carry out a person's groceries. In some ways, it was always good to get outside on a carry-out, even if to collect stray carts. At least in the parking lot you were, for the most part, out from under the constant scrutiny of the horde of managers who were working very hard to see that you worked hard. There was, however, over the long haul, no escape: you were doing time and were conscious mainly of how long you had to go until you got off.

In college, a new social situation and a heavy study load, I forgot about grocery, and, forgetting, felt I'd escaped. Not so. Before I knew it, my freshman year was over and I needed a place for the summer. My father had moved to Arizona; my mother was living in the desert. The only way I could live in Santa Barbara was to share an apartment with friends, and to do that I needed work. I called Jordanos—my only connection, my one working skill. Business picked up in summer, so I was assigned almost immediately and shuffled between stores. Summers between my sophomore and junior years were the same. I should have sensed something was wrong when, during my last year of school, dreams about forgetting to come in to work my grocery shift mixed in with the usual anxiety dreams of missing class or the big test.

I did not attend my college graduation because at the time my stepfather, a wonderful and generous man, was dying of cancer. I went to be with my mother and everyone in Santa Barbara, because he was in the hospital there. It is only obvious and inadequate to say this was a bad time for everyone. One morning, my mother gone to the funeral home, I was in a hotel room with my stepsister and her husband, a true and serious salesman. He had moved from soft-water sales to Gallo. He had no education beyond a year at community college, but he had drive, he had goals; he had business in his blood like a zealot has God. A numb silence in the air, and he thought he'd put that time to good use, enlighten me with his experience and views about life and business, both the same to him. Now that I had a college degree, what *was* I going to do? "Everyone needs GOALS," he proclaimed. "Needs to plan." Five or six years older, he really knew that he really knew what was what. I was stunned with Frank's death—something no job, no goals would rectify. The four years at college had gone in a blur, and so much change was imminent—politically, socially. I had no focus at all. I'd applied to one graduate school but was not accepted. The draft was looming. I was more than a little brain-weary.

I flashed back to a scene from *The Graduate* with Dustin Hoffman, his character, Ben, floating in the pool, drinking a Coors. Graduated from Berkeley, he's feeling pressure from everyone to do, or say he's going to do, something in line with their expectations. He has just survived a cocktail party in his honor to which his father invited all of his own friends. His father is a predictable business type, persistent in his advice—"Plastics, America's future," but he has lost patience with Ben's loafing. "Well Ben, what's it all mean, then? Four years of college, what does it mean?" Ben rolls over on the raft and replies, "I don't know. You tell me," and then pulls on his mask and snorkle and dives deep underwater. Every friend I talked to at that time understood that particular scene, related absolutely to the exasperation, the confusion. It wasn't just that we didn't know what all the work and ritual was for, what it added up to; our reaction—Ben's response—was also a first step away from the thoughtless traditions and petrified prescriptions that our fathers—smug in their blue business suits—stood for. In college, I had switched from a business major—my father's choice—to an English major and had told him of the switch long afterwards. Now especially, I didn't want someone's expectations, the New Jerusalem of profit and loss, foisted on me. So I answered my stepbrother-in-law with something I truly felt at that time, but also something I knew would really annoy him and shut him up. I said, "I don't have any Goals. I want to just live, hang out with my friends."

The adage about watching what you wish for because you may well receive it, was soon true. I spent that summer with my mother, helping with probate, fending off lawyers who descended like a passel of crows to play golf and peck pieces out of Frank's estate. I maintained the lemon trees, tamarisks, and oleanders around the house, and gave what emotional support I could. I came up with a teaching job for the fall—seventh and eighth grade in Torrance, a truly forgettable city. I obtained a position for the following school year at my old grammar school in Santa Barbara, Mt. Carmel. I interviewed with the Sister Principal, with the old pastor from my childhood, and moved back to town. I had enough money saved to make it to my first paycheck in September, and enrolled in graduate education classes that summer at the university, read, and took advantage of the sun and surf. When I called the school to ask what forms needed to be signed, what texts I could pick up, I was told I no longer had the job.

I had not been smart or experienced enough to ask to sign a contract when I was told I had the position. I had taken the spiritually committed at their word. Mistake. The teacher who had agreed to exchange seventh- and eighth-grade math for fifth- and sixth-grade English had backed out. I suggested that since she had broken her agreement and I was keeping mine, why shouldn't she be the one to lose her job? But she lived with another woman who also taught at Mt. Carmel, and if one were let go the other had threatened to quit as well. So, Sister Principal explained, she would then be out two teachers and still have no one to teach upper-level math. She had just hired a woman who could teach both. Good-bye.

I would be out of money in three weeks. I had to come up with work, and quickly. I called the other schools in town—way too late, nothing available. I called Jordanos and had an interview the next day. The first thing the woman did was hold up a drawing of acceptable and unacceptable employee grooming. If I got a haircut, they might have a position. I said of course, and added that I was looking for a journeyman's job, not a boxboy's, and did not mention teaching, college, or graduate classes. They offered a journeyman track with half boxboy hours. Take it or leave it. What choice did I have?

I found myself back at number 9 on Milpas Street, many of the same people still there; Gordon, the third man, was now manager. I found, too, that I was not given the hours promised, and was given no section to stock. My journeyman hours were only from six to nine in the morning, before the store opened. I had to wake up at five to be on time to mop the entire store. Occasionally, I'd be sent to another store and end up with journeyman hours all day. I needed to accumulate a certain amount of hours at that level to move permanently into a clerk position. At the rate I was going, it would take years. Once, replacing a checker on vacation, I stood for two weeks all day at the register. Only women were full-time checkers; men stocked, placed orders, gave orders, so management thought they'd given me a demeaning assignment. In fact, the best people in the store, the only ones I really liked aside from two boxboys my age, were the women checkers. I still remember Ann Avilla, Wanda, and Charlesetta Williams, who always treated me well, and joked around. They knew the caliber of the minds at the controls and always had practical tips about surviving in the store. They were reasonable and sweet and offered a series of momentary stays against the drudgery, but they were stuck there, even more than I. I didn't mind checking one bit, but after the two weeks, back I went to the mop.

I also filled in at the San Andreas store. One afternoon I was assigned to stock Jell-O and pudding. I hadn't been at it five minutes before Tom, the clerk whose section this was and who was filling in for the assistant manager, came over and started realigning all my boxes so not one centimeter of one corner of one box was out of square. He started in about the right way to stack Jell-O. I said, "Jesus Tom, it's just Jell-O, not a life's work." But I had insulted him; this was in fact his life's work.

He faced-up the end sections of lemon and lime, tore the brown wrapping off a bundle of mandarin orange boxes, and stacked two columns of those faceup. He tensed up along the neck and said, "Well, there's value in work well done," and walked off toward the back room. Value. Sweet Jesus! I thought. Not this work. Not this life. After that, it was back to number 9. A boxboy. Twenty-two years old, college degree, graduate classes, year of teaching, and I was schlepping groceries for two bucks an hour. I began to think about *goals*.

The managers had no intention of moving me along the track. I was kept on there as a boxboy when there were clerk openings at other stores. I had tried to look like a company man to escape the early hours and mopping and my status afternoons as oldest boxboy in the world. I proposed a section of organic items as in one of the L.A. chains. Wrong move. I was the weirdo, the one with hippy ideas, definitely not career grocery material. I checked out the LSAT test, asked one of my friends about Loyola Law School, where he was doing well. Wrong again. Gordon and the assistant manager began to give me trouble: "Hey counselor, clean up on aisle seven. Push the cart to the back and sort bottles, Your Honor." Nothing was going to change.

While I was unloading the salt truck in front of the store one morning, Tony Ramirez, manager of the liquor store next door, offered me a job. He was watching me stack the fifty-pound bags and said he thought I worked hard. I told him he was right. He needed a clerk at $2.50 an hour and pointed out that it was a much easier job. Tony seemed friendly, and he did not give off the sacrosanct attitude that came with working grocery. I quit Jordanos that week, happy to make fifty cents more an hour, thankful to have some morning hours to myself, and only one boss. My brain was about to atrophy, so I enrolled in an early-morning French course at city college. A more flexible schedule allowed me time, and that improved my overall feeling about life. I also began to teach tennis at a private school a few afternoons a week. I was writing the occasional inward and incomprehensible poem as had been my habit from college, and, terrible and infrequent as they were, these poems at least reinforced some sense of a life of the mind, a life beyond selling things. But soon, because I showed up on time and didn't steal the place blind, I was given more hours at the liquor store; often I pulled double shifts to fill in for Tony when he left town. This, finally, was only a small step above working grocery, a sideways move. I'd better get a *plan*.

One motivational factor was a new clerk, Don, a fellow down on his luck who worked like a dog. Tony finagled a lot of free hours out of Don. He only paid him for twenty hours a week, but had him in there more often, helping with the boxes out back, driving to the dump, stocking the beer case—Tony got Don to do all this just by giving him a free soda, a place to hang out, the promise of more hours. Don needed money, and since I had not had a Saturday night off for ages, I arranged for him to take my shift. That night a guy came in and browsed until the store cleared, and then asked for one of the tamales steaming in the Crock-Pot we kept on the front of the counter. As Don leaned over to take the top off the pot, the guy whipped out a bowie knife from beneath his coat, fixed the tip to Don's throat, and had Don up on his toes while he cleaned out the register. That throat could obviously have been mine. I needed to get out from behind a counter, to stop putting things in bags for no good reason under the sun.

About this time, my old friend Sozzi, back from Vietnam and recovered from illness and general shock, dropped by to say he was going to enroll at San Diego State and finish his degree. Looking through his catalog, I saw that the school offered a master's program in creative writing. So I thought about it for a week, recalled the clear image of that knife at Don's throat for not a damn thing more than $2.50 an hour, and decided to go to graduate school. My stepsister and her family would be nearby, and my mother often went to San Diego for the summer—there would be a safety net of sorts. I could sell my car and take a shot at it. Sozzi and I could split the rent and bike to school. I figured that even if I washed out as a writer, I would learn something about American poetry, avoid business, bosses, and brain-death for a few more years. It was time to wake up. I was still in my twenties. What did I have to lose, I wondered, except the nightmare of working grocery?

On My Own

My problem at fifteen was the same as every teenager's—getting around, point A to point B, acquiring some control over my own life. The year previous, I'd caught rides with friends—to games, dances, the occasional party. And once in a while I would be allotted one of the three designated spaces in a buddy's car for cruising—up and down State, the main street in town, or, along Cabrillo Boulevard as a full moon ignited the lines of surf. Out there, all four windows down, the savor of wind and salt air rushing in, all the atoms of my body pressed forward—against what I couldn't possibly have said—I sensed that finally something might be about to happen in my life.

But my father moved us, yet again—this time into the foothills, a good trek out of town, and I was no longer close to my one or two friends with cars. To me, the remedy to the problem was obvious—my own wheels! As always, my father pleaded financial impossibility and reminded me that at fifteen and a half I could not drive a car without a person eighteen or older along with me. I had a learner's permit, so the only motor vehicle I could operate by myself was a motorcycle. Fall semester would be starting soon, and I'd have to get to high school on my own.

An immediate solution presented itself by way of my friend Tuck Schneider, ten months older than I. He had been tooling around on a Honda 55 trail bike for the last few months. I needed a motorcycle. No. My father was "not going to condone the risk of that kind of reckless transportation." I suggested several re-payment plans, limited usage hours and days, various penalties for tickets, but he was opposed and continued to advance safety arguments and examples of maimed teenagers whenever I raised the subject.

But I was sold. This was the way to go. I rode double with Tuck and dug up all the information I could on Hondas and even the two-stroke whiny Suzukis. Tuck's Honda was easy—a three-speed job with a centrifugal clutch, and that meant there was no clutch handle to engage smoothly against the throttle— hence no real shifting maneuvers to master. Piece of cake. You simply twisted the throttle handle back all the way, stomped once, twice, or three times on the gear lever with your left foot, and you were in a different gear. Topping out, you could hit perhaps thirty-eight down a major hill. Couldn't be easier, and I had the hang of it in five minutes, winding the gears out, up and down the quiet oak-shaded road where Tuck lived. But, no sale! My father more or less told me not to ride with Tuck. The trail bike model had a single seat with only a rack behind it, so you really had to be desperate to ride double. But for a while, it was my only means of getting around, and somewhat surreptitiously, Tuck would drive us to his house or to a friend's, down to the beach, wherever we had to be. I was going slow, and without comfort, but at least I was going.

One day my mother called, and in the course of our usual conversation I managed to convince her that the motor bike idea was a good one. They were not powerful and so not very dangerous on that account, yet they were not that expensive, especially when compared to cars with initial cost, repairs, and insurance. And the savings on gas! These Hondas ran on a thimbleful a week.

I'd ride into the center of town with Tuck to the Honda dealership in the old Dal Poso tire garage. The showroom was jammed, five rows of bikes, small ones up to the 305 Super Hawks. A bright world of chrome, an intoxicating soup of leather, oil, wax, and rubber. Tuck would talk shop—clutch-plate replacement, customized accessories. He eyed a chrome fender for his front wheel to replace the stock red plastic one. We both enjoyed checking out new models, especially the big bikes. I found a blue number called the 110 Sport. It had, in fact, the same 55-cubic-centimeter engine as Tuck's bike but had more style, more bells and whistles. It *looked* more like a motorcycle—sleeker, more chrome, a sculptured gas tank, and a long bench-style black leather seat. The trail bike had knobby off-road tires, a frame more reminiscent of a bicycle than a motorcycle. The 110 Sport was lower and had a true "street" look, though it couldn't outrun the other.

I knew I wanted this one, and my mother understood my predicament. Since she was not around to help with transportation, she offered to buy the bike in place of Christmas and birthday gifts that year. I proposed it to my father, and I was amazed that his objections so easily disappeared. Mom sent the check for three hundred dollars, and I went down the next Saturday to buy the blue 110. I wanted Tuck along for moral as well as technical support, but he had something he had to do with his parents, so I went alone, my father dropping me off on his way to work. Although I'd ridden Tuck's Honda many times and could shift that trail bike in my sleep, the 110 had a clutch lever on the handlebars like on a real motorcycle. It took as much clutch release/throttle coordination to run as a standard shift in a car, and I'd yet to try that, having only wheeled around in our family's boat of a Plymouth automatic station wagon. Similarly,

I'd never ridden a bike with a real clutch. I was in the woods.
There I was, fifteen and a half, doing my damndest to appear
cool and on top of the situation, lying to save face. This was
important, a way I would "see" myself for a while, and I was
trying to bluff my way through it.

The salesman briefly differentiated the brake handle from the
clutch handle, the foot pedal for the rear brake from the gear
shift pedal—first down; second, third, and fourth up. Light
switch, cutoff valve on the fuel line to thwart thieves, papers
of registration and sale, and it all was over before I could even
think of risking embarrassment by asking, "Just how fast should
I let out the clutch?" He showed me where to store the papers
under the seat and headed right back to the showroom. I fished
around with the gear pedal until the amber bulb near the speed-
ometer lit up, which meant it was in neutral, then I kick-started
it on the second try. So far so good. I pulled in the clutch lever
and, just to be safe, coasted out of the lot to the traffic light and
crossed the street before letting out the clutch. The bike gave
a spurt forward, then the engine died. I walked it over to the
curbside, turned it off, then on, wiggled the gear into neutral,
kick-started it on the first try, felt confident, hopped on and
let out the clutch so fast that I barely managed to hang on as I
popped up and down—bucking bronco style—in first gear for
a block. Hanging on, stuttering forward and coming to a quick
stop, I looked as graceful as a pelican choking down a huge fish.
At the intersection I held in the clutch and turned off the key.
I knew people had to have been watching, wondering if this
crazy kid had any idea what he was doing. I knew the answer
to that. But to cover up my inadequacy, I inspected the bike—
seriously examined the gas cutoff valve, inquisitively turned the
headlight on and off, took a close and long look at the rear chain
sprocket, and wiped some grease on my jeans. I backed away,
looked perplexed, and rubbed my forehead with my hand as if
there were something malfunctioning with the systems and not
the rider. I sputtered across the downtown area a block at a

time, never getting out of first gear but dispensing at least with the mechanical examinations every time I killed the engine.

I then chose a less traveled street to ride out of the city and back into the suburbs of Montecito. Luckily, this motor bike was small enough that even when you pulled a wheelie—that is, popped the clutch so fast that the whole bike shot out from under you—you could catch yourself by sliding off the back and standing straight up in the street holding the handlebars at arm's length in the air while the engine raced and the back tire spun and bit into the asphalt, bouncing up, trying to take off. I managed to hold onto the bike. I was a strong kid, though perhaps not a very smart one, and I toughed it out. On the long quiet road home, I managed finally to shift into second and third with only small jumps and jolts. A trial by fire. It was dumb luck that I didn't send the bike flying beneath the wheels of some beer truck, into a roadside eucalyptus or ditch. For two or three days, I rode covertly—up and down our driveway before and after school, along untraveled School House Road during sleepy weekends—with a dark cloud of doubts about the glamorous fraternity into which I had marginally lurched pursuing me and the engine's tiny noise.

The turnover time between triumph and despair was almost negligible those teenage years, and in a matter of days I had the procedure wired, could downshift and speed shift to the RPM limit that small one-cylinder engine block could stand. Tuck and I were soon cruising the outlands of Montecito south into Summerland and north to Goleta and the airport. I was riding daily to and from school. This was independence. I was on my own. Often I'd just head out of the house and ride around with nothing more in mind than moving, just watching the air finger the hedges of pittosporum and eugenia that lined the roads. Usually I'd end up at Miramar Beach, sit there for a half hour or so complaining to the blue about a real or imagined romance—the quick, open joys and inevitable despairs that the waves seemed to echo, the hammerlock on happiness that wouldn't let up, the loneliness love left you always arm wrestling with. But that loneliness, that inflated sense of general grief, reinforced my sense of self and left me almost calm, content there just trying to form a single clear question about the gridlock of emotions knotting at the green base of my heart. I would, of course, do my pondering sitting on my bike, in my designated navy and red reversible bike jacket, one with a zippered inner pocket and a hood hidden in the collar. I'd unzip the pocket and pull out my pipe and Cherry Blend tobacco, light up never for one moment feeling pretentious, and think that despite all the emotional devastation of those days, I was now someone in the world.

Many times Tuck would come along and smoke a Tareyton or two. We could do what we wanted now. And though the surgeon general was just starting to figure out the effects of smoking and we had been somewhat warned, we paid as little attention to him as to any other adult, and felt, really, what could possibly hurt us? A day after Tuck had installed his new chrome fender, he took off from the beach a bit ahead of me. Not twenty seconds behind him, I came up to the railroad crossing to find him face down just across the tracks, his bike upside down in the road. He was conscious but in bad shape—his face scraped up with bits of gravel dug into his cheek. I went for help rather than try to move him. Tuck had built up a little speed crossing the tracks, and the front tire, recoiling from the bump of the rails, locked in the new fender, so when the tire touched down, it stopped the bike cold, and Tuck was pitched over the handlebars and onto his head. His cheekbone was broken in a couple of places, and he had to spend a couple of days in the hospital. No one, especially on little bikes, wore helmets in those days. He was in some pain, but considering he could have just as easily broken his neck, he felt more or less lucky, and when healed, even half heroic.

Still, for those first few months, and despite Tuck's example, I felt marvelous, still sped around feeling immutable in body and mind, captain of my fate as far ahead as I could see. That turned out to be about five months. Many of the other students began to drive cars to school, and rusted or primered, coughing oil and crawling, that was a sure level above small motor bikes in the parking lot. Tuck got a job and invested in a Honda 250 Scrambler, a twin-cylinder cycle that would do seventy miles an hour on the freeway with both of us on it. Big bikes had as much status as cars, and really big ones had more. Tuck often talked about a Triumph Bonneville 500, a monster of a machine as we saw it then. I had graduated to the point where I could use our family car once in a while on weekends, but I was still riding the 110 to school. A couple of times I even picked up my friend Orsua when his car had broken down, and the two of us, crammed onto that little bike, would ride across town in the dark to the Earl Warren Showgrounds for a dance. If you couldn't get there looking cool, you at least had to get there, and times when we doubled up on the bike, we'd park it a long way away from the entrance so no one would detect our humble transport.

A year later, I finally managed to buy an old Chevy, but I never lost my love for motorcycles. There was still a pronounced rush in riding a motorcycle—the air pulling at your eyes as you sped through it, the green and blue world in a blur and hum past your ears. Riding continued to send a charged atmosphere of particles through every cell; there was still a romance in the blood thrumming with acceleration. It still beckoned. And working at grocery, I had a couple friends with bigger bikes. One friend had a Scrambler set up for dirt racing. There was a figure eight track in the fields of scrub brush near the new arm of freeway that reached from 101 out to the university, and I gave that a go for a couple months—the knobs of the tires digging in the dirt, my boot dragging along the ground on the inside loops at the top and bottom of the track to keep the back of the bike from spinning out, the smell of licorice when you went too wide and a tire took a bite out of the wild fennel bordering the turns. But once you learned the tricks, it became repetitious.

Rarely did you exceed twenty-five or thirty, and even with a bandana bandit-style across your face, you ate dust going around in a circle.

Another boxboy at the grocery had a Honda 305 Super Hawk, tricked out with bored carburetor jets and a couple other electrical goodies that made it one rapid machine. His problem was that he'd picked up six tickets on it, and another one was going to cost him big. So on weekends, I'd swap my car for his bike, and we'd reexchange Monday at work. He had a safer means of transportation and I was flying. That summer between my freshman and sophomore year in college I spent a lot of time on that bike. I was supposed to be learning things, but caution and common sense didn't seem to top my curriculum. My favorite ride was out to the university north of town, where I'd flip a U at the gate and then start back on Ward Memorial Boulevard to 101. Where the boulevard joined the freeway, there was a sweeping ninety-degree turn banked perfectly into the on-ramp. I'd head into the turn doing ninety-plus miles an hour, leaning for all I was worth, and shoot down a tunnel of gravity, only an edge of two tires and the laws of physics binding me to the earth and my life. A bit of gravel, a spot of oil, or a gust of wind and I'd have been smeared along the roadway for a quarter mile— no helmet, boots, or protective leather clothes, just blue Sperry deck shoes, a short-sleeve shirt. Some color and stubble in the fields, that's all that would have been left of me. But I was sure I knew what I was doing, had a handle on it, a cool grip; I was one with the machine. Death didn't enter into it. The practical matter of someone suddenly swerving, making a stupid move with the brakes and precluding my best intentions and skills never came up. I didn't even wear sunglasses. I just rode out the G force through the turn, downshifted, cut it back to sixty, and pulled up in traffic as wind burned my eyes and my blood went crazy blasting through the air.

Back in college for my second year—no bike, no car—life slowed down. I began to see that I enjoyed literature more than anything else I was studying. This perception became even more clear after I failed accounting and bagged a C in economics. Facing statistics and business management in the spring, I realized not only that I had no chance of passing the courses, but that I couldn't care less about them. I switched my major to English midyear. Brother Cassian, the academic advisor, asked what my father would think of switching from business administration to English. I said I didn't know and had planned on telling my father after the fact. I pointed to my grades from the last semester, the only A coming in World Classics, an English/humanities course. He sighed, nodded his head, and signed the card. By the time I informed my father of the change, he was bailing out of paying for my college anyway. After my Christmas visit to his house in Arizona, he was driving me to the airport so I could catch my flight back to California. Just before I headed to the plane, he said, "Oh, by the way, tell your mother that I'm not paying for your college anymore." What could I say? I told her. Luckily, my stepfather was a very generous man and picked up the tab. He was a lawyer and thought a major in English as good as any other—being an educated person was the thing.

I'd done what I could to decide who or what I would be, but my father cutting off all college support had been beyond my control. A close call. For a while, all I could see ahead was grocery—dropping out of college with tuition owing, going back to the only thing I knew how to do, putting groceries in bags, stocking shelves, unloading water softener from the truck. I'd be living cheaply, riding some small inexpensive Honda through the morning dark, hands and face half frozen, to arrive early and mop the floors of the store.

This shook me. After Frank had agreed to pay my tuition, I truly felt lucky to be in college that spring, happy to be taking survey literature courses, breathing a few sighs of relief. Yet about the third breath, it hit me: I was nineteen, soon to be twenty, no longer that boy in the blue shirt doing ninety miles an hour, leaning into a turn wearing nothing more protective than Levi's, heading into his life as fast as he could for all he was worth. Contrary to all the impervious impulses effervescent in my blood and brain, I was not, it finally occurred to me, going to live forever. If there were such things as guardian angels—spirits who protect you and pull you back from the proverbial curb in the nick of time—I realized that by that point I had run mine ragged.

Or, if it was not quite so conscious a realization, I must have at least sensed I'd lost that subliminal message that had been cooking through my veins at seventeen. Moreover, I didn't need an accounting course to see that I only had two and a half years of relative freedom before I would be out looking for a job, working, if business statistics had it right, forty or more hours a week in a field unrelated to my major. Until then, I was going to enjoy myself—read literature for the pure pleasure and private edification of it. All my friends were business or political science majors, but I was determined to go my own way and was for the most part oblivious to the bleak financial consequences. I did, however, take on some practical directions that mitigated a little the reading of poetry and the filling up of my notebooks with my own stiff and pretentious verse. I took some courses in education, worked at teaching techniques and theory. But doing so, I knew too that I'd given something up, that that beautiful, crazy, burning passage in my life would soon be behind me, barely visible as smoke.

But not completely. I was taking a course with the head of the English department, Mr. James Townsend, a serious and exact man. I don't think I even half caught on to the ideas and nuances he was prompting us toward in our readings and discussions during my first year as a major. As well as sophomores, there were juniors in that class, and some seemed to know every difficult and hidden thing in the text, and I had no idea how. Along with half a dozen others, I received what was then known as the "gentleman's C"—a grade that meant you showed up, completed assigned reading and writing, but were essentially clueless. But I tried nonetheless and contributed often in class, though to my professor and the brighter students, my comments seemed to emerge from a fog. Still, I was eager, and that is how I ended up at my first poetry reading.

Mr. Townsend announced that William Stafford would be giving a reading of his poetry, and we were quietly encouraged to attend. I did not know Stafford from Sappho. I was a sophomore. T. S. Eliot was the most, and probably the only, modern poet I had heard of or read, and we had just finished a class on the "disassociation of sensibility." I loved "Prufrock" and "The Waste Land"—the images, high voice and music—but at that time had no access to or understanding of the conceptual grids and allusions. Stafford's reading was altogether different than what I had expected, and I was stunned. This was 1966 or early 1967, and he was reading much of his work from *The Rescued Year*. The poems were moving, clear, directly imagistic, human, and accessible to me. How could this be? Townsend encouraged us to ask questions of the poet after the reading, and, blithely as ever, I pressed in with a few other students and at the first opportunity blurted out a stupid question. "Do you think it is all right to use 'I' in a poem?" Obviously, I had been over Eliot-ized. Here was Stafford with his first-person, autobiographical style, violating what I'd just learned. He responded generously and without the least sign of annoyance, "Well, it seems to work for me. What do you think?" He was a man modestly confident in his own work so had no need to puff himself up or point out what an idiot I was. He knew what a poem was, had just proven this for fifty minutes, and was happy to let my own perceptions decide things for me. His example said a poem made its own way, its own life, in the hands of a poet; it sang and was human independent of theories, academic or private. It worked for me.

It would be five or more years until I realized that I could use "I" in my own poems in a more or less realistic sense, that I would not need to write only in imagistic codes with an appropriated prophetic rhetoric. Nevertheless, I absorbed something important about writing, about subject and the real driving centers of poems, even if I couldn't then put my finger/pen on it or articulate it to myself. It coursed in my veins, waiting to surface.

The poem that gave me that sense was Stafford's poem "Fifteen," a poem about a boy discovering a motorcycle by a bridge, on its side, its motor running. It is an initiation poem. One of its marvels is how well and how subtly Stafford turns or translates the experience, charges it with sexual nuance. The connection between the cycle and a woman is intentional. "I admired all that pulsing gleam, the / shiny flanks, the demure headlights / fringed where it lay." For a moment the speaker is also charged with energy and access to a new world; he leads the bike to the road and for the first time, looks forward in his life to the undiscovered territory of the body:

> We could find the end of a road, meet
> the sky on out Seventeenth. I thought about
> hills, and patting the handle got back a
> confident opinion. On the bridge we indulged
> a forward feeling, a tremble. I was fifteen.

And that, of course, was the problem. Fifteen—slightly too young, almost there, not completely in charge. The boy of the poem thinks to look for the rider, finds him just coming to, and turns the bike back over to him. No matter, it's a start, a first step. The poem transfixes that exact moment when life first presents itself to you in a tangible array of possibilities, when you first have a degree of control and, although teetering on a threshold, know that living electricity and movement as part of you. You take life and shape it in your hands, if only for that moment. You don't get exactly what you want, but you know it's you standing there, and you know a little more fully the world before you.

I was nineteen. Stafford's poem brought back that moment, the blood circling my heart like a July Fourth sparkler twirled in tight circles against the dark, every nerve revving up as easily as twisting back the throttle on a bike and hearing the whine and combustion blast past the baffles. This was the sensation that affirmed my life and took me out of myself at the same time, transformed me as I sped through the oncoming air, riding up Camino Cielo above town or cruising along the beach, the salt and mist off the breakwater stinging the night. It would take years to put this gift to use, to take a first step into my own imaginative life and hold onto it the way I gripped the handle-bars heading into a ninety-degree turn. But the poet had left it there, idling in the tall grass for me to pick up when I was ready, and for better or worse, run to the end of my own road.

Time and Again

What makes us go against our instincts, our best learned inter-ests? Though time and again my mother impressed upon me gentleness and a respect for life, though I knew in the back of my mind and in the humming cargo of my own blood that she was right, there I was at nine years old, living across the street from the foothills, armed to the teeth.

The mild coastal wilderness came right up to our drive. But what really had I to fear? What enemies lay in ambush across Alisos Drive among the lichen-covered boulders, the impromptu gatherings of oaks and ferns, the dry knee-high tides of grass? I knew the chipmunks among the thickets and the chicken hawks lazy on the air, heard the jays and wild peacocks complain through the burning twilight and dawn. What was I preparing for when I was allowed to roam all day across the creeks and hills—hunting knife and throwing knife in my belt, thirty-five-pound fiberglass bow in hand, and a quiver full of bullet-point arrows on my back? I possessed all the bravery needed to pin-cushion a rotten log with shafts, or with a friend fire arrows off into the seeming center of the sky, testing how close to us they would dive back down. But in the creeks, for no reason I could then know, I was the scourge of the blue-belly lizards sunning themselves there, and ran their slight bodies through from close range. When my last arrow shattered against a rock, miserable boy that I was, I unstrung my bow and looped the string around the neck of a dead lizard and dangled him by the crevices where his compatriots hid, and thereby drew them out; whereupon I brained them with a bash from the flat face of my bow. Oh, we had myths about blue bellies being poisonous, so we allowed ourselves the senseless kill. The two stripes along their undersides were as often yellow or green as blue, and they had no teeth, were small and wisely frightened of us; no one was ever bitten. But these were our self-proclaimed trails and creeks, and our unthinking myths somehow served to harden my boy's heart against such tenuous slips of life scampering in the afternoon light, out of my unconscious way.

Respect for life. The idea should have sunk in the year before, when one Sunday I went out the back door with a slingshot, and, loading a piece of gravel from the drive, shot at the first thing I saw. A common robin. It was about fifteen feet away, and I was surprised when I hit it—more surprised when it let out a cry as the pebble struck it broadside in the wing. I had not killed it, but its reaction was distinct, reminding me of a kid crying out and gasping for air at the same instant after being sucker punched in the stomach by a bully on the playground. The bird flew off, but I felt terrible all morning. I had not expected to really hit it. I was just carelessly fooling around with whatever device I had at hand.

Before that, there had been Christmas, and a foot-long silver World War II cannon that shot shells across the length of our living room. I already had metal tanks with movable rubber treads, turrets that pivoted three hundred sixty degrees, and legions of plastic soldiers in assorted combat poses. Like almost all boys I knew, I had painstakingly glued together models of battleships, aircraft carriers, submarines, airplanes ranging from a Sopwith Camel with mounted machine gun to a blue British Spitfire, a green Flying Tiger, and the new delta-winged jet—an arsenal of toys. This was de rigueur for the '50s. That same Christmas my friend down the street, Archie Korngiball, and I received matching sets of military gear—plastic helmet, canteen and .45 pistol on a utility belt, and a replica Browning water-cooled machine gun on a tripod, vintage World War I. We had acres of brush and hills and fields in which to run around pretending to kill each other, and did so happily the livelong day.

The last years of grammar school I outgrew this and left the hapless lizards and birds in peace in favor of sports. Yet many films still celebrated World War II and were offered for our general consumption. Certain classmates were always drawing bombers and jet fighters being shot down in flames on their notebook paper and swastikas on their cloth binders. But by eighth grade, almost everyone's thoughts had turned to dances, dating, records, and radio—the usual first rush of hormones and romance. Deciding who was popular and who was not, we were less obviously cruel. The early '60s were a holdover from the '50s. We were too young to have grasped what had happened in Korea, and those details and political lessons were long over by the time we were old enough to study history. Though Korea was our most immediate example, in high school we were still examining Hittites and the first iron weapons, the strategic importance of the Bosporus and the Dardanelles. The one modern history class—an elective—ended with World War II.

Right in front of us was Vietnam, but in 1965–66 it was more a social issue than a political reality for us. Among parents or on TV talk shows like *Joe Pine,* we'd hear something like "They should take all those long-haired hippies and send 'em over there with a bunch of flowers in their hands and see how they do." Yet going through our freshman year, we questioned little and were, for the most part, oblivious to Indochina. But not for long. At the beginning of our sophomore year of college we reported one Saturday morning to a hall at UC Berkeley where the redoubtable American institution of testing, the Educational Testing Service, was administering an exam for the draft board. The results of those three hours needed to add up to a score of 70 or above, or you traded your 1-S student deferment for a ticket to the jungles of Southeast Asia. I was terrified. I had, and have to this day, a severe mental block, learning deficiency, dislike for math, and having taken the college entrance tests, I knew two-thirds of the test would likely be math. I had scored very low on the SATs and was lucky to have been admitted to college at all. Although the draft board exam had not as much math as I feared, I barely squeaked by with a score of 71. My feet had felt the fire as I narrowly jumped over the flames.

Weeks prior to the big test, recruiting officers had set up tables in the halls of our classroom buildings—a ploy that would not be tolerated a few years later. In 1965–66, however, a more conservative national climate supported the war, so a military presence on campuses—whose avowed aims were educating and opening minds—was not seen as contradictory. Two marines stood just inside the door to Dante Hall in pressed blue coats and pants with red stripes, with white belts, gold swords and scabbards as polished as their buttons. They were closely shaved and had buzz haircuts. They drank their coffee black. Cocky, almost cheerful, they were confident they could talk students into joining the corps. "All you college boys are going sooner or later!" they'd almost yell at our backs as we walked by. "The corps will teach you to fight, to stay alive!" was their parting appeal to logic. Fearing the worst from the ETS, I stopped by the National Guard table to check out the reserve program. The recruiters there were all in wrinkled green fatigues and were decidedly less gung ho as compared to the marines. Reserves meant six years—six-week summer camps through college, a year of active duty, then a couple of years on reserve with two-week camps in summer. Purely from a practical point of view, I knew I wanted nothing to do with the military, but I wasn't so sure the feeling was mutual, so I was weighing one dark eventuality against another. Not even nineteen, I came close to being frightened into joining the reserves. I hadn't seriously begun to think things through—morally, ethically, philosophically—one of the main reasons for being at a liberal arts college. I mentioned the reserves to my father, and despite the fact that he had been proselytizing me for years with his conservative political agenda—everything from the domino theory, Communist infiltration of the UN, liberal senators on the Foreign Relations Committee, to the length of girls' uniform skirts—he advised against signing up. He said it was a good rule not to volunteer, not to ask for trouble. Delay as long as possible. Something else may turn up. It was the best single piece of advice he ever offered.

I made my 71 and continued college. Others were not as fortunate. Some failed the test, others gradually flunked out of school. At home, my friends attending city college had been kidding themselves about their studies for a year or more. With classrooms situated on a cliff top overlooking the beach, they could see daily right down to the sea. If a swell was running, some drove down with their surfboards. If the bay was calm and glassy, Schiefen would drive five minutes to his house, hook up his boat, and round up the usual crew for waterskiing. Eighteen, nineteen years old, living on the coast in southern California, it was next to impossible to focus on the future. About the time Sozzi, Bruno, Orsua, and Schiefen were getting notices to report for physicals in L.A.—the prelude, we all knew, to an induction notice—I was reading Locke and Hobbes. While they were either being pressured into enlisting in hopes of having some choice of assignment and avoiding the front lines with the draftees, or, while delaying, were in fact drafted, I was piecing together my thoughts about government and the war. I had the luxury of time to think. If, at nineteen, anyone had a "world-view," it did not then, even for a moment, include the possibility of dodging the draft by going to Canada. The choice was war or jail. No choice really. Before my friends had a chance to figure out who they were, what they believed, or what a life was worth, they were coerced—plain and simple—into playing a hand dealt from the bottom of the deck. Locke and Hobbes gave me a pragmatic notion about why anyone would choose to belong to a government/commonwealth—happiness and security. Right off, it made no practical sense to fight a war—especially one so monumentally removed from our national security—and die, as likely as not, to hold onto something death would deprive you of posthaste. More time, more arguments, more of LBJ's face on TV shoveling (as Robert Bly so aptly put it) the lies of war at us, and a perusal of theology, brought me to a firm and moral opposition to the war.

Schiefen pulled transport and Orsua, jet engines; neither would be sent out on search and destroy "missions" with M16s and bayonets. They survived and came home. They dodged their share of missiles and mortars, took fire along the road to Khe Sanh and Chu Lai, saw enough men die on both sides to skew their views and values for more than a little while. Another high school friend, De Vito, was sent into Cambodia. Once there, he mingled with the Montagnards, married the chief's daughter, and took up a loin cloth and a powerful supply of smoke. When he wouldn't report back, they had to send some force recon guys in deep to drag him out. He worked through post-traumatic stress for more than fifteen years, trying to make adjustments to the plain flat facts of his old world. Sozzi was given a radio and made to run through the jungle. Bruno went down in a gunship but managed to crawl free of the wreckage and hide, despite a sprained back, broken ribs, and a mangled hand. He lay in a rice paddy for fourteen hours before he was picked up. One summer after the war, when he couldn't find a ride, I drove Bruno up to

San Francisco for the seventh operation on his hand to make it finally 20 percent functional. From all of my friends I learned a lot about the war secondhand before the pressure was really applied and I had to make a decision.

College over, I took a job at a Catholic grammar school in Torrance and applied for a 2-S deferment for teaching. About this time, late 1970 and early 1971, opposition to the war was mounting and the system was running short on recruits and draftees, so the Selective Service canceled all teaching defer- ments. I was classified 1-A. By that point, I knew I wasn't going to Vietnam or any war, was not going to take a life or put my life on the line to further the economic interests of the military industrial complex and its shareholders, the political capital of politicians, or the "careers" of men like Westmoreland, who lied and knew he was lying to the American people. What I did was contact my friend in law school who was in touch with a battery of lawyers who were fighting the draft. For four hundred dollars they took you through all the appeals with the Selective Ser- vice System, counseling and everything right up to court; then you worked out payment depending on how long and involved the case was. I went directly to the Selective Service System in the basement of the post office to appeal my 1-A classification. I began to state my views as they conformed with the Con- scientious Objector classification and said I wanted a hearing and would appeal this right on up the line. The appeal board was staffed by citizens of the community, and until I reached court, I felt I could defend myself against the usual blood-and- guts scenarios and conundrums with which Republican bank vice presidents and local chamber of commerce types challenged C.O. applicants. But before I finished my third sentence, the agent said he would postpone my official appeal for a few weeks. A lottery had just been approved for the next year's draft, and after the first drawing, if I did not have a good number, they would process my appeal. He said that if I received a number over 245, the chances were good that I would not be called, and over 285 my chances were very good.

I walked out feeling lucky and unlucky at the same time. I at least had more of a chance than I had first thought, an uncomplicated chance, if I could for once get really and truly lucky. I sat on the beach for the rest of the afternoon, looking out to a blue point where I couldn't tell sea from sky. I wondered about my karma. Had I done anything at any time to deserve, more than the next guy, to be that lucky?

Word of the lottery spread quickly. On the night of the drawing, I ended up at a friend's duplex with about ten or twelve others. Everyone arrived with a bottle—no wine, no beer, no mixers; this was straight, hard medicine to celebrate or feebly console. In black and white we watched a big plastic globe being turned; inside were markers for three hundred sixty-some dates (they were covering leap years and every contingency). They pulled birthdays out and lined them up on slots—one at a time, a long, slow process, which reminded me of a documentary film in which men were burning leeches off their legs. This was crazy. Bingo. Bobbing and weaving with fate, ducking death's long left hook. No choice. Your birth date, your number, could as easily pop to the top first as three hundredth. Sweat it out or adiós!

A couple of fellows whose numbers came up early left. I hardly knew these fellows, but felt awful for them, suspecting the ludicrous nonsense to which all the bodies would add up. The media was the message. What message did the first 245 receive from the TV that night about their lives, their worth? This was obscene, but certainly no more so than witnessing the war on TV every evening for years in filmed footage and body counts, with commercial interruptions. I was halfway through a bottle of gin on the rocks when I cleared 245. One or two pulled numbers in that limbo between 245 and 285. I was 314. I sat my glass, whose contents had not produced much numbing effect, down on the kitchen counter and went for a walk outside along the cliff top to shake myself, clear my head and heart a little, just to hear the reassurance of the waves, take in the salt savor of the air. That was it. Something had come up. It looked like I was free to live my life. Many were not.

Four and a half years of graduate school followed, then years of part-time teaching, finding my way as a writer, making a living by teaching freshman composition. Yet it's amazing how youth buoys you, how much you can bear. I scraped by rather cheerfully. Finally, in 1980, I landed a full-time position at the University of California, Santa Barbara, and though the work-load was very heavy, I found time to write. I rented a room from my stepbrother, who had bought a fixer-upper, and there was a nice field out back with a white horse, a dilapidated Italianate villa on the rise, which blocked out most of the freeway over-pass. We had tamarisks bordering the field, trumpet vines along the fence, agaves across the street, jade plants and cabbage roses by the garage. I had a view out on it all, a very good group of people to work with, and that was conducive to writing, to appreciating my life.

One day, driving back to Santa Barbara from Santa Cruz, where I'd gone to visit my friend the poet Gary Young and to go over some recent work, I saw a jackrabbit along the side of Freeway 101 outside of Santa Maria. In 1982 there were still stretches of the road along 101 covered by nothing more than scrub oak and chaparral. The rabbit was not ten feet from the right lane, and as I saw it a memory flashed up in full detail about the one time I had ever gone hunting, just a little farther down the road in Los Alamos. The scene came back so vividly that I pulled over to the roadside and jotted it down, knowing that it had to mean something, that it would probably work its way into a poem sooner or later.

I was eighteen that summer and had been invited by my friend Harry to go hunting. Harry's father owned a ranch, and it was dove season. I'd never eaten a dove, killed a bird, or for that matter fired a shotgun. Still, it seemed something young men did. Without giving it much thought, I said I'd be happy to go. I borrowed a shotgun from another friend, even bought a cheap

hunting vest to look the part, one with back pockets for birds
and rows of slots on the front to fill with shells. We parked the
car near the base of a short run of hills and took off hiking over
some deer paths. We reached a small summit and paused to load
up. Just then, Harry yelled, "Here they come," as doves scat-
tered from a large oak tree upwind. We blasted away and doves
began falling out of the air like planes in the war films from
our youth. Some streaked in long horizontal paths like Japanese
Zeros smoking down on that TV program from childhood *Victory at Sea*. Others scissored the air in splashes of confusion,
a tumble of off-kilter grey feathers. But they weren't all dead.
With thumb and forefinger, Harry showed me how to squeeze
the last air out of their slight necks, but I just couldn't. Our initial salvos must have scared the rest off. We hiked around a bit
more, then separated and took different trails. Walking a gully,
I heard a spray of shot rain down on the oak leaves above my
head. I yelled out that I was downrange and to have an idea, but
heard nothing in reply. Later, when I was walking a path with
the shotgun over my shoulder, it discharged into the air. Earlier,
Harry would have been walking right behind me. Again, later,
forgetting which way the safety was off or on, I discharged a
round into the dirt, inches from my foot.

Harry and I met up, sat in the shade and drank some water,
our jackets weighed down with doves. We talked a little about
the regimentation of the Catholic school we had both attended,
the beautiful girls there who had eluded us. We must have felt
smug, self-possessed, must have thought we were someone all
right. The fear and guilt of religion had scared him so thoroughly, Harry told me, that until he was seventeen, he figured
there was no way to avoid spending eternity in hell. Now that
the grip was broken, if he ever had kids, the last place they
would go would be a parochial school.

We were still floating on the cheap grace of youth, alive in the
heat and high summer, with the vague and great expectations of
young men, so the subject of the war and draft never came up.

We counted out our doves, swore we would cook and eat them, and headed back down to the car. Just before we got back, something moved in the raw dry grass. Then, with the first twitch of two tall ears, we together blew the ever-loving Jesus out of a jackrabbit until we couldn't tell fur from dust from blood.

I wrote down that entire incident in five minutes, so completely had it played back in my mind. That rabbit caught my eye; it was a messenger from a world almost lost, a world I needed to reconsider and make sense of for my life. A few weeks went by, and a combination of several things helped put my notes in perspective and give me a poem. One week both *Newsweek* and *Time* had apocalyptic photos on their covers and gave coverage to the nuclear freeze movement—a strong political cause between 1982 and 1983. An artist friend had a new bumper sticker on her VW that read simply FREEZE OR BURN. On our small cement patio, I had recently noticed that a family of lizards had started sunning themselves as we rarely sat out there. Also, there seemed to be a connection between the mind-set of nuns and the strict Catholic upbringing we had had and what I'd seen of the military. Hellfire and intimidation, the arbitrary values assigned to one life, one belief over another—the rules and a mindless power.

The poem I wrote was a simple narrative about hunting, and all I finally had left to do to make the body and ideas turn together and take on a larger focus was to give the poem a title relating to the nuclear freeze movement. It needed a title against which the action and event could react and so stand without embellishment and be a mindful emblem of our lesser selves. The events then, would speak for themselves. "Why I'm In Favor Of A Nuclear Freeze" came to mind and served to signal the argument whose rhetoric would be absent from the body of the poem. That was all I had to do to "get" the poem right, all, that is, except ask myself why the hell we had killed that rabbit so coldheartedly, and answer, that it was because we had the guns, because we could.

Something I Could Live With

The mining analogy has always seemed a good one. A writer, especially a writer in the first few years, often has to work through half a hillside of worthless material before hitting a slender vein of ore. There's a lot to uncover, and unless you are one of the exceptionally talented, there's always the danger of getting avalanched, of being swept away with eagerness and ambition and proclaiming pyrite to be gold. The saying sometimes attributed to Hemingway reminds us that every writer needs a good friend with a "shit detector." That's direct. And true, in my experience.

In the early '70s, there were a lot fewer MFA programs and fewer applicants; that is the only way I can account for my acceptance into the writing program at UC Irvine. For even then, with the ego and enthusiasm of youth, I knew my work did not fall on the "really talented" side of the scale. But, having worked for two and a half years on an M.A. in creative writing at San

Diego State, I must have deserved some reward for my dogged endurance and willpower. I was a standard-bearer for that camp and drove close friends crazy with endless revisions. Still do.

But where was I then heading? We all were heading, we thought, toward a book, and following that, of course, fame, riches, a stretch limo, and a three-movie contract. For nothing more than the sheer brilliance of our poems we would be invited to dine with the famous and drink the wines of princes. In truth, the former was as likely for most of us as the latter. Only one of the many young poets I met at UC Irvine would emerge from the program and those years with a book. Gary Soto had been a quick study as an undergraduate and arrived for the workshop with poems already published in the sorts of journals that the rest of us would not publish in for many years if ever. So it was not too surprising when he won the United States Award for 1976 from the University of Pittsburgh Press for *The Elements of San Joaquin,* a book I still to this day find to be a remarkable first book.

One reason Gary and I became friends, I think, was that his roommate at the time, Jon Veinberg, a fine poet and incisive critic in his own right, told Gary that my comments in workshop were worth thinking about, that he should pay more attention to criticism. Jon and Gary lived in Laguna Beach, about a twenty-minute drive from the campus. They rented a two-bedroom apartment right across from the beach. It was a little ramshackle, the second story of a wooden complex the color and apparent condition of driftwood, but plenty good enough for the times. The apartment complex was called the "Poet Ghetto" because a number of other second-year people in the writing program also lived there. The rent was amazingly cheap, even for then—two hundred dollars a month and fifteen yards from the Pacific, with a long balcony overlooking the waves. The three of us would sit out on that porch, praise the Pacific, and drink tall plastic tumblers of Cribari Mountain Chablis, on ice—a wine so green and full of tannin that you had to mitigate it with ice to get the first glass down. Those first sips puckered your mouth and made you feel you wouldn't say a kind word about anything for a week. But one tumbler full and you were acclimated, and because a half gallon cost only $1.49, we sang its relative praises as we chewed over revisions of poems and first drafts. Although we all critiqued each other's work, I usually weighed in with the longest poems and the most revisions. I had been given a ream of legal paper by a good friend at the U.S. District Court in L.A., so I used extra-long paper—in retrospect, it was a disastrous gift for the overwriter I was. I can distinctly recall the reaction when early one evening I arrived with my tenth revision of a poem about taking my niece to a convalescent home. Jon and Gary looked at me with a packet of those long sheets under my arm and put up their hands in that sign of the cross used in movies to ward off vampires. Then Jon held out his arm like a traffic cop stopping traffic and twisted the top off a fresh bottle of Cribari, insisting we sit on the porch and take in the sunset and salt air with a glass or two before we took up any business. In no time we were in a more mellow mood and skipped our own work to talk of favorite poems and to defame our enemies against the backdrop of the flaming horizon, although in truth we were not important enough to have enemies beyond one or two theorists who filibustered our workshop in defense of theoretical constructions they insisted were poems on the cutting edge.

Our second and last year in the program, Soto won the book prize. About the same time, I put together a manuscript and, among a thousand or more others, sent it off to the Yale contest—one snowflake in a flurry. You had to be very arrogant or crazy to think yours might win. I was somewhere in between the two. I knew I wouldn't win the contest. What I did hope was that my manuscript would make it into a final round and that Stanley Kunitz, who was the judge that year, would perhaps think enough of it to recommend it elsewhere. That is exactly what happened. Olga Broumas won, but I received a very kind card from Kunitz saying that my poems had "strength, structure and dignity." I've never forgotten that, bless him. Deserved or not, those few good words from Kunitz went a long way in helping me keep my head above those raging waters of rejection in which most all young writers are aswim. Kunitz recommended my book and one other to Texas Tech University Press, but after a few months the press wrote to say my manuscript had lost out to the other by half a vote by the readers.

Of course, I was disappointed, but a little more than a year later I was relieved. Well, if not exactly relieved, I at least understood that the manuscript was not really of publishable quality. Soto and Veinberg helped me realize that, despite the fact that I had published a lot of the poems in little magazines and had come close to winning a contest. That next year, and the year after, I stayed in the area, living in Costa Mesa and becoming a "freeway faculty," that is, teaching part-time at several places. Besides tutoring twenty hours a week at UC Irvine, I taught composition, Intro to Lit, and creative writing courses for Saddleback Community College in Mission Viejo, Costa Mesa, and Laguna Beach. I also took on a composition course for Orange Coast College, a four-hour section on Mondays—a real No Doz effort—and I taught in the Poets in the Schools Program every Thursday in a high school in Anaheim. The majority of my classes were evening or late afternoon, and I even had one basic English course for mostly Laotian students at 7:30 on Saturday mornings down in Mission Viejo. Somehow I found time to write. Five or six mornings a week, I was at my old "Cadillac" of a manual typewriter, a reconditioned office Royal. It weighed a ton and would bow the card table when I set it up in the small dirt patio outside my studio apartment. But it had great key action and never once broke down. I still had a supply of those legal sheets and kept the revisions rolling.

On vacations and long weekends, I'd grab a stack of new drafts and revisions, a bottle of Cribari or a recent Wente Brothers I'd found on sale, and drive up to Fresno where Veinberg and

Soto were living. During one of these visits Jon suggested a title for my manuscript that he thought united themes and details. I thought he was talking about a second book, but as we worked through the manuscript, it became clear that most of the poems were not worth saving. The confessionalism that had been the rage when we were in school looked not only strained and inauthentic, but just plain exaggerated and embarrassing. There was already more than enough emotional complaint in current poetry to go around. It was second-rate work, two years' worth, and luckily Jon's shit-detecting equipment was cranked up to ten that day. I chucked out about three quarters of the book, added new poems, and had a working manuscript once again.

Jon was renting an old farmworker's house in the middle of a huge fig orchard. That night, though it was late October, we put on our jackets and sat out beneath an umbrella tree and a full moon. To soften the demise of so many sheets of poems, Jon opened a Louis Martini Pinot Noir and left it to breathe on one of those tables made from the wooden spools of telephone company cable. There was a long corridor of eucalyptus through the orchard, and we took a walk down the center of it while the wine opened. We returned as the moon began to sink and sat out on old kitchen chairs. As I watched that moonlight float away, all those eucalyptus leaves in the dark, it didn't seem like such a big deal to let a few dozen bad poems drift off into the merciful silence. The pinot noir was blood-thick and curranty and took the chill off the evening.

The title Jon suggested, "Last Rites," seemed perfect: the poems, though largely tied to family and landscape, were still working through a lot of Catholic imagery. The only problem was that I had no poem by that title. I soon came up with one. Soto had made suggestions based on imagery from some recent drafts, and I got a longish one going in four sections with an environmental slant. The images were concrete; it seemed tight, focused. I sent it back and forth to Jon and to Gary, and they re-

sponded with switches, cuts, and tweaks. It improved; it went
into the manuscript in the last position, but something in the
back of my mind kept nagging at me that it wasn't right. I re-
wrote, but it still was forced; it read like someone with a little
talent trying too hard. I'd run up against a wall, so close to
finishing the book, and what was really a second book at that.

One Saturday morning, after hours at the typewriter with
no appreciable results, I jumped in my car and drove over to
the South Coast Plaza, a huge shopping mall off Freeway 405.
My intention was simply to change scenery and imagery, relax, shake things up, and get my mind off that title poem in its
rigor mortis. I passed the wine shop I often went in just to look
around, as everything there was pretty much beyond my means.
I stepped in to find they were going out of business and having
a great sale on the inventory. I had my first Visa card with me
with its hundred-dollar limit paid up. I charged ten bottles of
wine at between two and three dollars each, all French. Two
wonderful Volnays, a couple whites, and several of the Beau-
jolais, which lay down—a Morgon, a Moulin-a-vent, Fleurie,
Brouily, and Macon Rouge. I also found one bottle of my favorite
wine, a Vosne-Romanée. It was four dollars, the most expensive and no doubt an off year, but for a Romanée-St. Vivant, a
steal. I headed home with a box, and in my studio apartment,
beneath the sink, I set up my first "wine cellar." It was a sunny
afternoon, and I decided to celebrate my good luck.

I took my card table outside and placed it under the waxy
shade of the pittosporum tree. I cut up cheese and bread, added
a few olives to the plate, and put it on the table. My real question
then was which bottle to open. I wanted to save the Vosne-
Romanée for an occasion. So I picked a Volnay because I had
two of them, opened it and put it out on the table to breathe. I
went back in, brought out a chair, and then almost as an after-
thought, went back and brought out the recalcitrant title poem,
the typewriter, and a couple of fresh long sheets of paper just in

case something turned up, suggested itself through the interplay of the leaves and the light blue afternoon. But I was determined to sit back, take my time, and enjoy the few hours.

I poured a large glass, held it up to the sunlight, and let one rich source flow through the other, hoping that flow might somehow reach into me and provide a little inspiration for the poem's lead-heavy feet. There was no one to impress but myself, so I took a taste and whistled it in. The wine was soft, full, and generous. The fragrance of the pittosporum blossoms was on the air; the little snacks were satisfying; a few strings of ivy ascended the side of the house catching the sun; the bird-of-paradise preened in the light; life was good. I finished the food, poured a second glass, took the poem out from beneath the plate and started from the top. I had the thirty-fifth draft in front of me but was now relaxed enough to just scan it and let the rush and subtle tide of the wine wash over me. I recast lines and made cuts, keeping a rhythm that dictated what went, what was added or compressed, what stayed as it was. I went straight through, the rhythm admitting another level of language and music into the poem; then I poured a third glass for the final polishing. The stiff, willed poem now seemed to have a voice and movement, to loosen up and sing a little, however modestly. I was content. No, I was glowing. For an hour or more I felt immutable, almost accomplished.

And I was not wholly deceived. Over the next few days, as I went back over the poem, I didn't change a comma. This was not a revising method I ever used again, nor one I especially recommend, though apart from work, I would recommend a good Volnay anytime. Yet it seemed to be what was then called for to move beyond a plateau where I was mired, stuck, hamstrung and still hammering. It helped me give the poem over to an easy but more compelling rhythm, a music, which, when we're lucky enough, I think, finds us, speaks in us where we write and live.

The poem was published in a little magazine. The book was issued by a small publisher of poetry, won no prizes and received little notice. Nevertheless, it was writing true to my best abilities at the time, true to the way I then saw things and heard them. Although I lacked eight-tenths of what most would call a career, the book was done and not all that bad. It was something I could live with. I sent copies to Jon and Gary, who approved. With their help, I had dug out, overcome a small mountain of bad writing and had a little something to celebrate. I had moved past the days of Cribari and was breathing a little easier. I saved the Vosne-Romanée and shared it with them on our next visit.

My Father's Body

My father. Who knew about my father? I didn't. Ever. He was a man who kept his distance from everyone. After I was eight or nine, I don't remember him having any friends, no pals or couples coming over for dinner or to visit. I know my mother found him a cold fish most of their married life. At some point in my presence, they must have embraced, been affectionate, but if so, it happened infrequently enough that it left no mark on my consciousness; I have no memory of them ever touching.

The last time I touched him was in 1983. We shook hands. I was leaving Santa Barbara the next day to drive a U-Haul trailer with all my possessions to western Kentucky where I'd taken a job at a state university. He offered dinner at Arnoldi's, a family-style Italian restaurant and one of the city's oldest, a chance to get together with my stepbrothers and Nancy, my stepmother, a chance to say so long for a while. Although we had been living in the same town for the last three years, we had seen each

172

other rarely. He was always working real estate, I was teaching, and, realistically, we did not have much to say. We had narrowed topics of conversation to cars, music, and a little sports— eliminating politics and his far Right agenda. Years had passed, the late '60s and '70s were gone for good, and an amiable truce existed, but there seemed no reason to visit too often and press our luck.

So, after ravioli and a modest Chianti, we walked out of Arnoldi's in the late summer of 1983. Stopping by the sandstone wall, under the red glow of neon spelling out the restaurant's name, he stuck out his hand, and, after hesitating a second, I shook it. He said something about driving safely, calling. I remember being surprised, standing there with my father's hand in mine, only able to say, "Sure," and "Thanks." He was not a big man, about five feet nine inches, average build, but I remember his hand feeling heavy, harder than it was. I looked down, and it was the same hand I remembered from childhood—fingers short, the skin very white with freckles.

Although he never worked at anything but sales, his hand felt thick, like a gardener's or carpenter's. That was strange, especially because he always took care of his hands. Mornings when I was seven or eight, before school, I'd find my father at the dining room table with a nail file—the only man I've ever known who owned one, though I suspect "grooming" kits were common in the '40s and '50s. We'd be getting ready to leave, and he'd come out in his wing tips, camel hair sport coat, and knit tie, put his left hand on the table, spread his fingers wide, take the file in his right hand and round the nails into crescent moons, with smooth curving strokes, sanding his nails to just the right length. Then he'd stand there and hold his hand out away from him to admire it before he attended to the other.

When we had last shaken hands I couldn't say. For just a second, standing outside the restaurant in the dark, I thought perhaps he figured he might not see me for a while, so he made this unusual gesture—at once friendly, affectionate, and at the same time formal. Here was a man who didn't show affection, so this was demonstrative for him, but then it was only a hand-shake after all, the same business gesture he performed several times a day. After the initial shock of it, I dismissed the sentiment I had momentarily attributed to that handshake, and didn't worry much. After all, we were both going to be around awhile, so why worry?

I inherited that feeling from him, the feeling that I was going to live forever. He professed belief in the Catholic Church, its metaphysical structure, an afterlife, though he never attended mass. He believed mainly, I think, in himself, deeply and unconsciously so. Believed that there, in the rush of experience, haphazard as we all were in a physical world, his body would be a coefficient of his will: he was impervious, lucky, and would remain so if careful, reasonable. Only airplanes presented an imminent prospect of death. Staying alive was logical as he saw it.

After flying hundreds of missions during World War II, after landing DC-3s *with* the wind for fun, after navigating from Africa to South America with a fuel stop on that speck in the Atlantic, Ascension Island, which many planes missed, he figured he'd used up all his grace in the air. His only friend from the war, Howard, had been killed giving his last training mission to a cadet flyer, so when my father put his feet on the ground in the states in 1945, he never again got into a plane.

Other than that, his was an implicit belief, not an arrogant one, like believing there would be air to breathe. His body would not fail him—it never had. There had been that momentary lapse during the war when he caught malaria, and now and then it returned for a night; every year or so there was a small flash-back in his blood and cells. He would sweat out a fever all night, and I vaguely recall going in my parents' room in the morning as a child and seeing him wrapped in the soaked sheets.

Finally, there was, in fact, nothing prescient about that hand-shake beyond the fact that my father and I never shook hands, didn't touch at all. It just never happened, so it was an incident that stayed with me for years—eight years—until he died, and I realized that was the last time we would ever touch.

Apart from that handshake, I remember touching my father only two times. Once when I must have been three or four years old, some Sunday morning out walking, we stopped on the courthouse or post office steps of some small town in one of the middle eastern states. I ran up the steps in my three-quarter grey coat, and he caught me in his arms. My smooth child's face rubbed against his day-old beard, that sanded texture marking the moment, the connection that, unknown to me at the time, would have to do for a long while. On the other occasion, I was ten and threw a jacket I refused to wear at my mother; he pushed me up against the wall of the dining room, his left hand at my throat, telling me I should never act that way to my mother again. I was conscious enough at the time to realize this uncharacteristic outburst was about him filling in the prescribed offices of The Father, which he rarely did. My antics had backed him into the corner of role-playing, into making a show of strength. He was, I thought, more interested in asserting his view of conduct than in any offense to my mother, yet I realized my behavior was enough out of line that I'd best keep quiet and let it pass. A little more than a year later they divorced.

I think his affection was really kept in reserve for himself. His mother, though also not an emotionally demonstrative person, had made him the center of her attention and emotion to the exclusion of his father. The light, so far as he could see in his life, was always focused on him. He was a man who would comb and recomb his hair several times a day, a man with charge accounts at Silverwoods and closets of tailored Hart, Shaffner & Marx clothes—tweed, camel hair, and herringbone jackets—a closet full of Florsheim wing tips and tassel loafers, shirts from the laundry always pressed with stays inserted in the collars. You couldn't tell the bills were not paid by looking at him. I remember my mother wearing the same red cloth coat all my early years at school, remember having to wear through a pair of socks to prove the soles of my PF Flyers were shot. I knew this about him, if I knew little else.

He was, I suspect, an attractive man and had some way with women. Looking back into my child's mind and sense of things, it's so dark down many of those hallways, I can never be sure. But there seemed to be friction there even though parents try to keep it from children. Years later, my mother told me of one woman he was seeing on the side, a rich woman. My mother got hold of the woman and told her that if she wanted him, really wanted him, she could have him, but it was going to cost something for my mother and me to be taken care of. That ended that one. I do have clear recollections of being out to dinner and my father asking my mother if she saw that woman across the room staring at him; almost unconsciously, with his open hand, he smoothed back one side of his hair.

Due to the interruptions of the war, a family, different radio jobs in different states, he took about eight years to complete his college degree and attended three or four different schools. Yet for all that time, he never went in for a party or a wild time. He was conscious of his body and good looks and never believed in drinking or going to bars. Before he went into radio, before he married my mother, he studied acting and voice at a drama school in Cincinnati run by Tyrone Power's aunt; he sang with big bands. Because he was always so well dressed, he had no problem picking up part-time jobs working in men's stores, even in small towns. Strange though, what you don't know.

A year after his death I received a note from the sister of one of his "best" friends from the small town in Ohio where my father had grown up. Her brother, Hughey, had died in 1988, and she was writing to find out what had happened to my father; she had been thinking of the old days, she wrote, and said that my father and Hughey had been close more than fifty years ago, that Hughey played piano and my father played the saxophone together in some small group. Though I had heard him mention Hughey, one of two friends he ever spoke of, I never heard him talk of playing the saxophone. That was about as far-out as he got, I suspect; he did not want to carry around that image of himself. The woman wrote that Hughey had moved to Canoga Park near L.A. many years ago. I found it strange that, since we were only an hour and a half away, we never once visited Hughey or got in touch.

My father did keep late hours though. When I was a child, and into the beginning of my teenage years, he worked at his radio station almost all the time and was rarely home in the evening, always with the excuse that he had to go back to work. It didn't take too long for my mother to figure out why. He was in fact seeing Nancy, the woman he hired as secretary, who was giving me piano lessons on the weekends in her home, the woman he would eventually marry and with whom he would spend the rest of his life. My mother hired a private detective, and that was the end of my piano lessons and the marriage.

When I was eight, I do remember him doing some physical labor, out working in the yard, shirtless and in tennis shorts, the summer we moved into our new house on Alisos Drive in the foothills of Montecito. We bought, along with nine other families, a ten-acre parcel of land; each family built its own house, cleared the land themselves as much as possible on acre lots. My father didn't look anything like a bodybuilder or football player. He was white, square, and looked as regular as any other grown-up, from what I knew. One day he was working with a pick and must have hit an oak tree root, because the pick rebounded from his downswing and hit him on the forehead. It was close. A knot formed and there was some blood. A little harder and who knows? I was frightened for him, and, though I can't remember it now, I must have given him a hug. He seemed a bit dazed, not so much by the blow itself as by the realization of what had just missed happening. My mother sat with him on a boulder, ministering to the skinned portion of his forehead, a red patch the shape of a quarter. It was a frightening moment for all of us. Like most kids, I thought my father was invincible.

A couple years later, when I had grown some and become accomplished at tennis, had started to play tournaments and help the pro teach, I played with my father for the last time. We used to play as a family when I was very young, but at about ten or eleven, I was playing better than he, and realized his service motion was not very good. Still using one of those old Bancroft bamboo rackets, he had a flat western grip and would slide his right foot up and stop with both feet together behind the service line before he started the swing with his whole arm rather flat and stiff, very much the way a jai alai player would make an overhand throw. He didn't manage the proper weight transfer or get the racket down in a back-scratching position and then snap the wrist over and through the ball. He came to a few of my tournaments and leaned against the fence, both hands gripping the chain link while he told me about hitting both serves flat and hard, not hitting the can opener or American twist for the second serve, but we never played again. He worked all the time, weekends included, and at the very least had to be out of shape.

More than ten years later, when I was home summers from graduate school and teaching tennis in city programs, I noticed that he was thinking about getting back into or maintaining some physical shape. He would take walks for two miles each evening. I don't know that he had any specific health warning then. It was vanity as much as anything, because he had started to expand a bit about the belt line. But he was serious about his health, had quit smoking cold turkey one day and never looked back. By the end of his life, he hadn't smoked for more than thirty years. He was always taking handfuls of very good vitamins and got me into the habit from my early twenties. He even took a series of shots supposed to clear the veins and arteries of cholesterol, and was taking a supplement developed by a heart surgeon for bypass patients to help repair arteries. He never said there was a problem, never saw a heart specialist. More than likely, he figured he was practicing prevention, determined to live and live and live.

He must have been in his late fifties when he started the hair transplants. Because I was away at college, then at graduate school, I saw him mainly during summers, and he must have gone through the processes largely between my visits home. One summer, however, I saw the means of it all—the mess of liquids and potions, the showercap-like apparatus, the dark pencil-dot plugs of hair healing into his scalp in the front of his head. He would spend most of the evening after supper in his bedroom with all that embarrassing paraphernalia on his head. This was the largest blow to his ego, the loss of hair. But a year or two later, all the treatments done, he had managed a head of white hair he could keep in place. He let the sides and back grow long and looked for all the world like a TV evangelist. For years at the end of his life, he had long, almost eccentric hair. This, I thought, was an ironic twist on vanity, a turnabout from the late '60s and '70s when I had long hair like most everyone, and for that he had denounced me to my stepbrothers and stepsister as crazy.

The last couple of years of his life he looked fine and so seemed to feel fine. He kept up his walks, had a room full of slacks, sport jackets, and suits, a large gold medallion and chain he wore outside his shirt and tie. He had two sports cars on lease, a nine-thousand-dollar Rolex on his wrist, and he worked every day selling big-ticket real estate. He wore glasses larger than Aristotle Onassis's, which probably cost as much. Except for the allergies that had always plagued him, he was doing fine. Seventy-one, and other than malaria in the war, never sick a day in his life. He would not think of life insurance, retirement and the like. What was the point if you were going to live forever?

When I came back from Kentucky to work at the University of California at Santa Barbara, I saw him every other month or so for the next two years. I was about to turn forty. My right hamstring and hip started to tighten, and that was the end of my running 10K's, or any real distance. My warranty had started to expire. I had no retirement money put away. I would never be able to afford a house in my hometown, where the cheapest stucco bungalow from the '40s went for close to three hundred thousand. So I took the first tenure-track job that came up. It came up in the East, and I was gone again. But I was back west on vacations as often as possible, and in the summer of 1990 saw him briefly for dinner. We had a pleasant enough time, and I walked out feeling that things were as they always would be, the same thing he must have been thinking.

That December I was out West again, giving some readings and job canvassing, but he and Nancy were gone to Scottsdale for their customary Christmas trip, so I missed seeing him. Early in February, my stepbrother Alan called saying my father was seriously ill, in the hospital, and I should come. I flew out right away but was too late.

What was really too late was treatment. My father had had what he thought were bad allergies and then the flu. He had gone several times to his allergist, who had not run tests but prescribed more medication. The day before Nancy took my father to the emergency room, the allergist took an X ray of his lungs and pronounced them clear; they were, in fact, badly infected with a strain of pneumonia that was getting the best of all his bodily functions. When he was sitting in front of the fire that evening in a sweater, his feet and hands were still so cold that Nancy took him to emergency. Admittedly, the doctors immediately found the pneumonia and started him on massive antibiotics; he remained conscious for two days. When I arrived, he was in a coma and on every life-support machine the hospital had. The doctor told us that my father had suffered "multiple organ collapse"—the heart had only been pumping at one-quarter capacity for days; hence the systems were shutting down. It was doubtful they could revive the organs. They had

him on a machine to breathe and work the heart, and were starting dialysis, though that was risky with the drugs and his high
blood pressure. The cardiologist said he thought it was something like a "microvirus" that had attacked the heart, caused the
systems to fail.

Neither Nancy nor I ever received a good, straight or complete explanation of what the "microvirus" was. In addition to
the three assigned by the hospital, a series of doctors came, un-
invited by us, to look at charts for five minutes and shake their
heads; there was nothing they could do. Several did this for several days while his body was being run by machines. What we
did receive were bills for about five thousand dollars for each
extra doctor, bills Nancy later paid with the last money left in
their accounts—there was no life insurance, no retirement, no
nothing.

He lay in a coma for over eight days until the doctors gave
up and turned the machines off. In all likelihood he had not
been there at all after the second day. Nancy went in every day
and talked to him and held his hands and massaged his fingers,
fingers that, puffed to the size of small sausages from the kidney failure, I did not recognize. I could only visit his room for
a few minutes each day, though I spent hours in the visitors'
room staring out the window to where the pier and breakwater
reached out into the sea and mist rose off the water and mixed
with the light.

Nancy had to fight hard to be there in the intensive care room
with him as much as she was, and probably, had I been able to
stand it, I would have stayed longer each time. There was not
much I recognized; there was jaundice and bloating, the weak
glaze over the eyes the one time they were half open. Hands and
arms and abdomen were swollen, all the tubes and machines
man can imagine hooked into him, heart monitor beeping on
cue from the lung machine. With the illness and distention of
his body, with my own fear and an emotional backlog, I could
not go up and touch my father. Though I did at one point speak

and say I was there, I could not take his hand. I was just over-whelmed, and felt badly for him, especially knowing he had no idea what had hit him. I could imagine the terror and sense of betrayal he must have felt as he sensed his life slipping out of his hands.

Nancy and I agreed: no funeral. It had nothing to do with any-thing we were invested in emotionally or spiritually. We chose cremation as the best thing to do on all counts, except perhaps what he might have wanted—perhaps the body preserved? But it made no sense to us, and, of course, he had never spoken of it. I did agree to go see a spiritualist friend with Nancy— a medium, an old and somewhat famous man, an honest man. Whether you believe in a spiritual continuum or not, if you met George, you would say he is honest and believes in what he does. There are many "psychics" who prey on people's grief and have them coming back for sittings at hundreds of dollars a throw, promising to tell them more next time; the world has always been full of charlatans. I have wavered between belief in an afterlife, and, in darker modes, a skepticism that subscribes to energy fields and something as atomically reductive as "the force."

When Nancy phoned George about trying to make contact with my father, George said his guides, those spirits who used him for a channel, said that my father could not communicate yet. George promised to call if and when things were propi-tious, when my father was available. Someone out only to take money from gullible people would have had us up there in a flash and would have manufactured something, had us back a second time, a third.

A number of months went by, and when I was next out to the coast, it seemed we might be able to have a sitting. Nancy was still eager to see George, so we went. George said through his guides that it had taken my father some time to realize he was not just having a dream, some time to "wake up" to the "other side." The first greeting George conveyed was that he, my father, Nancy's husband, sent us his . . . well, "good wishes, affection," George correctly adding that my father was not the sort of person who would say he sent his "love." There were just a few messages for Nancy, and his parting words were that in the spirit realm now, he was younger than his son, in a youthful version of his body, a body glowing in the life image of his late twenties. The message was calm, meant to reassure us, almost happy.

At that tenuous distance between worlds, between realms, that was the last thing I would hear. The message was from him; that much I knew.

What's Fair?

Somewhere in the collected wisdoms we're advised to let go of our grievances, told that to progress even modestly on the path of contentment, we should accept what has happened. No matter what we have worked diligently for or think we justly deserve, the world is as it is; we should enjoy our lives as best we can. I think I would benefit if I adopted this approach. Certainly the stress level and hammerlock on the heart would ease if I accepted daily outcomes no matter how contrary they run to my wishes and designs. Only so many lucky stars out there under which to be born and everyone contending for those few spots. I'd feel better, perhaps even be a better person, if I could just give up my complaints about what *should be* the case.

Yet I'm not sure this is good advice for everyone. From the first moment I met him, my friend Peter Sozzi was defined by his defiance, his underdog posture, his active lack of tolerance for hypocrisy. Sanguine, quick to anger, he knew when he'd been had and would blurt out the unsettling truth into the nearest face. Early on in grammar school, Peter could recognize the official line, the language of rule and regulation used to keep him from making his point, getting his way. I wouldn't be the first to say that lives appear to develop patterns, karmic tracks if you will. When it came to luck, an even break, Sozzi always seemed on the other side of the fence, fortune's loyal opposition. He was the first kid I knew to know in his bones things could be otherwise, and as often as not, *should* be otherwise. He ridiculed class and from the start was opposed to people thinking they were better than others for no reason beyond money or popularity. He resented the hands life kept dealing him, and survived on his willpower and outrage, his sense of justice diminished at the personal level. His dynamic and forceful nature, his mercurial temperament, forged his metal, made him who he was, and for the most part, enabled him to finally come out the other side.

The first day I saw him, he came screaming down from the embankment in back of the swings, arms waving over his head, leading seven or eight girls and boys yelling past me—hair messed up, shirttails out, swinging their sweaters helicopter fashion in the air. I was seven, new in a Catholic school, and this was as close to anarchy as I would come for many years. Perhaps because I was a new kid or had—unknown then to me— made friends with one of the more popular kids in class, perhaps because I was just there at the start of recess and Sozzi and his crew needed to fly by someone to assert themselves—I had no idea. Given the choosing up of social cliques even in the lower grades, it was quickly clear to me that Sozzi was not among that most popular group. He led this pack he called a skunk army. He did not enjoy popularity and acceptance, so he would have this, minor terrorism and acting out on the playground.

Peter was, I soon discovered, about as friendly on a one-to-one basis as anyone else, except when he was crossed, and he had the lung power to let you know when that was. With one younger and four older sisters, he no doubt felt he needed to carve out some space of his own. His oldest three sisters had gone through our school and were model students who made good grades. His closest older sister, Michele, a few grades ahead of us, was the angel in the Christmas play the following year, and she was a good choice. At eight years old, what do you really know? I knew an angel when I saw one, and she was beautiful. So Peter was often known as Michele's younger brother, and he didn't make the high marks of his other sisters and was a long way away from the paragon of comportment that Michele was. He was not a "kiss-up" and often, after coming in from recess or lunch, was sent back out to wash up or comb his hair. In the middle years of grammar school, Peter was among a group of us who were slower learners, kids who never received A's for anything, who once in a while attained B's, but most often C's. Sister Vincent de Paul, the principal, repeatedly told us, and our parents echoed her, that we were "not applying ourselves." Our real concerns were kickball, baseball work-ups, and later on, the forbidden free-for-all football game, "kill-the-man-with-the-ball." In the younger grades we focused on the "seasons"— marbles, yo-yos, kites—which were our "sports."

One recess Peter and I were playing a game of marbles, "chase" as opposed to the old-fashioned game of shooting marbles out of a circle. One player would shoot a marble somewhere over the field, and the other would chase after it, the players alternating shots. This was a game of strategy more than anything else. You could not allow your marble to land too close to your opponent's, and you'd hope instead that he would leave his marble in range so you could hit it on your next shot. Usually you used a "shooter" marble, most often a "half-pint," which was not quite double the size of a regular marble but half the size of a "boulder." Half-pints were usually agates, rare enough even in the '50s. The victor would receive a marble of the loser's choosing from his bag, usually the common "cat's-eye." However, sometimes a game would be played for "purees," for "boulders," or for "shooters," and the one losing would have to give up a prized possession.

Peter and I pursued each other across the dirt and ended up by the old acacia tree at the top of the field one day. We kept our distance, positioning our shooters behind chips of bark and roots, which protected them from a hit because all shots were fired from ground level. (We allowed none of the silly rules that younger players did, such as "bombs," which, when called, enabled one player to walk over to the other's marble and, standing above it, attempt a hit by dropping his shooter from eye level. No, we were rigorous competitors.) Finally, just as the bell rang to return from recess, Peter took a long shot, got lucky, and ever so slightly hit my marble. I saw the graze of stone on stone, though mine hadn't really moved at all, and Peter's rolled back to rest a quarter inch away. I knew it could be contested and, though I knew better, I claimed it had stopped just short—no hit. We were under pressure to be in the classroom before the second bell rang, no time for protracted argument or appeal to friends, none of whom had seen it anyway. I picked up my agate shooter and Sozzi picked up his, but he was mad. He'd won fairly, but I was not giving in, not giving him his due, not about to hand over my blue and white half-pint, which looked—as we would discover by the end of the decade—like the earth spinning in space. He looked me square in the face, blood rising in his cheeks, and yelled that he had made the hit, had won, and I knew it, and I was cheating him. I stonewalled the issue as we raced back to the room, and that was that. In a day or two, it was forgotten and we were onto something else. We were kids. Every few hours there was another focus, one immediate triumph or tragedy after the other in the crucible of a schoolyard.

I expect that to this day he has no memory of this episode, but I do. It has stayed with me, whenever I think at any length on Peter or those years. I suspect that it is more than guilt, which, being Catholics, we were well schooled in. It's also probably more than a sense of fair play, though, in fact, that instance is my only memory of cheating at any game, ever. I always enjoyed playing games too much to want to fix the outcome and thereby deny myself a possible real victory. No, not just guilt. It had as much to do with Peter and an empathy I felt for someone who tried hard, who was deserving, and who was denied success for unfair or arbitrary reasons. I sometimes felt in a similar position to Peter's. Parochial, isolated, winning and losing were every misery or joy we knew, and by cheating Peter I had— it seemed then—added significantly to a friend's bad luck and unfair turns of fate.

Peter didn't have much time with his father, and this too I understood on some level, as I grew and became dimly aware that I too had spent little time with mine. Peter's father was a lemon rancher with some acres just past Summerland, south of Santa Barbara toward Carpinteria. He worked the ranch himself, long hours all week. With a large family, there were no new cars, none of the baseball gloves or footballs that some in our class had. One Saturday, Peter's father hosted our Cub Scout pack on his ranch. We were interested in seeing how things grew and worked, and his father would pop in and out of our tour, which was guided by Mrs. Sozzi and Peter's older sisters. He was a gentle white-haired man who seemed fond of his son. I saw him occasionally after mass, standing around a bit nervously out in the courtyard of the church as the other men lit up smokes; he'd given up his Chesterfields after a heart attack almost ten years previously. He died, it seems now, suddenly during our seventh-grade year. The older sisters were married, and Peter's mother could not keep the ranch going. The family moved to a little stucco house on the west side, and Peter had to switch to Dolores School because it was closer, and perhaps a bit cheaper than Mt. Carmel. Peter had no father, no inheritance. I didn't see him again until high school, a few years later.

At Bishop High, the class system was not just composed of those who were or were not popular or thought to be "personalities"; it also broke down into economic strata, some racial groupings, and this was often connected with grades and achievement, and often, ever so subtly, with volunteer work in support organizations like Dad's Club and Key Club. I didn't see it then, but in retrospect, and as Peter later pointed out to me, it existed. Clearly, some were expected to do well and did, and some were not expected to achieve and almost no matter what effort, did not. One classmate, whose older brother had been student-body president and all-around great guy, always fared well with grades and social rewards. He was quiet, neat, mild-mannered as a pharmacist. Although of average intelligence, he had good-will and expectations behind him, which kept him cresting the B range in grades, though no doubt he studied diligently. Sozzi's lot was different.

Peter told me that at the end of his junior year, Big A, as our principal was known, told him directly that he would not make it, not amount to anything, and to his face said he was lacking in character, had no future: "Mr. Sozzi, you can't surf all of your life. Your family has given two daughters to the Church. What contribution do you think you're going to make to society?" Peter had no father to volunteer time for the Boosters Club. Peter did not sport the button-down, pressed pants, and penny loafers look. He was a surfer and wore T-shirts, Pendletons, clean but wrinkled flannel shirts, blue Keds deck shoes, and white Levi's. He did not "dress for success" like the A students. He drove a '57 Chevy wagon, which under most circumstances would have been a cool ride, but his was a beat-up eight-cylinder automatic with a rusted muffler. The miserable flat white paint was flaking off from an engine fire that had burned up the hood, and the old coat of forest green underneath was showing through pinto pony style. The tires were bald, and the engine burned a little oil, but he kept it going, if only on threats and promises.

If Peter lacked anything, it was the disposition which told us that to get along, you had to go along. He wasn't going. He certainly did not lack character, and may have had one of the strongest in our class. He questioned authority at almost every turn, especially in religion class, which was mandatory for us. He would point to war, poverty, the immediate death in his family, as well as to social injustice, and say that if God was merciful, he was sure enough selective about who saw that mercy. While these are rudimentary polemics opposing the existence of a benevolent deity, they were not all that worn in 1964 and were certainly bold and singularly expressed in a Catholic high school classroom. It took conviction and fortitude to express those objections then. Time and again, Peter complained about receiving low or average marks because of his outspokenness, because he would not conform, and not because he didn't have the information or ideas down on paper. Because teachers had pigeonholed him as a low achiever, he maintained that he couldn't receive a high mark on an essay test no matter how complete his responses were. Many years later, recounting this one night over beers when we were both attending San Diego State, his passion and detailed memory of civics and history tests convinced me that this had been the case. Also, his basic intelligence was evidence that he was more than a C student. He had studied hard in high school, easily as hard as I had when we compared notes, yet my grades were always better. I fit in more with the main achiever stream in presentation and appearance; I volunteered for some of the service clubs, looked the expected part. I know that for no good reason, he received a raw deal from Catholic school.

And yes, as it had been foretold, grades did affect your immediate future. Also, your ability to pay figured in. My SAT scores were terrible, but my father, for a while, could pay the tuition at a Catholic college, and I had decent grades and solid recommendations from the teachers and so was admitted. Peter had been so put down, so consistently told he could not do college work, I don't think he even took the SATs. Besides, there was no money for college, and so for him, as for many others with potential and the intellectual tools in place, it was city college—high school with ashtrays as many referred to it.

The city college overlooks the ocean, and from many places

on campus it's easy to check the conditions of the surf or wind. When the wind was down and a swell running, Peter and some of his same friends from high school would head north with their boards to Sands or further to Jalama instead of to calculus or English class. The Pentagon was cranking the war machine up to ten, and the draft pressure increased. Before the Selective Service System began to harass students in four-year colleges, it began to search through student deferments for those who were slipping behind in units or those who had plummeting GPAs in two-year community colleges. Peter and the rest did not have philosophy by that point, had not worked over political and moral reasoning with their own lives at the center of the question. Canada was not an option, really, in 1966–67. The media only published the relative truth of a daily body count. They did not dare dig deep enough to uproot the corrupt political and economic motivations or expose the rationally and morally bankrupt policies that fueled the administration. Johnson would fall, but that would come later. Westmoreland wanted to keep his job and promote the distant purposes of Colt Manufacturing, Dutch Shell Oil, General Dynamics—take your pick—but this would not come to light until the '80s. For now, Peter was again swimming against a current of lies, and there was no truth to set him free, to give him a real and fair chance at education.

Like many, Peter came home one day and reached inside the mailbox for a letter that opened, "Greetings: You are now a member of the United States Armed Forces. . . ." He was drafted, sent directly to Vietnam, handed an M16, and sent into the bush. His luck did not improve much by being made a radio man, running the front lines with a 1 APRC 25 radio pack squarely on his back like a big bull's-eye. But the bottom-line luck, that last-ditch brand of luck half connected to his tenacity alone—staying alive—stuck with him. On patrol, coming to a rise in the path, Sozzi's unit came face to face with a contingent of Vietcong coming the other way. His buddy Jacobs sighted the VC point man just as the point man spotted him; Jacobs took a burst from the AK-47 in the sternum at the same instant he fired his grenade. The point man was blown to bits, and Peter caught Jacobs in his arms as he fell back, but Jacobs was no longer there.

Not long after that, Peter's battalion was caught in a firefight, completely surrounded by VC. Ninety percent of the battalion died or was medevaced before some sorry support came in almost too late to get the living out. Peter figured he'd stretched his luck to its thin limit.

He mustered out at Fort Sill, Oklahoma, where he spent the last few weeks of his hitch. After returning home to Santa Barbara, just as he must have begun to feel free of the daily dread and worry for his life, he came down with a high fever and muscle pains. At Cottage Hospital, the doctors were perplexed and figured it was some exotic virus he'd picked up in the jungle. For a week he became progressively worse. When we first went up to see him, he was conscious, alert for only a couple minutes before he again slipped into delirium; he was burning up in his blood even though strapped to a refrigerated sheet. After days of sending his blood around to UCLA, USC, and elsewhere, UC San Francisco identified the infection as Rocky Mountain spotted fever, something he'd undoubtedly contracted from a tick bite at Fort Sill. At that point, he was only hours from death, but once the condition was identified, the doctors were able to administer treatment and he recovered.

For the ten days previous to the treatment he was in fever and delirium, calling up strikes from deep in his unconscious, reporting troop movements, sniper fire, incoming, enemy strafing attacks. His eyes glazed over and yellow, he thrashed about, ducking, diving from mortar attacks, shouting into some invisible transmitter, "The VC are gonna overrun us if some of you jockeys can't lay down some fire pretty damn pronto!" He laid down a consistent combat patter reliving all his war, our war. He brought it home for the nurses and doctors and for those of us who could bear to visit. In short, he was made to do it twice—fight an unfair and worthless war all over again. For nothing.

For a while, he lived at his mother's house, then rented a small apartment. We'd often ride bikes around town together, and I'd ride with him up to his doctor's appointments. He had to see about a lingering muscle spasm or nerve twinge, which the doctors seemed incapable of curing or about which they were just not that concerned. When serious argument came up about the war those days, Peter was usually quiet, distant. Asked for an opinion then, his response was, "You don't know. You just don't know." Of course, he was right—we had not gone, were not going, did not, and finally would not know. After a while, I had some idea of the rock and the hard place he found himself between. Day by day and minute by minute, he had struggled to stay alive, to do whatever it took to keep breathing and be in the world for better or worse. The immediate truth was staying alive, keeping your head down. Larger truths? You just didn't have time for those; in the middle of that morass, there probably were no such things. Two years of your life, nine months to a year on the line, you still had to justify your immediate living life. To then speak out against it all, against the corruption of government and the military, against a foreign policy whose grasp of reality rivaled that of the Emperor's New Clothes—that would have been enough to drive you into a frustrated silence when the subject came up. And it did.

By this point in time, I, like Peter, was drifting. I'd finished college, taken a few graduate classes, even taught a year of seventh and eighth grade at a parochial school in Torrance. I was just getting by teaching tennis part-time, working at a liquor store, living Friday to Friday. One night, Peter stopped in to say he was going back to school to complete his B.S. in business administration. For no reason I could see, he'd decided on San Diego State—the closest state college with good surf, I guessed. He'd spent a year or so just cruising, getting acclimated to the world again, and he was now resolved that this was the right thing for him to do. His resolution spread quickly to me, and I decided to pursue an M.A. in English and head down to San Diego with him. Peter was again a catalyst. Without him proposing a return to school and San Diego State, sharing an apartment together, I'd probably have bounced around a lot longer.

The summer after our first year there, early '70s, he decided to take a road trip in a van with a couple of friends, head out and see the U.S.A. Then, it was still possible to do so cheaply, travel and camp, meet some generous people along the way. But bad luck hit quickly—the van's engine blew outside of Yellowstone National Park. But this was good luck in disguise. Perhaps the spin on fate was changing? There was nothing for Peter to do except find work immediately, and it was early enough in the summer that there were positions still not filled in the park. Because Peter was a veteran and had a Purple Heart (he'd sustained a slight flesh wound from a flying shard of pottery), he rose to the top of the list and was given a starting position as park ranger.

He stayed on through late summer after the others had headed back. He returned to San Diego State but soon transferred to Cal Poly at San Luis Obispo for a new major in Natural Resources Management, which dovetailed perfectly with his summer work at Yellowstone. He did well and graduated and then made a home in Gardiner, Montana, and began a career with the National Park Service. But the job had its drawbacks: most ranger contracts did not extend over the winter, so he had to cast around for other positions until the park opened in the spring. Some winters he turned up a stint at the Channel Islands or at Point Lobos, and others he had to winter out in Montana. He and his wife Barbara faced months of thirty below, getting up every two hours during the night to load wood and keep the stove from failing and their trailer from freezing up. But as he moved up in seniority after several seasons at Yellowstone, he put in for a transfer and moved to Salmon, Idaho, as head ranger on the river, in charge of float trips in summer and general conservation of the river and lands year-round. His job with the Park Service secure, Peter and Barbara adopted a son, and four years later a daughter. Hitting middle age, he made peace, more or less, with the breaks. Certainly he loved the clean and pure environment, the meaningful vocation he'd worked through a lot of trouble to find.

Nevertheless, it was Idaho. Like me, like many of us, he keeps coming home to Santa Barbara, and he is as vociferous as anyone about the ruination and exploitation of the town—the expansion for the developers and the nouveau riche up from L.A. He's mad as any of us about never again—barring a big lottery win—being able to live in his hometown. He grew up on the coast when the air and sea, beaches, mountains, and trees were available to all regardless of cash or class. He was a surfer at heart, and the beach had once been clean, the waves free, and that basic feeling of freedom ran through him as purely as light. Never, it seems, again.

Our class in high school had been a small one: 130 or so graduated in 1965. Most of us got along well, knew each other, and for years a core group stayed in town and kept in touch with the rest. Those living out of town came home often. Every five years the class reunion is well attended. I remember best our five-year and our twenty-five-year reunions. In 1970 everyone there was under the influence of the conservative early '60s—business suits, fancy dresses, moving ahead in the company, supporting America by supporting the war. Only Sozzi, I, and two or three others had swung over in opposition to the war and were more or less in sync with the counterculture. We came in jeans, our hair was long, and we were opposed to a lot. Along with Peter, I felt we were right about not going along with the majority then, and history has proven us so. Let me be clear: Peter had had to go much further than I to come to that position; he had risked and suffered a great deal more to arrive at that point than most of us. We were not representative of the group that night; we had no suits or haircuts, no wallets with foldout pictures of our children. But it was good to be in the group and at least socially oppose the manifestations of society that supported that war. We had a good time nevertheless, just being there and seeing what it had all come to so far.

Twenty years later, and we were happier at that reunion. In some ways, happier than ever to be there and just see each other, to drive or walk around the town, to be alive and have familiar points of reference because so much else had begun to slip away. That July, 1990, Peter and a few others came into town early and spent a couple days hitting the waves. I missed a get-together at Schiefen's, the usual meeting place, and an evening of beers and nostalgia. Peter, I heard, had put a few away and was in rare form, decrying, in love and bitterness, the conspicuous consumption, the residual Reagan/movie star presence in Santa Barbara and Santa Ynez, the high tide of BMWs and Mercedes, restaurants, and convention centers. Still, there was the sea and friends, and the hills and parks; the streets were resplendent with jacarandas, acacias, coral trees, and fifteen kinds of eucalyptus despite a recent fire that had cleared a black swath almost to the sea.

At the reunion itself, Peter was recalcitrant, truculent, hard to talk to. Hangover? Some of the same folks in the same social cliques after all this time? More likely it was simply that for the first time the reunion was held in the old high school gym instead of at one of the local hotels. Those bricks had soaked up a lot of bitterness and bad reminders, and though all that had happened twenty-five years ago, now that we were in our forties, it was somehow not that long ago. Peter wanted more— wanted to feel happy here, wanted to be at ease and free to love it all without reservation here in his hometown. The old gym was a bit of a red flag. Just for once, he wanted things to feel right, to finally be fair.

Sic Gloria Transit Mundi

The earliest photograph I have of myself is at nine months. I'm seated on the front of the long white hood of my parents' '47 Pontiac, my mother standing to the side of the car having just placed me there. The car is parked on a hilltop overlooking Humboldt Bay in northern California, where I was born, and the horizon is about level with the hood of the car. There I am—all the sky behind me, my arms stretched out to either side for balance as if I was riding a surfboard on a big wave.

I actually began surfing, taking my lumps and cuts off the rocks and barnacles, in the summer of 1961 after we had graduated from eighth grade. However, the summer before, I had already discovered the energy and power, the almost magical force field surrounding a surfboard. My friend Harry Fowler, who had a house right on the beach and with whom a bunch of us had been bodysurfing and skin-diving for the last few years, had built a surfboard from a kit. There were few people surfing in 1960—the popularized lifestyle and upswing of interest in the sport was barely beginning. Throughout the '40s and '50s only a handful of "old men" surfed—guys often in their thirties who rode huge boards in old photos of Hawaii. My father told me that he had surfed on a mahogany board that belonged to the natives along the Gold Coast in Africa when he was stationed there during the war.

By 1962 or 1963, a lot of teenagers had taken up the sport, and it became a sort of social phenomena, enough so that Hollywood even began including it in teen films. Fabian, Frankie Avalon, and even Elvis himself were "surfin'" in their films—that is, standing on a plank in a soundstage in Burbank with a fifteen-foot wave from Makaha or Huntington Beach projected on a screen behind them. They stood with their feet parallel so they could face the camera for a shot from the waist up, a fan blowing in their faces and barely a lock of their greased-down hair moving. In addition to striking that awkward position on the board, they put their arms stiffly out to the side, balancing like rank beginners though they were shown riding powerful and fast-breaking surf. One director, realizing how unrealistic these scenes must look, had Elvis or Fabian, I forget who really, look over his shoulder as a surfer cut in back of him on the same projected wave, which was even more unlikely. I saw these clips in previews and coming attractions—no real surfer would be caught dead at a Beach Blanket Bingo flick!

Somehow, surfers as a group began to be seen as juvenile delinquents—"juvies" as we knew them—or the older ones were seen as vestigial beatniks. Although there were jerks in the water and some fistfights over who cut whom off the wave of the day, although some cars were broken into and the occasional beer can flung among the rocks, the majority of the surfing population was interested only in the sport and the experience. Indeed, in the '60s, the sport was more popular than at any time since. Weekends, with a big swell running at Rincon Point south of Santa Barbara, there would be over two hundred people in the water. I've never seen that many out there since. And though it was mostly boys, there were some good women surfers out, too, and some older men. When Rincon was breaking, there was a crowd. John Severson's *Surfer Magazine* was a forum for a "clean-cut" view of the sport. Bimonthly, it published the most awesome surf shots available at the time. *Surfer* also offered an absolutely "bitchin'" collection of surf posters—black-and-white photos with a blue or green wash, telephoto shots of the big names in the best poses: Ricky Grigg in a bottom turn at Sunset Beach, Pat Curren on his big gun slicing across a wall at Waimea, and the famous one of Paul Straugh in his patented crouch, locked in the curl, one knee bent under him and his left leg stretched forward so that his toes reached over the nose, "hanging five."

About this time, Phil Edwards emerged and made his reputation surfing the Banzai Pipeline—eight to twelve feet pumping left-breaking waves that were smoking! This was the new hot spot in the islands. Waves formed quickly and hollowed out over a coral reef not far offshore. Wave after wave curled into perfect tubes, hence the name "pipeline." Edwards was the first to really have the place "wired," dropping in quickly with an angled turn, trimming up the board pronto, crouching, disappearing for seconds at a time before being spit out the end of the wave with the spindrift and spray. He cranked a big knee-drop bottom turn on a slower wave face then grabbed a rail as the wave broke over him and he shot the curl—never wiping out. Wiping out there, we were told by Severson narrating his hit surfing film, meant landing in only two to three feet of water, meant meeting up with spikes of coral on the bottom. You could come out looking like a sponge—hence the other half of the name—"Banzai." We all sent away for the poster of Edwards on the Pipeline as soon as it was available. We were fans.

Harry had all the posters up on his wall and a subscription to *Surfer Magazine*. He was the first to be really consumed with a passion for surfing, and the rest of us became interested through him. Harry saved up to buy that surfboard kit, with a balsa wood plank, fiberglass, resin and catalyst and pigment. He shaped and sanded the blank on intuition, anchored the wooden skeg, or fin, into the tail block, cut the glass cloth, mixed resin and catalyst and "glassed" the whole thing. After it dried for a couple of days, he sanded down the edges of fiberglass that stuck out, the bubbled or globbed resin spots, then mixed a finish coat of eggshell-blue pigment and applied that. Only nine feet long, but the board weighed a lot with a balsa wood plank, all that resin and ten-ounce glass. Compared to the other boards we'd ride in years to come, it was thick and slow, but at age twelve or thirteen, just starting out, it looked stunning.

One day that summer between seventh and eighth grade, Harry had to go somewhere with his folks and he let me use the board. There were no waves that day, and had there been I would not have had the first notion of what to try to do, would have made a fool of myself in front of lots of kids I knew there on Miramar Beach. I made a fool of myself later, but in front of fewer folks. That day, it was just hot and the water was cool, especially further out from shore where the hotel anchored a raft. What was easy enough was paddling the board; all you had to do was balance lying down in the middle so that the nose skimmed an inch or two above the water as you stroked. I took it out to the raft, back into the shore, picked up Virginia Cortez from the beach and paddled her out to the raft. I was cool. The only guy around with a board—something new, a sure status symbol, I came to realize after giving a few people rides. Next weekend swimming out to the raft, some kid asked, "Aren't you the guy with the blue surfboard?" I had to explain that, no, it belonged to my friend. A short-lived life in the lights.

Harry wasn't interested in status or being seen. He was serious early on. No waves broke where everyone hung out on the beach. More and more often when we came by to see if he wanted to ride bikes downtown to buy 45 records or go skin-diving or play some Kingston Trio albums, Harry was gone—

down to the beach, to Shark's Cove, or up to Hammond's Reef. For a while, we thought it was something he'd get tired of before too long. But one day at school, I heard that our friend Phil had gone with Harry to Shark's over the weekend and had mastered standing up in only one afternoon. How difficult could it be?

The next Saturday, I walked down to the beach to watch them surf, and, peer pressure aside, this looked like fun. I wanted to give it a try, and began asking my father about buying a board. He, of course, said no. There was tennis practice, transportation problems, and there was the hoodlum reputation of surfers among the middle-class community. One of my tennis partners had a friend with an old board for sale cheap. Extra yard chores, my life's savings, and a month later I bought that board for thirty dollars. Though the foam had yellowed from age and there were dings on the rails, it was not too waterlogged, and once it was dried out, Harry helped me patch it up. He still had glass and resin left from his kit, materials that in coming years would become second nature to me, but which then were exotic and arcane. Patched, a finishing coat applied, my first surfboard was old and beat up, but it beamed out a special light to me.

By this point, Harry had a new nine-foot-two-inch Yater, his old board having lost its skeg and served its time. There were few surf shops those days and most were in L.A.—Velzy/Jacobs, Dewey Weber, Gordon and Smith. In the Santa Barbara area, there was only Reynolds Yater's shop south in Carpinteria, but it then made, and has continued for over thirty years to make, one of the best boards anywhere. That board moved! Harry moved on it, always catching the best waves and beating out the crashing sections of beach or point break. My board was also a Yater, really the premiere name on our part of the coast. Mine even had a "split stringer" running the length of the board. Instead of Yater's standard "stringer"—the strips of wood epoxyed down the middle of the foam for strength—which was an eighth inch of redwood with a quarter inch of balsa, mine had three strips of redwood. A quarter-inch strip ran down the center with two eighth-inch strips alongside until they reached the tail block and dovetailed out to the rails, the one center stringer continuing down to the end. Precious few of those around, old sun-yellowed foam or not. To get this on a new board would cost a lot. My board was yellow and used, but it was a classic and more than fine for learning.

Harry was happy to have his friends take up surfing, and he helped each of us along, though by that time Phil had become fairly competent. The dings on our boards patched up, we hoisted our boards and headed for Shark's Cove, a small bay on the other side of Fernald Point. Then, Shark's had more of a beach, and also a breakwater extending out into the bay that gave good form to the waves. The waves were all "rights"—the best wave for left-foot-forward surfers—and had, except on the few days when a swell ran over head-high, a slow break that was great for learning. Even though there was more sand on the beach in those days, the shallows were mostly rocks, and you rode over the rocks or fell off your board onto them.

The day I went out to learn, I put in a good four hours on the rocks. Phil and Harry were catching waves, standing up and riding smoothly and confidently into the beach. They were helpful about the lineup—where to position myself in relation to the swell—and told me when to start paddling in order to catch a wave. In no time, I had the hang of catching waves; it was not that much different from bodysurfing. But there was not much they could tell me about how exactly to stand up and get your balance once you caught the wave and it was sweeping you forward in its trough. You just pushed yourself up on the moving plank, scrambled to find your feet, and things developed from there. After an hour or so of trying, actually standing up and fighting for balance, I yelled to Harry to witness the fact that I was up and riding the thing. Just then I "pearled," the nose of my board digging under the wave as I shot forward, landing on my back on the rocks as the board, continuing straight on, ran over my leg with its skeg. I was not discouraged. I had made it up, not as fast as Phil, but I would do this. I would be as cool as everyone else. I would be tough. I lasted the afternoon but never rode a wave all the way into the beach. I had mastered catching a wave, getting up and riding a few feet before "wiping out." But it was great fun, an exhilaration of speed, light, air, and water, and I was "psyched." Next day out, I was up every time and soon made it all the way into the beach, one time even managing a turn so I rode across the breaking face of the wave instead of straight into the beach in the "soup." In a few weeks I was moving my foot to the rail to make a hard right turn after taking the "drop," and could also manage a passable "kick-out" to pull out of a bad wave or pull back over the wave once it had given out. I even managed to "walk" to the nose to trim the board out and pick up speed and then backpedal to keep the board from "pearling." I'd arrived. At least on waist- to shoulder-high waves I was kinetic, moving with the blue motion of the waves all that summer from Miramar Point to Shark's, as glad as the fish or birds gliding by.

At fourteen, we were wonderful in our bodies, and completely hooked on surfing; nothing could keep us out of the water. We went out all winter regardless of weather. Harry and Phil had wet-suit tops for warmth, and I had one whose zipper broke after two weeks. Even without a wet suit, we were out surfing in February, in frigid waters, buoyed by the antifreeze of youth coursing in our veins. Wet suit or not, the water off southern California is cold in winter. I have a clear recollection of surfing then. You'd stand in knee-deep water, rubbing wax on your board, passing the requisite five minutes of pain until your legs went numb so you could then paddle out to the break and sit on your board, concentrating on the next set of waves coming in. If there was a swell running, we'd be out even in rain, figuring we were wet anyway, so why not take advantage of the storm surf? Even our friend Peter Cooney started surfing. Pete was at most a hundred pounds, and even the smallest wet suit left him plenty of room to shiver. He'd come along every time and catch a few small inside waves before having to go in to the beach and warm up at a driftwood fire. Pete had picked up a used Dave Sweet nine-foot-two-inch board, and for some reason that board hauled. Every time he had to go in I'd borrow it. It trimmed up perfectly for nose rides in the two- to four-foot tubes we rode at Miramar or Shark's.

Phil became a "big gun" guy, bought a board from O'Neill's Surf Shop in Santa Cruz—a longer one with a narrow tail block especially for big waves. Harry and I both bought new boards as well—Eichardt's balsa boards were the rage for a while; IKE's, the orange decal placed on the nose of the board declared. Harry ordered a nine-foot-six-inch and I ordered a nine-foot-eight-inch. His board cut cleanly across the water while mine was a log—just the breaks I guessed, though I knew he was the better surfer. Yet mine was sure, solid in the bigger waves, and by then, Harry and Phil were for moving on to bigger surf. Rincon Point, just south of Santa Barbara, was one of the premiere surfing spots anywhere in the world and was included in all the surf films.

Rather than stake out a lineup in the bay with the crowds, Harry preferred to paddle out to the Indicator, the most dangerous break, the furthest beyond the point, where waves first formed in a hot breaking "section"—a part of the wave that walled up all at once and that required a lot of speed to surf through. Harry could handle the Indicator, could shoot the section into the bay, riding the nose. Naturally athletic, Harry did well in the usual sports at school, but surfing was where he touched the light and knew the body as something fluid and intuitive.

Paddling out to get into position at the Indicator took fifteen minutes—stroking through incoming sets and soup, rolling under big "outside" waves, avoiding surfers streaming down at us on the curling face of a powerful tube. Against my better judgment, that is, despite a sense of FEAR that rolled around in my stomach like a handful of ball bearings, I went along with Harry and Phil.

Some days, I'd be out all afternoon and take off on only three or four waves, making sure they had good shape because on a fifteen-foot wave, when you stop scratching for all you are worth and feel that pause as the wave picks you up, lifts you like a leaf in the wind, it's like going from a dead stop to being strapped on the front of a Mac truck charging down the highway at sixty-five miles an hour. You take the "drop" and the whole world falls out from beneath you as you dig your heel into the tail block with nine-tenths of the board in the air, hoping you can hang on to the bottom, crank a quick turn, and trim the board up to shoot the section. It's electrifying skimming across a wall of water, flat out a couple feet from the nose, knowing you'll "make" the wave into the shore break. You paddle back out into the lineup hooting, waving your fists above your head, yelling the nonsensical code all surfers used then—"Stoked! Bitchin'! Cowabunga!"—no matter how incoherent. There was no way to feel more alive in the world, in the elements, and almost out of your body.

Almost out to the Indicator once, I grabbed a monster "outside" wave as I was one of the few in position—everyone else having taken the previous wave. The grey salt spit off the top of the wave blew back and blinded me as the wave sucked out over the point. I "took gas" as I tried to handle the drop. It was then I experienced the "washing machine": you were tossed around in the soup; the white water, six to eight feet of it, churned and held you there for a minute, or more. A quarter mile from shore and so spun around that you couldn't tell up from down when the power of the wave dissipated and released you, you just hoped you swam the right way—that is, toward the surface and not toward the bottom. I did. But when my head burst above the water, there was four to five feet of soup rolling right for me with a half dozen boards flipping around in it. I gulped a lungful and dove down to come back up once that passed. It was a long process bobbing into shore like that, ending up doing the "rock dance," the last hundred yards over rocks, kelp, and barnacles.

After a winter of battling the huge sets at Rincon, waiting an hour or more for that one wave with shape, a wave not loaded with people on your right cutting you off or on your left hollering "coming down," I began to consider other places to surf. Except at the Indicator, there was no room to maneuver, to cut back and climb, to stall out a little before running to the nose. The ecstatic waves in which you crouched down, cocooned in gold light, the green film tubing over your head, were few and far between. If it was a sunny weekend, you just stood there moving slowly forward, surfers on your right and left. You could have been in a Beach Blanket Bingo movie you stood there so still.

I was fifteen and life still looked pretty good. Surfing offered an immediate glory, and I figured I could reach it on smaller waves without risking my life. Crowds aside, surfing Rincon on a big day meant placing more value on staying alive than on having fun. There, I rarely had the confidence to risk it all, go for the Paul Straugh position on the nose with twelve feet of Pacific churning like a locomotive right on my tail block. One roll in the washing machine on a big day would do. I knew my limitations as a swimmer and decided to stick with the breaks where the swims in were short.

Later, during high school, we moved from Montecito out to Hope Ranch, so I started to surf there. The waves had exceptional shape, good breaks left and right. A number of my old tennis friends surfed Hope Ranch, so I knew enough of the locals to be comfortable. About the only thing to worry about were the "gremmies"—mean little kids who couldn't surf well but had an attitude. They'd take off in front of you even though you had position and were locked into the curl or the wave of the day. If you really got on their case, they'd bail out right in front of you, hoping that their wrecked out boards corkscrewed in the soup and came down on yours giving you a couple of good dings.

We'd drive to school in the morning with boards strapped to racks on top of our cars, leave them like that in the parking lot all day, and come out after classes to find them still there—pretty innocent times. It was still hot through September and October, and a bunch of us would head right to the beach after school. About the only really dangerous time I had at Hope Ranch Beach was on one of those lovely warm afternoons. I was sitting outside the break a little with my pal Scott Spencer, waiting for a set to roll through. I noticed a lot of guys to our right all taking the same not too spectacular wave in to the beach, some just riding straight in and not even trying to make the wave left or right. I yelled over to Scott because suddenly we were the only two in the water; the others were standing on the beach and pointing at us. Scott backed up on his board, did a 360-degree turnaround, lifted up and looked over his nose and pointed and gestured about four or five times before I saw what he saw—some black fins about twenty yards beyond us. What went through my head was the shot from a Severson film where a twenty-foot shark was swimming inside the break at Rincon—the film offering the audience a freeze-frame of the shark silhouetted inside a cresting wave. Luckily, a set of waves was coming, so we both scratched in as fast as we could, catching the first one, not even trying to stand up, just proned out all the way to the sand. "Killer whales," the other guys on the beach said, almost laughing at us. As we looked out, shivering a bit just standing there in our trunks, we could see the black and white markings of the whales as they cruised just outside the breakers. Killer whales love to eat seals, and sitting on your board, waiting for a wave, you look a bit like a big fat seal. We stood there and watched awhile, laughing a bit, but still shivering.

Over the years, we moved to beaches to the north to escape

the crowds—Sands, Haskells, Mar Mesa. Not long out of college, most of us stopped surfing regularly. In and out of town, it was hard to get together and be lucky enough to find a swell running when you were there. I was going to graduate school and teaching tennis full-time in the summers. There never seemed to be time. At the end of the '70s *Apocalypse Now* came out, and one of my favorite scenes was the surfing sequence with a couple of young California surfers who had been drafted. There they were, at the mouth of a river in Vietnam, Robert Duval's character's air calvary unit going in to take a VC position so they could drive a boat up the river, and he had the boat and the surfboards airlifted in. He wanted to see these renowned surfers do their thing. Napalm, mortars, rounds of automatic fire all over the place, and Duval's character stands there in his green Yater T-shirt, saying to the nervous and hesitant privates, "Son, you surf or you fight." They hit the waves—knee- to waist-high lefts and rights, big boards, riding the nose, and nostalgia washed over me despite the ludicrous situation.

I moved back to Santa Barbara in 1980 to take a teaching position at the university there and found it easy to buy one of the old "long boards." I picked up a classic Jacobs ten-footer for only thirty-five dollars. Small boards were in, and no one wanted these dinosaurs, but that board was really the only thing that would float me and my memories. If I were to have a chance of getting back into surfing—and the weather was right for it— I needed the old board. I went out a few times with a high school buddy, John Craig, a fireman. His occupation afforded plenty of time off, and he had kept up with his surfing as part of his physical stamina program, which the fire department demanded. Nice work if you can get it. We went south one day to the beach at La Conchita, just before the oil piers. While I was catching some rays on the beach, he took his daughter out on my board and they rode tandem on it. They looked like a film clip from the late '50s or early '60s as they caught a slow rolling wave, got up, and John tried to lift his daughter up on his shoulder as they rode in. Three years later I moved away to another job but kept the board in a friend's garage in town. Returning to the university only a couple years later, I found Santa Barbara even more expensive than it had previously been. One month, things very tight, I discovered that the old long boards had made a comeback, were now classics, and I put an ad in the paper. I sold the board for $125 to the first person who came by, and for the moment felt lucky to have the money, but soon I wished I'd kept it. It wouldn't be that long until I'd see how much of an emblem it was, how much of what I'd been was wrapped up in some fiberglass and foam. Whether I ever used it again or not, its value over the long haul would easily have outweighed the ready cash.

Through the generosity of my cousin, in 1992 I was able to spend most of the summer in Santa Barbara in a condo she had not rented. After another grinding year of a state college load, another inactive eastern winter, it's doubtful I would have had the energy to try riding some waves even if I'd held onto the board, but it would have been wonderful to try. I spent most days just walking on the beach, the very beaches where I'd spent so much time and energy, so much youth, surfing eight or ten hours a day—a wise use of time, it now seems to me.

The city put the freeway underpasses in after twenty-odd years of debate. This demanded moving two blocks of shops next to the freeway and also signaled the development of lower State Street, an area formerly filled with car dealerships, liquor stores, cheap hotels, and pawnshops. Fancy coffee and croissant shops, upgraded hotels, beach rentals, more and better Mexican restaurants filled the area—all the facades shiny in new pastel pink, terra-cotta, and turquoise. Out on Stern's Wharf, the bar above the Harbor Restaurant had changed hands and was now called Longboard's Grill. A few old-style big boards glistened high on the walls like large marlin or sailfish. Some were tipped out from the wall at angles, and there was a neon wave curling along the wall as you went up the stairs into the bar. Drinks were served with a plastic replica of a long surfboard instead of a swizzle stick. Not everything had gone to hell.

I went in search of Yater's surf shop. My green Yater–Robert Duval T-shirt was starting to sport more air than fabric in places and I needed a new one. I thought, too, it would be interesting to see what the new boards looked like. Yater's was one of the businesses that had to move for the freeway, and I found his place in the back of a new shop whose main business was beach clothing. But overhead, suspended from the ceiling, was a collection of almost mint-condition long boards from the '60s, as beautiful as the classic cars in any museum. Hard to know if they were for sale or show, but they were the real things— Velzy/Jacobs, Dewey Weber, Bing, and Hobie—with original wide stripes of red and blue pigment. Even with the foam a bit sun-yellowed, they still were magical floating there above me in the air. In the very back of the room there was one rack of new boards, all Yaters. They were magnificent. All big boards in the old shape and style, nine feet six inches to ten feet, glossy green as the thin lip of a wave. They were absolutely faithful to the original Yaters—the standard redwood and balsa stringers and a clean light green cast to the resin, medium rails for smooth easy turns, the same triangular decal about a foot or so up from the tail block. I checked the tag—$535 each. Were I living there, God help me, I would have bought one, adding to the Visa bill beyond my means, even knowing that I might not ever get it in the water again. They were just that beautiful and took me back to a place and time when a pure movement through water and air was all the world.

The night before I had to leave to drive back East, I went down to the breakwater about six o'clock. I'd heard a group of old friends were still gathering there on Wednesday evenings under the pretense of fishing. A couple of them actually had poles, none of which, however, were snapped together or in use. Mainly, they were there to be there, to have one, perhaps two beers over a couple of hours and look out to the sea and islands, to the sun-backed salt air, to gaze west up the valley where sun sifted down the Gaviota Pass and across the town glowing between the Mesa and the foothills. Harry was there. It had been a few years. I told him about the new Yaters, their beauty, their cost. He shook his head but said he could believe it. I asked if he got out much anymore. With working a full-time engineering job, with a family and a house, he didn't hit the waves that often.

But he still had a board, a Yater from a few years back. Hadn't had it out in a while actually, but he knew where it was, checked the level of the dust every now and then. I trotted out my usual litany of complaints, mostly about not being able to live in the West, especially in my hometown. At one point we had to admit that, strange as it was in our minds, having known each other since we were six years old, we were in fact middle-aged. Our politics, once very different, seemed to have moved closer together: we disbelieved the same things now, shared a general disappointment.

What did he want, now that he had a career, some semblance of success? He wanted to surf—just be on the beach, retired. To hell with the money, the forty hours a week that are really sixty-five or seventy, the finally insignificant whole nine yards of working your life away to pay for the house you live in and keep up for the bank. At this point in life, it was getting simple. You'd gone soft a little, not inside—not where a low flame of anger and desire burned blue. But you'd gained something bordering on bitterness and love, because what you were lucky enough to begin with was wonderful and intangible, something to hold onto with your heart. Now you needed something as basic as land. And, barring that, all you'd have to cherish would be the intangibles still slipping like water through your hands. You could come to the same place once a week and stake a silent claim on the air. You could see the glory of the world shining out there, and you could hold your arms out as best you could for the fading embrace of sky—doves scattering from the eucalyptus, the feckless array of clouds, the spray splashing randomly over the breakwater. You're left with the ocean, the surface glassy with its charge of light. You have a board in the garage just in case you forget. You have one evening a week to watch it all pass away among friends.

Credits

Buckley, Christopher. "Days of Black & White. *The Lowell Review* no. 1 (Summer 1994). Copyright 1994 by Christopher Buckley. Reprinted by permission of author.

Buckley, Christopher. "Working Grocery." *The New Press* 10, no. 6 (Fall 1994). Copyright 1994 by Christopher Buckley. Reprinted by permission of author.

Buckley, Christopher. "Work-Ups." *Creative Nonfiction* 1, no. 2 (Fall 1994). Copyright 1994 by The Creative Nonfiction Foundation. Reprinted by permission of The Creative Nonfiction Foundation.

Special thanks to Francis Orsua, Steve Schiefen, Tuck Schneider, Peter Sozzi, and Harry Fowler for their time and help in researching these essays;

Jeanne and Tony Lehman for their support during the beginning of this book;

and Luanne Smith and Nadya Brown for proofing and editing suggestions.

Western Literature Series

■ ■ ■

Western Trails: A Collection of Short Stories by Mary Austin
selected and edited by Melody Graulich

Cactus Thorn
Mary Austin

Dan De Quille, the Washoe Giant: A Biography and Anthology
prepared by Richard A. Dwyer and Richard E. Lingenfelter

Desert Wood: An Anthology of Nevada Poets
edited by Shaun T. Griffin

The City of Trembling Leaves
Walter Van Tilburg Clark

Many Californias: Literature from the Golden State
edited by Gerald W. Haslam

The Authentic Death of Hendry Jones
Charles Neider

First Horses: Stories of the New West
Robert Franklin Gish

Torn by Light: Selected Poems
Joanne de Longchamps

Swimming Man Burning
Terrence A. Kilpatrick

The Temptations of St. Ed and Brother S
Frank Bergon

The Other California: The Great Central Valley in Life and Letters
Gerald W. Haslam

The Track of the Cat
Walter Van Tilburg Clark

Shoshone Mike
Frank Bergon

Condor Dreams and Other Fictions
Gerald W. Haslam

A Lean Year and Other Stories
Robert Laxalt

Kinsella's Man
Richard Stookey

Cruising State: Growing Up in Southern California
Christopher Buckley